The Island of Happiness

For Linda Nochlin, with love
—Natalie

The Island of Happiness

Tales of Madame d'Aulnoy

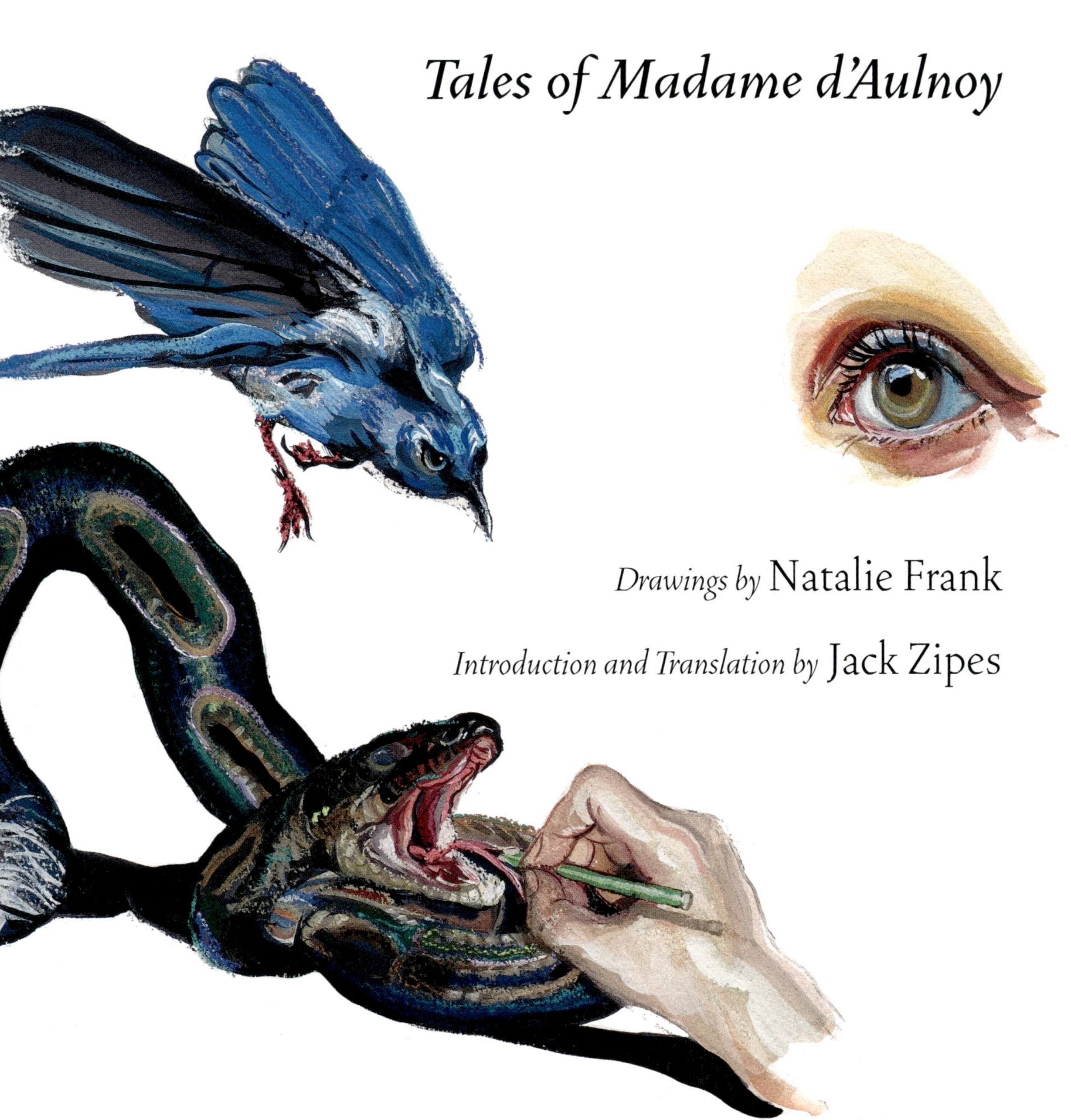

Drawings by Natalie Frank

Introduction and Translation by Jack Zipes

Published by Princeton University Press
41 William Street, Princeton, New Jersey 08540
6 Oxford Street, Woodstock, Oxfordshire OX20 1TR
press.princeton.edu

Library of Congress Cataloging-in-Publication Data

Names: Aulnoy, Madame d' (Marie-Catherine), 1650 or 1651-1705, author. | Frank, Natalie, illustrator. | Zipes, Jack, 1937- translator, writer of introduction.
Title: The Island of Happiness : tales of Madame d'Aulnoy / drawings by Natalie Frank ; translated and introduced by Jack Zipes.
Description: Princeton, New Jersey : Princeton University Press, [2021] | Stories translated from French into contemporary English.
Identifiers: LCCN 2020017876 (print) | LCCN 2020017877 (ebook) | ISBN 9780691180243 (hardback ; acid-free paper) | ISBN 9780691213668 (ebook)
Subjects: LCSH: Aulnoy, Madame d' (Marie-Catherine), 1650 or 1651-1705--Translations into English.
Classification: LCC PQ1711.A85 A2 2021 (print) | LCC PQ1711.A85 (ebook) | DDC 843/.4--dc23
LC record available at https://lccn.loc.gov/2020017876
LC ebook record available at https://lccn.loc.gov/2020017877

British Library Cataloging-in-Publication Data is available

Design: Marian Bantjes
Editorial: Anne Savarese and Jenny Tan
Production Editorial: Sara Lerner
Production: Steven Sears
Publicity: Alyssa Sanford and Amy Stewart
Copyeditor: Jennifer Harris
Jacket: Marian Bantjes & Natalie Frank
This book has been composed in Vendetta and Respira

Printed on acid-free paper. ∞
Printed in China
10 9 8 7 6 5 4 3 2 1

Contents

The Hopeful, Hyperbolic Countess d'Aulnoy

Who was this exceptional woman, Marie-Catherine Le Jumel de Barneville, Comtesse d'Aulnoy, pioneer of the literary fairy tale in France? Why is much of her life a mystery, even though she was a major writer and socialite in Paris during the 1690s and the beginning of the eighteenth century? What brought her to write what she allegedly considered trifling tales, "bagatelles," which nevertheless drew the admiration of aristocratic and bourgeois readers and were turned later into popular chapbooks and books for children? Why did she coin the term *conte de fées* and more or less initiate a fairy-tale vogue during the absolutist years of Louis XIV?

Born in 1652 into a wealthy aristocratic family in Barneville-La Bertrand, Normandy, Marie-Catherine had a close relationship with her mother and her maternal aunt, who educated her and told her numerous folk tales. More than likely, she also heard stories from her nannies and servants. In addition, she became proficient in English and Spanish and demonstrated a broad knowledge of medieval French and Spanish literature. Her mother married her off at age thirteen to François de la Motte, Baron d'Aulnoy, thirty years her senior and a notorious gambler and libertine. By the time Marie-Catherine turned eighteen, she had given birth to three children.

In 1669, due to the baron's financial difficulties and dissolute character, his relationship with Marie-Catherine and her mother, Madame Gudanne (who had remarried after her first husband's death and changed her name), deteriorated to the point that mother and daughter implicated Baron d'Aulnoy in a crime of high treason (*lèse majesté*), punishable by death. They recruited two accomplices, Jacques-Antoine de Courboyer and Charles de la Mozière, and the baron was arrested. The plot backfired, however, when the baron proved his innocence: Courboyer and Mozière were charged with calumny and executed. Mme Gudanne escaped charges by fleeing France, while her daughter, young Mme d'Aulnoy, was briefly imprisoned with a newborn daughter—her two other children had died in infancy. By 1670, Mme d'Aulnoy was pardoned because her role in the conspiracy could not be proved. After she was released from prison, she separated from her husband and temporarily entered a convent for refuge, which she left by 1672. During the next thirteen years, she traveled a great deal and allegedly spent time in England, Flanders, and Spain, where her mother lived and worked as a double agent for the French and Spanish governments. Otherwise, Mme d'Aulnoy would occasionally return to Paris, but there are no records or clear evidence about what she did during this period of her life. It remains a mystery.

What we do know is that around 1685, she bought a house on the rue Saint-Benoît, and was gradually accepted into Parisian high society. By 1690, she published her first important novel, *Histoire d'Hypolite, comte de Duglas* (*The Story of Hypolitus, Count of Douglas*), which was a great success and contained her first major fairy tale, "L'Îlle de la félicité" ("The Island of Happiness"). She followed this book the same year with a pseudo-memoir, *Mémoires de la cour d'Espagne* (*Memoirs of the Spanish Court*), and in 1691 with her travel/epistolary narrative, *Relation du voyage d'Espagne* (*An Account of a Journey to Spain*), which included another fairy tale, "L'Histoire de Mira" ("The Story of Mira").

Once fully settled in Paris, d'Aulnoy became one of the most popular and notable authors of her time. She was invited to various literary salons and established her own salon on the rue Saint-Benoît, where she often read her fairy tales aloud before they were published. It became customary at d'Aulnoy's salon to recite fairy tales and, on festive occasions, to dress up like characters from fairy tales. She was regarded as a talented storyteller and published her fairy tales in several volumes: *Les Contes des fées*, I–III (1696–97); *Les Contes des fées*, IV (1698); and *Contes nouveaux ou les fées à la mode*, I–IV (1698). Altogether, she published twenty-five fairy tales during her lifetime. She was the first to establish the literary fairy tale as a genre. Indeed, she was more responsible even than Charles Perrault for the extraordinary vogue of French literary fairy tales that swept Parisian cultural circles from 1690 through 1705.

On the basis of her writing—in addition to fairy tales, d'Aulnoy published historical romances, novels, devotional books, and memoirs—she was elected a member of the Academia dei Ricovrati in Padova, and she continued to be active in the literary field by publishing such works as *Sentiments d'une âme pénitente* (*Sentiments of a Penitent Soul*, 1698) and *Le Comte de Warwick* (*The Count Warwick*, 1703). In addition, d'Aulnoy managed to make time for intrigues. In 1699, she is said to have assisted her friend Mme Ticquet, who attempted to assassinate her husband, a member of Parliament, because he allegedly had abused her. He survived the attempt, and Mme Ticquet was beheaded. D'Aulnoy was not charged with any wrongdoing.

In 1700, d'Aulnoy's husband, the notorious baron, died. Although he had never divorced her, he had disinherited her before his death. Nevertheless, she continued to maintain her salon and participate in the cultural life of Paris until her death in 1705.

Many mysteries about her life remain unsolved. She published nothing until 1690, at age thirty-nine, and there are no reliable records about what she did during her years of travel, from 1672 to 1685. In fact, it is unclear how she supported herself or who fathered two of her daughters, born in 1676 and 1677. It is possible, since she was an only child, that she inherited a good deal of money and received support from her mother from 1670 to 1685, when she bought her house in Paris, and that she later earned money through her writing. What seems clear is that she was an independent young woman of thirty-five when she left Paris, and that she began writing her first three works toward the end of the 1680s. Moreover, these works, *The Story of Hypolitus* (1690), *Memories of the Spanish Court* (1690), and *An Account of Travels in Spain* (1691), were highly diverse. Her first fairy tales, "The Island of Happiness" and "The Story of Mira," are very different from her later ones and yet foreshadow many of the themes and concerns found in the later stories. Both are surprisingly dystopian narratives and stem from oral traditions, so the style and language are not as hyperbolical or euphemistic as in the later tales.

By 1690, d'Aulnoy had become an idealist and moralist. She was exclusively interested in the aristocratic classes and how they suffered from the decline of the nobility—that is, she believed that the upper classes were declining because of the corruption of civil manners. What interested her most of all was the status of women, the power of love, ethical behavior, and the tender relations between lovers. Without love and the cultivation of love, she believed, an ideal and just society could not exist. In even her earliest fairy tales, d'Aulnoy was a severe judge. King Adolph dies in "The Island of Happiness" because he chooses pride and glory over his love for Princess Felicity; the princess dies in "The Story of Mira" because she is too proud and narcissistic and must be punished by the gods. In these tales, d'Aulnoy's privileged king and princess could have lived ideal lives if it had not been for their character flaws.

It is evident from "The Island of Happiness" and "The Tale of Mira" that d'Aulnoy had not yet conceived a plan to write a series of fairy tales or to experiment with the genre. In fact, it was not until 1697 and 1698 that she was to make a name for herself as the writer of *contes des fées* when she published *Les Contes des fées*, fifteen tales within two frame narratives, *Don Gabriel Ponce de Leon and Don Fernand de Tolède*, followed by *Contes nouveaux ou les fées à la mode*, nine tales within the narrative frame of *Le Gentilhomme bourgeois*. If she had particular reasons and causes for writing these tales, it is likely that they were prompted by her disillusionment with the court and politics of Louis XIV, as well as by her experiences in the literary salons of Paris.

France endured a major crisis around 1688, and conditions began to deteriorate at all levels of society. Indeed, even the aristocracy and haute bourgeoisie were not exempt. As Louis XIV waged costly wars and sought to annex more land for France, taxes for all classes became exorbitant. At various times during the latter part of his reign, terrible weather led to years of bad harvests, and the continued wars added to the devastation. The steady increase of debt, taxation, and poor living conditions resulted in extreme misery for the peasantry and austerity for the bourgeoisie and aristocracy. Moreover, as Louis XIV became more orthodox in his devotion to Catholicism, he became more rigid in his cultural taste, and more arbitrary and willful as absolutist king. His reign, which had begun during an "Age of Reason," turned reason against itself to justify his desires, tastes, and ambition for glory, and this solipsism led to irrational, destructive policies that were soundly criticized by the highly respected Fénelon, the archbishop of Cambrai, who became the moral conscience of the ancien régime during its decline. Given these dark times, and the censorship that prohibited writers from criticizing Louis XIV directly, the fairy tale became a means to vent criticism and at the same time to project hope for a better world. D'Aulnoy clearly was drawn to imaginative literary works by educated writers as well as to magical folk tales from the common people, and adapted them for members of her social class.

From the late Middle Ages up through the Renaissance, peasants told a variety of folk tales, legends, and fables among themselves at the hearth, in spinning rooms, and in the fields. Priests also used vernacular tales in their sermons to reach the peasantry. Literate merchants and travelers transmitted these tales to people of all classes in inns and taverns. Storytelling was popular at royal courts. All kinds of tales were told to children of the upper class by servants and governesses. They were remembered and passed on in different forms and versions by all members of society and told to suit particular occasions—*as talk*. Gradually, however, this talk became elevated, cultivated, and, by the seventeenth century, considered acceptable in Italian and French salons. By 1696, printed fairy tales were in vogue: the literary fairy tale had come into its own.

Though it is impossible to fix a date for the rise of the literary fairy tale in France and the exact reasons d'Aulnoy was attracted to this genre, it originated in the conversation and games developed by highly educated aristocratic women in the salons of Paris, beginning around 1610 and remaining popular through the beginning of the eighteenth century. Deprived of access to schools and universities, French aristocratic women organized gatherings in their homes to which they invited other women and men to discuss art, literature, and other topics important to them, such as love, marriage, and freedom. These women, called *précieuses*, tried to develop a manner of thinking, speaking, and writing to reveal and celebrate their innate talents and to distinguish them from the vulgar elements of society. Most important was their emphasis on wit and invention in conversation. The women who frequented the salons constantly sought innovative ways to express their needs and to embellish the forms and style of speech and communication they shared. The folk tales they had heard as children became a source of amusement and served as models for the occasional lyric and the serial novel. Speakers in the salons endeavored to portray ideal situations in the most effective oratory style, which set the standards for the *conte de fées*, or what we now call the literary fairy tale.

By the 1690s, the "salon" fairy tale became so acceptable that women and men began writing down their tales for publication. Most of the notable writers of the fairy tale learned to develop this literary genre by going to the salons or homes of women who wanted to foster intellectual conversation. D'Aulnoy based her stories on the oral tales she had heard as a young girl or read in Giovan Francesco Straparola's Italian collection, *The Pleasant Nights* (1550–53). She might also have known Giambattista Basile's *The Tale of Tales* (1634–36) and other French and Spanish literary works that circulated in the salons.

The transformation of the oral folk tale into a literary fairy tale was not superficial or decorative, however. The aesthetics that the aristocratic women developed in their conversational games and in their written tales varied in style and content, but these tales were all anti-classical and written in opposition to the literary establishment that championed Greek and Roman literature as models for contemporary French writers to follow. Instead, early French fairy-tale writers used models from French folklore and the medieval courtly tradition. In addition, since the majority of the writers and tellers of fairy tales were women, these tales displayed a certain resistance toward male rational precepts and patriarchal realms by conceiving pagan worlds in which extraordinarily majestic and powerful female fairies had the final say.

Until the publication of *Les Contes des fées*, no French author had used the term *conte de fées*, which is key for understanding the unique quality and appeal of d'Aulnoy's tales. Translated literally into English, the term means "tale about fairies" or "tale of the fairies." In other words, the fairies were to become the central figures or protagonists of magical tales, replacing the gods and goddesses of Greco-Roman myths. Moreover, d'Aulnoy never refers to religious principles of the Judeo-Christian tradition. Her tales are entirely secular, and the destinies of aristocratic heroes and heroines are determined by the fairies, who uphold the moral principles of the French civilizing process. These somewhat arbitrary principles of the civilizing process are generally summarized in quaint moral poems at the end of each tale. They are the laws of the fairies, and woe to anyone who defies them, even though d'Aulnoy and her friends could not enforce them in reality.

D'Aulnoy and many other gifted women authors of fairy tales, such as Marie-Jeanne L'Héritier de Villandon, Catherine Bernard, Charlotte Rose de Caumont de la Force, Henriette-Julie de Castelnau, Comtesse de Murat, and Mlle de Lubert, developed fairy tales that pronounced their social views of civility. The aristocratic writers often used the term *fée* among themselves and created an atmosphere in the salons in which they could freely exchange ideas that challenged the hypocrisy and immorality of Louis XIV's court. Of course, they did not direct all their criticisms at the court, but it was clear that their strange metaphorical language and codes, filled with hyperbole and euphemisms, were intended to create utopian narratives in opposition to the status quo.

Of all the women writers, d'Aulnoy was the most critical and judgmental. For example, "Finette Cendron" and "Belle-Belle, or the Chevalier Fortuné" reveal how conspiracies and corruption ran rampant at royal courts, and how courageous young women with integrity could withstand abuse and betrayal to become queens in their own right. D'Aulnoy was fond of transforming traditional folk tales into long, sophisticated literary tales intended for upper-class readers. In "Finette Cendron," for example, which could be translated as "Clever Cinderella," she begins by alluding to the abandonment motif of "Hansel and Gretel" and then also includes her own version of "Cinderella." The dissolute villains are Finette's parents, who lose their kingdom because of their decadent characters. Concerned only about their own fate, they abandon Finette and her sisters in the woods. In addition, her malicious sisters constantly betray her, and ogres threaten to kill the three princesses. All are greedy and treacherous, but they are not punished in the end, because Finette, encouraged by her fairy godmother, believes that a magnanimous soul gains more vengeance through generosity than through punishment.

This is not the case in "Belle-Belle," in which a cross-dressing and multitalented young countess, six extraordinary peasant types, and a talking horse add a great deal of humor to a tale about another king who loses his kingdom to a brutal emperor. Once again, the source for this fairy tale is a folk tale about "How Six Made Their Way through the World," in which a soldier and his lower-class compatriots gain vengeance on an unjust king through magic and force. In d'Aulnoy's tale, however, the major conflicts are fought by aristocrats. Instead of punishing an incompetent king, who is always described as the most handsome and charming in the world, d'Aulnoy decides to make the king's sister and Floride, her lady-in-waiting, the evil characters. Both are in love with Fortuné, whom they think is a young man. Blessed by a fairy and her extraordinary companions, Fortuné accomplishes numerous difficult tasks to assist the king, whom she loves, and she becomes even more desirable in the eyes of the king's sister, the dowager queen, and Floride. When they are rejected by Fortuné, because she is in love with the king, they plot her murder. When their plan fails after Fortuné is exposed as a young woman, Floride poisons the queen and then commits suicide. Here we have vipers at the center of the king's court, and an incompetent king whose kingdom is restored to him by an androgynous heroine.

D'Aulnoy showed no mercy when displaying the negative side of the so-called nobles and gallants of the aristocracy. In "The Blue Bird," for instance, the poor King Charmant is punished brutally by the vicious queen/mother-in-law because he refuses to wed her ugly and slovenly daughter, Truitonne ("trout"), and seeks instead to marry Florine, the queen's stepdaughter. The malicious stepmother asks the evil fairy Soussio to transform Charmant into a blue bird and has Florine imprisoned in a tower. Using her characteristic hyperbole and melodrama, d'Aulnoy brings Florine and Charmant together as the princess desperately contemplates suicide:

> The blue bird listened attentively, and the more he did, the more convinced he became that it was his charming princess who was doing the lamenting.
>
> "Adorable Florine," he cried, "wonder of our days, why do you desire to terminate your life so hastily? Your misfortunes can still be remedied."
>
> "Ah! Who's that speaking in such a consoling way?" she asked.
>
> "An unfortunate king," replied the bird, "who loves you and will never love any other than you:"
>
> "A king who loves me!" replied Florine. "Is this a trap set for me by my enemy? But what would she gain by it? If she seeks to discover my sentiments, I'm ready frankly to own up to them."
>
> "No, my princess," replied the bird. "The lover who's speaking to you is incapable of betraying you"—and as he uttered these words he flew to the window.
>
> At first, Florine was alarmed at the appearance of such an extraordinary bird, who spoke with as much sense as a man and yet had the small, sweet voice of a nightingale. The beauty of his plumage, however, and the words he uttered soon reassured her.
>
> "May I be permitted once more to behold you, my princess?" he exclaimed. "Can I taste such perfect happiness and not die with joy? But, alas, how this happiness is troubled by your captivity, and the condition that the wicked Soussio has reduced me to for seven years."
>
> "And who are you, charming bird?" the princess inquired, caressing him.
>
> "You've pronounced my name," said the king, "and you pretend you do not know me?"
>
> "What? The greatest monarch in the world, King Charmant?" cried the princess. "Can the little bird I hold in my hand be you?"
>
> "Alas, beautiful Florine, it is but too true," the bird replied. "And if anything can console me, it's the feeling that I chose this pain instead of renouncing my love for you."

This is a high comic scene, and yet it signifies how much emphasis d'Aulnoy placed on tender love and faithfulness just as the scene, in which Charmant is trapped and wounded by swords, knives, razors and daggers, reveals d'Aulnoy's fondness for sadistically testing the integrity of her heroes and heroines. Many of her tales involve the metamorphosis of her protagonists into animals, and here the influence of Apuleius's second-century story "Cupid and Psyche" in *The Golden Ass*, in which a prince is turned into a donkey for insulting Isis, plays a major role in d'Aulnoy's works, as do the beast/bridegroom variants widespread in Europe.

The plot of this popular tale type generally begins with a childless royal couple, desperate to have a child even if it is an animal. Consequently, the queen gives birth to a hideous beast (pig, donkey, boar, serpent, hedgehog) who demands to marry a young woman when he grows up. Once the beast weds a young woman, she is put to all sorts of tests to prove that she is worthy of him, for he is a handsome prince at night and a ferocious beast during the day. She has no idea what he actually looks like because they sleep together in the dark. His bride must swear to keep his secret but succumbs to the questioning of her curious sisters and/or mother and divulges it. They encourage her to see what he looks like. Then she either burns his animal skin or drops wax from a candle on him as she tries to see him. The beast/bridegroom is enraged because he must continue to live a dual existence as animal and man, and flees. To prove her love for him, his "true" wife must travel the world for three or seven years to win him back.

The French writers played a significant role in popularizing this tale type, especially Mme d'Aulnoy, who was evidently familiar with different versions of beast/bridegroom folk tales and reworked the "Psyche and Cupid" story in several fairy tales: "The Ram," "The Beneficent Frog," "The Green Serpent," "Gracieuse and Percinet," and "Prince Lutin." The two most important versions are "The Ram" and "The Green Serpent," and it is worthwhile to examine some of the basic changes in the motifs and plot that break radically from the male tradition of "Psyche and Cupid." D'Aulnoy, after all, prepared the way for the standard literary version of "Beauty and the Beast," written by Mme Le Prince de Beaumont in the eighteenth century. D'Aulnoy wanted to make the fairy tale part of the living practice of the aristocratic salon, and her tales were elaborated in the parlor games that she and her contemporaries (mainly other women) played before they were composed. In the conscious composition of the tales, she clearly intended to present a woman's viewpoint on such topics as tender love, fidelity, courtship, honor, and arranged marriages. She contributed to a discourse on manners that she shared with an intimate group of people whom she hoped would embrace her ideas.

Mme d'Aulnoy was by no means a rebel, but she was definitely an outspoken critic of what we would now call patriarchal values. As a member of the aristocratic class who had experienced the benefits of changes in education and social roles for upper-class women, d'Aulnoy's tales placed women in greater control of their destinies than they were granted in fairy tales by men. It is obvious that the narrative strategies of her tales, like those she told or learned in the salon, were meant to expose decadent practices and behavior among the people of her class, particularly those who degraded independent women.

"The Ram" and "The Green Serpent" are d'Aulnoy's two most interesting commentaries on the manners a young woman should cultivate in determining her own destiny. The power in all her tales is held by fairies, wise or wicked female figures who ultimately judge whether a young woman deserves to be rewarded. In "The Ram," the heroine is punished by a relentless fairy. Based on the King Lear motif, this tale has Merveilleuse, the youngest daughter of a king, compelled to flee the court because her father believes mistakenly that she has insulted him. She eventually encounters a prince who has been transformed into a ram by a wicked fairy: she is gradually charmed by his courteous manners and decides to wait five years, until his enchantment is over, to marry him. She misses her father and two sisters, however, and through the ram's kind intervention, she is able to visit them twice. The second time, she forgets about returning to the ram, who dies because of her neglect.

In "The Green Serpent," the heroine Laidronette acts differently. She runs away from home because she is ashamed of her ugliness. Upon encountering a prince, who, as usual, has been transformed into a monstrous creature, in this case a serpent, by a wicked fairy, she is at first horrified. Gradually, after spending some time in his kingdom of the pagods, exquisite little people who attend to her every wish, she promises to marry him in two years, when his bewitchment will end, but she cannot see him until then. Even though she reads the story of "Psyche and Cupid," however, she breaks her promise and gazes upon him. This enables the wicked fairy Magotine to punish her, and only after Laidronette performs three near-impossible tasks, helped by the fairy Protectrice, is she able to transform herself into the beautiful Princess Discrète, and the green serpent back into a handsome prince. Their love for each other persuades the wicked fairy Magotine to mend her ways and reward them with the kingdom of Pagodia.

The issue at hand in both fairy tales is fidelity and sincerity, or the qualities that make for tenderness, a topic of interest to women of the time. The focus of the stories is on the two princesses, who break their promises and learn that they will cause havoc and destruction if they do not keep their word. On the other hand, the men have been punished because they refused to marry old and ugly fairies and seek a more natural love. In other words, d'Aulnoy sets conditions for both men and women that demand sincerity of feeling and constancy, if they are to achieve true love. Nothing short of obedience to the rule of "fairy" civility will be tolerated in d'Aulnoy's tales.

Of all her tales, "The White Cat" is perhaps d'Aulnoy's greatest declaration of respect for the aristocratic woman and also female autonomy that challenges the power of the fairies and retains "fairy" utopianism. Combining two well-known oral tale types of "The Frog Princess" and "Rapunzel," d'Aulnoy recalls the idyllic setting of the "Island of Happiness" when she transports the youngest prince, in search of a little dog for his father, to the white cat's realm. Her castle is the most magnificent castle ever seen. The gate to the castle is made of gold covered with carbuncles, and he is pushed onward by invisible hands and voices that sing:

Be not offended by the hands you see.
Have no fear in this beautiful place.
There's nothing here except a lovely face,
Nothing at all that your heart might flee.

The young prince is dazzled by the white cat, who has astonishing powers and great dignity. He falls deeper in love with the white cat each time he encounters her, and actually wants to stay in her kingdom, unlike Adolph in "The Island of Happiness." In short, he is willing to wed an animal just as the princesses in d'Aulnoy's tales are ready to marry beasts. (Ironically, the beasts generally have better manners and tenderness than "real" people do.) The white cat has her own tale to tell before she agrees to marry the prince, however, and we learn about her mother's betrayal of the fairies when she, as princess, fell in love with a king who climbed the tower in which she was imprisoned after rejecting the terrible dwarf whom the fairies had chosen for her husband. In her hyperbolic manner, d'Aulnoy has the fairies order the king to be devoured by a ruthless dragon in front of the princess's eyes. Then they change the princess into a cat, who must remain this way until she finds someone who resembles the king she had once loved. In the comic ending, the young prince must cut off the white cat's head and tail so that she can become a ravishing queen who is so rich, powerful, and generous that she divides the six kingdoms that she rules among the young prince's father and two brothers.

Magical transformation and magical justice are never explained in d'Aulnoy's tales. The exaggeration of the imagination for just causes is celebrated. Moreover, the hyperbolic and euphemistic style of d'Aulnoy's language is intended to stun and surprise readers. Though originally designed for aristocratic and bourgeois readers, d'Aulnoy's tales have had a stronger and wider appeal than she anticipated because her incredible stories demonstrated how social and political conditions could change, especially if the fairies roamed and ruled the universe. In short, d'Aulnoy imbued her fairy civilizing process with a strong dose of compassion, tenderness, and ethics, and perhaps the moral of all her fairy tales comes down to one blunt statement: Don't mess with the fairies!

Jack Zipes

Bibliography

Madame d'Aulnoy

Relation du Voyage d'Espagne. Ed. R. Foulché-Delbosc. Paris: Librairies C. Klincksieck, 1926.

Travels into Spain. Ed. R. Foulché-Delbosc. London: Geourge Routledge & Sons, 1930.

Contes. 2 vols. Ed. Philippe Hourcade. Paris: Société des Textes Français Modernes, 1997.

Secondary Literature

Dewald, Jonathan. *Aristocratic Experience and the Origins of Modern Culture: France, 1570–1715*. Berkeley: University of California Press, 1993.

Duggan, Anne. "Feminine Genealogy, Matriarch, and Utopia in the Fairy Tales of Marie-Catherine d'Aulnoy." *Neophilologus* 82 (1998): 199–208.

———. *Salonnières, Furies, and Fairies: The Politics of Gender and Cultural Change in Absolutist France*. Newark: University of Delaware Press, 2005.

Farrell, Michèle. "Celebration and Repression of Feminine Desire in Mme d'Aulnoy's Fairy Tale: *La chatte blanche*." *L'Espirit Créateur* 29.3 (Fall, 1989): 52–64.

Hannon, Patricia. "Feminine Voice and the Motivated Text: Madame d'Aulnoy and the Chevalier de Mailly." *Marvels & Tales* 2.1 (1988): 13–124.

———. *Fabulous Identities: Women's Fairy Tales in Seventeenth-Century France*. Amsterdam/Atlanta: Rodopi, 1998.

Lau, Kimberly. "Imperial Marvels: Race and the Colonial Imagination in the Fairy Tales of Madame d'Aulnoy." *Narrative Culture* 3.2 (Fall 2016): 141–179.

McLeod, Glenda. "Madame d'Aulnoy: Writer of Fantasy." *Women Writers of the Seventeenth Century*. Ed. Katharina Wilson and Frank Warnke. Athens: University of Georgia Press, 1989. 91–118.

Palmer, Melvin. "Madame d'Aulnoy's Pseudo-Autobiographical Works on Spain." *Romanische Forschungen* 83.2/3 (1971): 220–229.

———. "Madame d'Aulnoy in England." *Comparative Literature*. 27.3 (1975): 235–253.

Seifert, Lewis. *Fairy Tales, Sexuality, and Gender in France, 1690-1715: Nostalgic Utopias*. Cambridge: Cambridge University Press, 1996.

———. "Animal-Human Hybridity in d'Aulnoy's 'Babiole' and 'Prince Wild Boar.'" *Marvels and Tales* 25.2 (2011): 244–260.

Seifert, Lewis and Domna Stanton, eds. *Enchanted Eloquence: Fairy Tales by Seventeenth-Century French Women Writers*. Toronto: Iter, 2010.

Stanton, Domna. "The Fiction of Précosité and the Fear of Women." *Yale French Studies* 62 (1981): 107–134.

Tucker, Holly. *Pregnant Fictions: Childbirth and the Fairy Tale in Early Modern France*. Detroit: Wayne State University Press, 2003.

Warner, Marina. *From the Beast to the Blonde: On Fairy Tales and Their Tellers*. New York: Farrar, Straus and Giroux, 1995.

Zipes, Jack, ed. *Beauties, Beasts, and Enchantment: Classic French Fairy Tales*. New York: NAL Books, 1989.

———, ed. *The Great Fairy Tale Tradition: From Straparola and Basile to the Brothers Grimm*. New York: Norton, 2001.

A Note on the Translation

With the exception of "The Tale of Mira," all the translations of Mme d'Aulnoy's tales originally appeared in my book *Beauties, Beasts, and Enchantment: Classic French Fairy Tales* (1989), in which I used James Planché's somewhat anachronistic translation, *Countess D'Aulnoy's Fairy Tales* (1885), as the basis for my work. Though I believed Planché's work to be dated, his renditions contained a certain idiomatic style that captured the highly mannered style of Mme d'Aulnoy. Moreover, as an expert in clothes, customs, and architecture, Planché provided accurate descriptions of the garments, buildings, and manners of late seventeenth-century France.

Consequently, his translations provided an excellent reference point for my work as I honed and tightened the tales. One of my major challenges involved translating the verse morals that appear at the end of d'Aulnoy's tales. In most cases, I sacrificed meter and style to meaning and tempered the lavish tone. In this book, I have carefully revised all the tales and corrected minor errors.

Since I first translated d'Aulnoy's tales, Professor Volker Schröder of Princeton University has uncovered important documents about Mme d'Aulnoy's life in *Anecdota*, an online source for rare texts and images. I have used his invaluable work to correct certain facts about d'Aulnoy's life. In addition, I wish to thank the two anonymous reviewers of my text for their suggestions and corrections in both the introduction and translations.

Jack Zipes

Drawing Mme d'Aulnoy

I came to the world of Madame d'Aulnoy because I wanted to draw tales that I read as unequivocally feminist. The wily heroines of d'Aulnoy's stories test the limits of acceptable behavior for women and appropriate roles for female characters in fairy tales.

Women in d'Aulnoy's tales are smarter and more vibrant than in those of her contemporaries and more active and unusual than those of her antecedents. They flirt with boundaries and power dynamics between men and women, frequently connected to the relationship between animals/gods and humans. Love and power, intertwined, enable women to seduce, triumph, change form, and tell their own stories. They undertake active pursuits: saving kingdoms, embarking on journeys, speaking their minds. They also fall prey to human complexities: hubris, jealousy, disgust, and vengeance. They test physical and emotional frontiers in their journeys and conflicts. A suitor's arrogance destroys happiness; kindness and cunning, combined with perseverance, triumphs; jealousy poisons families and separates lovers. Frequently, women activate their lovers' metamorphoses from animals to humans, and humans to animals. Women's virtue often is rewarded, and conversely, men's vice often is punished. In traversing class lines and in interspecies love, d'Aulnoy uses the humor of cross-dressing and animal-smitten women to overturn then-conventional ideas of femininity. D'Aulnoy engages her female characters in many types of performance: they perform as animals, as women, as men, as fairies, as nature, and as stepsisters, lovers, wives, daughters, and mothers. They possess self-knowledge, and this ownership is tantamount to power.

Depicting the stories of d'Aulnoy, in drawing and painting with gouache and chalk pastel, is the culmination of my exploration of fairy tales with my mentor and collaborator, Jack Zipes. I first worked with fairy tales in *Tales of the Brothers Grimm. Drawings by Natalie Frank* (Damiani, 2015). Though these tales are the original versions prior to their twentieth-century sanitizing, they are avowedly not feminist. Instead, they are firmly rooted in a nineteenth-century mindset favoring princesses waiting to be wed and little girls punished for veering from the forest path. My drawings for this series imbued a feminist perspective that reimagined these tales. I recast the heroines with more agency and, at times, more threat. Amplifying their attributes made them bolder and more in control of their own stories. My work with Zipes on *The Sorcerer's Apprentice* (Princeton University Press, 2017) deepened my fascination with fairy tales, the role of women in them, and the tales' evolution as memes. Drawing d'Aulnoy's stories was a departure from my previous work. The tales have boldly imagined heroines and a brightened palette that allow my role as artist to be more personal. In d'Aulnoy's work, I see connections with my own twenty-first-century ideas about femininity, sexuality, and power: her themes are timeless and her heroines, daring.

Performance and role-playing are pivotal to the ways in which women challenge power dynamics, engage with transformations that straddle human and magical worlds, and provoke revelations that spur character development. D'Aulnoy creates female characters that play out a full range of women's actions and reactions, striking in their depth and complexity, especially among traditional and current conceptions of what a fairy tale is. Just as d'Aulnoy's female characters develop from pivotal moments—transfiguration, falling in love, despair, shots of courage—my female figures are defined at fulcrums, under physical and emotional duress. Just as her heroines cross between the banal and the spectacular, I also am drawn to times when unexpected change collides with everyday life. In these images, I can capture a figure in motion. I am also captivated by the complex ways that violence and sexuality are performed by and on women's bodies, an undercurrent of these stories.

As author, d'Aulnoy inhabits other bodies, simultaneously acting as voyeur and participant in her characters' stories. I undertake a similar and sensual pursuit: drawing itself is a performance. I bring forth life by squeezing, rubbing, creating, and destroying bodies; casting characters; constructing images; and building scenes. When I draw, I begin with the form, a sketch in a single color, that delineates the movement of the figures, the interplay between them, and the composition as a whole. I enhance the figures and their space, again and again, until a scene emerges, akin to d'Aulnoy's verbal aggregation. My drawings, like her stories, arise out of the layering of drawn and painted passages both representational and surreal. An abundance of animals, magical transformations, fairies, and jewels are her paint; the layering of chalk and gouache are mine. D'Aulnoy's stories read as combinations of painterly scenarios in sequence. As I read them, vivid images come; color sensually floods over me.

I first became aware of my synesthesia, a neurological interconnectedness of words and colors, when I began to read the Grimms' tales. Literature always had elicited images and colors for me, but the Grimms' brought forth complete compositions: drawing became a direct record of images in my head. When I drew d'Aulnoy's tales, which are lengthy, developed narratives with baroque flourishes of writing, her florid prose manifested in evocative color. Her sentences are melodic and bursting with description.

D'Aulnoy's stories are lush with objects that emit movement of pigment and light: jewels, ribbons, sunsets, flowering meadows, dew and rainbows. My associations with words and language are hyper-colored daydreams—ones that I am able to manifest immediately through my own hands. I create movement, bright, sumptuous, and nonsensical juxtapositions of color, teasing the eye with a visual hum. Much of my pleasure in reading comes from this translation of d'Aulnoy's and her characters' performances into my drawing, which feels like the retelling of a secret.

Performance and play, in the magical and natural worlds, unmask larger themes of self-reliance and human vulnerability; these manifest in distinctive ways in my thirty-three drawings. In "Finette Cendron," "Belle-Belle," and "The Blue Bird," I am interested in the heroine's strong sense of self and comfort with vulnerability, which ensure success; conversely, in "The Island of Happiness" and "The Ram," Adolph and Merveilleuse's human weaknesses are their undoing. In drawings with assertive heroines, I focus on scenes in which these women demonstrate their individuality. My Belle-Belle is dressed as a man; her clashing feather vest, vivid cowboy boots, riding pants, and tied-back hair mark her as the antithesis of blasé femininity. In the second drawing, she dances with a male version of herself. Her lower body, bare and feminine, embraces her upper body, clothed and masculine. I focus on the fluidity of her gender and identity. Whatever might belie her gender, I erase or negate. In the subsequent drawing, various superheroes become actual parts of her body, and in the next drawing, she transforms into a new hybrid of king and queen. Last, I draw Belle tied to a stake, her torn-open shirt exposing her breast; her confrontational stare defies both the king and queen. Her image is far from that of a typical fairy-tale heroine. With her pose, I evoke the image of Saint Sebastian, martyr and symbol of steadfast courage and justice. Belle's most potent characteristic is her own vulnerability.

Finette Cendron's success revolves around her constant state of active wakefulness. In the first drawing, she rides, and in the second she lies awake, while one unpleasant sister sleeps and the others stares upward, light in hand, unable to see. I picture Finette looking at the viewer, aware, even in repose. Next, Finette conjures the magic of the acorn tree, leading her stepsisters to the ogre and ogress's kingdom. Her head and patterned dress dominate the space; her less compelling sisters pictorially recede. In the fourth drawing, Finette dangles her foot on the threshold of the page's border, stepping into the viewer's space, testing the boundary of the image. Like the savvy one-eyed ogress who continually outsmarts her husband, Finette outwits her stepsisters. It is Finette who plants the decisive ax blow in the ogress's neck; she becomes even bolder as the story continues. In the final image, Finette assumes the crown of a leopard with a border of spots, royal purple because she is queen. An underdrawing of black gouache reveals her jagged grin. One snaggletooth juts out against her rouged lips; she is both a lady and a stealth huntress, regal in her patience and fidelity to herself.

"The Island of Happiness" juxtaposes the natural and eternal with the human and ephemeral. To begin, I present Felicity with a soft, floral palette. She is at one with the natural world. Her rose-colored dress, garland-laden hair, and pink skin unite her with the beds of flowers among which she stands. I put forward Adolph, a mere mortal, naked, ashamed, and covering his genitals. Uncloaked, he reveals his human frailty. In the joint portrait of Felicity and Adolph, her head transforms from pink and alive to blue and cold: there is an air of death in her eternal life. He is a caricature. I focus on her face and body throughout: I am interested in the devastating effect that mortality and human weakness, despite her eternal youth and beauty, will have on her body and spirit. In the final drawing, she lies on a yellow ground with black staccato lines. The ground is barren, despite its lushness, and the hand of time, purple and greedy, reaches over her. A black entryway into a mausoleum beckons the viewer. Her fate of eternal confinement after experiencing flawed, human love, represented by harsh vertical and horizontal lines, is the true prison.

In drawing "The Green Serpent" and "The White Cat," which show the fatal cost of curiosity and greed, even if love and fealty triumph in the end, I explore the violence that often accompanies a fairy-tale ending. I picture the cat with her retinue in the court hall and also as a huntress with her suitor diminutive on his hobby horse. The cat's final transformation is captivating in its goriness. I replicate the fragmentation of her body through a mélange of body parts, human and feline, with mismatched features of size and exaggeration. In the final drawing, she springs out of her own body with a cat's ferocity, heightened by the black space and her frenetic, chalk outline. In these drawings I try to capture what it looks and feels like to be trapped in a body, human or animal. I appreciate the ways that d'Aulnoy's characters exhibit gender and physical fluidity and the way they embrace the grotesquerie and beauty in physical and emotional transformations. I use a lurid palette, bodily fragmentation, and collaged images to present multiple versions of an individual at once.

My favorite tale, "The Tale of Mira," is the most unequivocally feminist of all of the tales of d'Aulnoy. Mira is a beautiful woman who murders men with her eyes—a feminist ghost story for the ages. She is, in turn, killed by her own unrequited desire of the strapping shepherd. Laced with dark comicality, the story engages clichéd depictions of conventional femininity in the fairy-tale genre. Mira's striking beauty is lethal because it is not passive. Absurdist humor also defines the treatment of the objectified shepherd, who becomes a heroine of sorts. Men rarely are trivialized as mere love objects, but unlike Mira, the shepherd seems to have no qualms about his objectification. Mira is tortured by her toxic effect on men; her male equivalent does not possess this depth of feeling. A traditional fairy tale warns of the dangers of unrequited love; this one warns of the violence that occurs out of unreciprocated lust, poking fun at the seriousness of a tragic fairy-tale story.

I render Mira's full lips and clownish nose to accentuate the macabre: her feminine beauty is weaponized. Her eyes glow pale cerulean, the color of the splitting sky, which she controls. She is possessed, and her giant arms block the landscape, an armature for the cascading men who disintegrate into fractured eyes and limbs, murdered by her beauty. Her body is swollen and her stomach, elbows, and hands push against the edges of the drawing.

She asserts her powerful presence through her towering form. All of the characters in this tale are undone by either the physical allure or disdain for the body. In death, Mira is fortunate to exist, formless, as a ghost.

D'Aulnoy turns this short tale into a farce. The narrator steps outside the fairy-tale narrative gone awry and breaks the fourth wall with an ode to her own hunger. The fairy tale is thus thwarted twice: once by Mira's dangerous beauty, and again by the narrator, abandoning the romanticism of the tale to attend to her own needs. I repeat Mira's image, once in light and again in darkness, to echo this break in narrative continuity. As much as the soft pinks, blues, and cascading blond hair frame Mira as a fairy-tale heroine, her corporality, rendered twice, in fleshy strokes of pastel and modeled gouache, exaggerate what it feels like to be human, cursed to experience the indignities of a physical body.

The fairy tale also turns a sharp lens onto itself. As much as d'Aulnoy personifies animals and nature in her tales, here she endows the form of the tale itself with self-awareness—the most notable characteristic of her fiercest heroines. This is a story of femininity with which I identify.

Natalie Frank

Fairy Tales

The Island of Happiness

RUSSIA is a frigid country where one rarely sees the beautiful days of a mild climate. Its mountains are usually covered with snow, and the trees are so loaded with icicles that when the sun casts its rays on them, they appear to be garnished with crystals. There are forests of enormous grandeur where white bears wreak terrible havoc, and the people are continually warring with them. Although they manage to kill the bears, it is not without difficulty and danger. Thus, in Russia, hunting bears is considered both the most noble and most ordinary occupation.

Once upon a time, a young prince named Adolph governed the Russians. Born under a lucky star, he was so handsome, polite, and intelligent that it would have been difficult to convince anyone that a person so accomplished lived in a country so coarse and savage. He had not yet turned twenty when he undertook a great war against the Muscovites and showed dauntless courage and remarkable leadership. When he allowed his army to rest, he himself did not rest. Instead, he went on that dangerous quest for bears.

One day, when he was carried away once again by his noble passion for hunting, he led a large retinue into a vast forest. He roved all over until he finally got lost. Just as he realized that he was alone, that it was late, and that he no longer knew where he was, a storm took him by surprise. He guided his horse down a wide track and vainly blew his hunting horn in order to alert some of his hunters. All at

once, the scant daylight that was left was transformed into the most obscure night, punctuated only by lightning. The thunder made a terrible noise as the rainstorm increased. The prince at first took shelter under some trees, but he was soon compelled to leave that spot. The rain continued to fall in torrents, and the paths were flooded. Deciding to get free of the forest and to seek some shelter from the tempest, he struggled with difficulty to reach open fields, where he found himself even more exposed to the inclement weather. He looked all around him and noticed a light in a spot that was very high up.

So, he headed in that direction, arduously climbing by foot and leading his horse to the top of an almost inaccessible mountain. His way was obstructed by a multitude of boulders and sheer cliffs. For several hours, he pressed on, sometimes on foot, sometimes on horseback, until he found himself nearing a cave. Through the opening, he saw the light that he had already observed. He hesitated before entering, for he thought it might be the hideout of some robbers who frequently ravaged the countryside and who could rob and kill him. However, since the souls of princes possess a nobility and pride that sets them apart from other men, he reproached himself for his fear. Into the cave he advanced, hand on sword, ready to defend himself in case someone was bold enough to attack him.

Because of the noise he made when he entered, an old woman, whose white hair and mass of wrinkles revealed how ancient she was, emerged from the rear of the cave. As she approached him, she was visibly astonished.

"You're the first mortal I've ever seen here," she said. "Do you know, sir, who dwells here?"

"No, my good woman," Adolph responded. "I have no idea where I am."

"This is the abode of Eole, god of the

winds," she stated. "This is where he retires with all his children. I'm their mother, and you've found me alone because they are all busy, each one doing good or evil in the world as is his wont. But you seem drenched from the rain that has just fallen. Let me make a fire so you can dry yourself. I'm afraid, though, that I cannot offer you much here. The meals that the winds have are very light, and men need to eat something much more solid."

The prince thanked her for the kind welcome and approached the fire, which leapt into flames almost immediately because the West Wind had just entered and blown on it. No sooner had he arrived than the Northeast Wind and many northerly gales returned to the cave. Eole was not tardy, and Boreas, the East, Southwest, and North Winds followed. They were all damp and had puffed cheeks and unkempt heads of hair. Their manners were not very civil or polite, and when they ventured to speak to the prince, they all but froze him with their breath. One recounted that he had dispersed an entire navy. Another recalled that he had caused many ships to perish. A third had kindly saved certain vessels from pirates who had wanted to seize them. Many of the gales reported how they had uprooted trees, knocked down houses, and overturned walls. In short, each one boasted of his exploits. After listening to all of them, the old woman suddenly showed signs of great uneasiness.

"Did any of you encounter your brother Zephir during your adventures?" she asked. "He's already late, and I confess I'm worried that he's not going to return."

While all echoed that they had not seen him, Adolph noticed a young boy at the entrance of the cave. He was just as handsome as Cupid. Indeed, he had wings made of white feathers mixed with the color of flesh that appeared to be fine and delicate and in perpetual motion. His blond hair fell carelessly in a thousand curls to his

shoulders. Roses and jasmine crowned his head, and he had a pleasant, jovial air about him.

"Where have you come from, you little rake?" the old woman cried huskily. "All your brothers are here. You're the only one who takes his time and who doesn't care at all about how much I might worry."

"Mother, I had no intention of returning so late." he said, "I know that you don't like it. However, I was in the gardens of Princess Felicity. She was taking a walk there with her nymphs. One made a garland of flowers for her. Another nymph, who was lying on the grass, opened her mouth a little, and this gave me the freedom to approach her and give her a kiss. Several were dancing to songs. The beautiful princess was in an orange orchard, and my breath swept up to her mouth. I dallied around her and played gently with her veil. 'Zephir,' she said, 'I like that! You make everything so pleasant! I'm going to keep walking as long as you tarry.' ... I must confess that such sweet words uttered by such a charming person captivated me, and I was no longer my own master. I would not have been able to leave her at all if I had not known how this would displease you."

Adolph listened with such great satisfaction that he felt sorry when Zephir fell silent. "Permit me, charming Zephir, to ask you where the country is that the princess reigns?" he said.

"It is the Island of Happiness," responded Zephir. "Nobody, sir, can enter it. People have exhausted themselves in trying to find it, but their fate is such that they do not know how to find it. They have traveled all over in vain. Sometimes they even imagine that they have found it because they often arrive at other small ports possessing calm and tranquility. Many people remain there happily, but these floating islands are quite mediocre compared with the Island of Happiness. People soon lose sight of them, and only desire, which allows mortals to hope for just a shadow of repose, keeps them searching. Every day I see distinguished men perish nearby."

The prince continued to ply him with questions, which Zephir answered with great precision and intelligence. It was extremely late, and the good mother ordered all her children to go to their corners of the cave. Zephir offered the prince a bed in a spotless place less cold than the other caverns of this grotto. A small spot of fine grass grew there, covered with flowers, and Adolph threw himself down on it. The rest of the night he spent with Zephir, talking about the Princess Felicity.

"How I'd love to see her!" he said. "Is it so absolutely impossible? Couldn't I succeed with your help?"

Zephir told him that such a venture would be very dangerous, but that if he had the courage to abandon himself to

Zephir's guidance, he imagined there might be a way; he would put him on his wings and carry him through the vast ethereal regions. "I have a cloak that I can give you," he continued, "and when you put it on with the green side showing, you'll be invisible. No one will be able to perceive you, and this is absolutely vital for your protection because, if the guards of the island, who are terrible monsters, see you, they'll capture you, no matter how brave you may be."

Adolph had such an urgent desire to begin this great adventure that he accepted everything Zephir proposed with all his heart, no matter what danger he faced. No sooner did the sun begin to shine in its chariot of mother-of-pearls than the impatient Adolph woke a still dozing Zephir.

"I've given you hardly any time to rest," the prince said as he embraced him, "but it seems to me, my kind host, that it's already time to depart."

"Let's go, then," Zephir responded. "Far be it from me to complain. Let me thank you instead, for I must confess that I'm in love with a proud and pert rose, and I'd be in a good deal of trouble with her if I weren't there to see her as soon as it turns daylight. She is in one of Princess Felicity's flower beds."

So saying, he gave the prince the cloak that he had promised him. He wanted to carry him on his wings, but he did not find this way comfortable.

"Sir, I'm going to lift you," he said, "just as I lifted Psyche on Cupid's orders when I carried her to the beautiful palace that he had built for her."

So he took the prince in his arms, and after positioning himself at the edge of a cliff, he rocked for some time in a steady motion until he spread his wings, took off, and began soaring through the air.

Although the prince was courageous, he could not help being afraid when he found himself aloft in the arms of a young

adolescent. To reassure himself, he recalled that Zephir was a god and that Cupid him self, who seemed the smallest and weakest of all the gods, was the strongest and most awesome. Thus, abandoning himself to his destiny, he collected his wits and gazed attentively at all the places they flew over. But how was it possible to count the places? There were so many cities, kingdoms, seas, rivers, fields, deserts, woods, unknown territories, and diverse peoples! All these sights transported him into such a state of wonderment that he was unable to speak. Zephir told him about the names and customs of all those inhabitants of the earth. He flew gently, and they even took a rest on top of the formidable Caucasian Mountains, on Mount Athos, and on many

others that they found along their way.

"Even though the beautiful rose whom I adore," Zephir said, "will sting me with her thorns, I can't cross such vastness without giving you the pleasure of admiring these wonders for the first time."

Adolph expressed his gratitude for Zephir's kindness and, at the same time, his concern that Princess Felicity would be unable to understand his language and he unable to speak hers.

"Don't fret over that," the god said. "The princess's knowledge is universal, and I'm convinced that you'll speak the same language soon enough."

He flew until that desired island was in sight, and the prince was so struck by all its beauties that he readily believed that it was indeed enchanted. The air was thoroughly perfumed with dew from the excellent waters of Nafre and Cordoue. The rain carried the scent of oranges. The water gushed up to the clouds. Rare trees filled the forests, and the ground was covered with extraordinary flowers. Streams as clear as crystal flowed all over with a sweet murmur. The birds sang concerts that were superior to the music of the great masters. Exotic fruit grew there naturally, and throughout the island one could find tables covered with all the delicacies that one could desire.

However, the palace surpassed even all the rest: the walls were made of diamonds, and the ceilings and floors were made of precious gems that formed compartments. Gold glittered everywhere. The hands of the most gallant fairies made the furniture. Everything seemed so natural that one could not help but admire the magnificence and assortment all the more. After Zephir set the prince down in a pleasant green lawn, he said, "Sir, I've kept my word, and now it's up to you to do the rest."

They embraced each other, and Adolph gave him thanks befitting such a favor. Since the god was eager to see his mistress, he left him in those delightful gardens. Venturing down several alleys, Adolph saw grottos made expressly for pleasure. In one, he noticed a white marble statue of Cupid so well made that it must have been the work of some divine sculptor. Instead of flames, a jet of water spurted from its torch, and the god was supported by grotto-work and seemed to be reading verses engraved on lapis lazuli. These proclaimed: "Love is the greatest of all blessings. Love alone is able to fulfill our desires. All other sweet things of life become dull if they are not mixed with love's attractive charms."

Adolph entered a honeysuckle arbor, where the sun could not penetrate the charming shade. Here, he lay on a carpet of grass surrounding a fountain, and he yielded to the sweetness of slumber, for his heavy eyelids and exhausted limbs begged for a few hours of rest.

It was close to noon when he awoke. He was disappointed to have lost so much time, and to make up for it, he rushed toward the palace. As soon as he got near enough to it, he began to admire its beautiful features at a more leisurely pace than when he had been farther away. It seemed to him that all the arts had competed with equal success to contribute to the magnificence and perfection of the building. He could view everything without being seen because he continued to wear the cloak on the green side. The prince searched for a

long time to find a way to enter the palace, but either the vestibule was closed or the doors of the palace were on the other side of the palace, for he saw no way to enter until he noticed a pretty young nymph opening a window made entirely of crystal. At the very same moment, a dwarfish gardener ran to the spot, and the nymph let down a large gold filigree basket that had many ribbons and bows attached. Then, she ordered the gardener to gather flowers for the princess, and the gardener promptly did as she was told. Consequently, Adolph threw himself on the flowers in the basket before the nymph had pulled it up to the window. (It should be noted that the green cloak that made him invisible also made him as light as the wind.)

As soon as he was inside, he entered a large salon, where he saw wonders that are difficult to recount. The nymphs were there in large numbers. The oldest among them seemed no more than eighteen, and a great many seemed to be younger. Some were blondes; others, brunettes, and all had remarkable white, fresh complexions with beautiful features and regular teeth. In short, the nymphs could pass for the most perfect people imaginable. Adolph could have stayed in the salon all day admiring them if his curiosity had not been aroused by numerous voices marvelously harmonizing with some exceedingly well-played instruments. He advanced toward the chamber from which this pleasant harmony came, and as he entered, he heard the most touching words sung in a manner equally tender.

When first the prince had entered the salon, he had thought that nothing could equal the charms he saw there. However, he was wrong, for the musicians surpassed their beauty by far. Due to some miracle, he understood everything they said even though he did not know the language they used in this palace. He was standing behind one of the prettiest nymphs when her veil slipped to the ground. Without realizing that he would undoubtedly frighten her, he picked up the veil and gave it to her. Since the nymph did not see a soul, she uttered a great cry, and perhaps for the first time, someone had become afraid in that beautiful place. All her companions gathered around her, asking her urgently what the matter was.

"You're going to think that I've been seeing things," she said, "but I assure you that my veil that just fell to the ground was returned to my hand by some invisible force."

Everyone burst into laughter, and several nymphs pranced toward the princess's chamber to amuse her with this story. Adolph followed. Thanks to the green cloak, he crossed invisibly through the rooms, galleries, and chambers until he finally reached the abode of the princess. She sat on a throne made of a single carbuncle more radiant than the sun, but the eyes of Princess Felicity far outshone the carbuncle. Her beauty was so perfect that she seemed a daughter of the heavens. Moreover, she cast a youthful aura of majestic confidence that aroused love and respect. She was dressed more in a gallant than a magnificent fashion: her blond hair was decorated with flowers and a scarf, and her robe was made of gauze mixed with gold. Around her frolicked many small cupids playing a thousand different games. Some took her hands and kissed them; others climbed her throne with the help of their companions and placed a crown on her head. The pleasures were also playing about her. In brief, everywhere the prince turned his eyes, he was struck by the most charming things imaginable, and he stood there like a man entranced. He could hardly stand the princess's explosive beauty, and he could not think of anything but this person whom he already adored. Indeed, he became so agitated and excited that his green cloak fell to the ground, and he became visible.

The princess had never seen a human being, and so she was extremely surprised. In turn, when Adolph saw that he had exposed himself, he threw himself respectfully at her feet.

"Great princess," he said, "I've crossed the universe to admire your divine beauty. I want to offer you my heart and devotion. I hope you will not refuse me."

The princess, who was normally vivacious, remained silent and confused. Until

then, she had never seen anyone as remarkable as this creature, whom she believed to be unique in the world. This thought convinced her that he was the Phoenix, the rare and vaunted bird. Feeling she was right in her mistake, she said, "Handsome Phoenix—for I can't believe that you are anyone else but Phoenix—since you are so perfect and don't resemble anything on my island, I'm extremely grateful to have the pleasure of seeing you. It's a great shame that you are the only kind of your species. If there were many more birds like you, they would fill beautiful bird cages."

Adolph smiled at her gracious naïveté. He did not want the object of his already great passion to remain mistaken for long because it might lead to misconceptions. Therefore, he took care to tell her everything about himself, and never has a pupil learned her lessons so quickly. In fact, she was ready to give them after just learning them.

Her natural intuition went further than what the prince could tell her. She loved him more than she loved herself, and he loved her more than he loved himself. The two lovers felt everything that love has to offer in sweetness, everything that the mind has to offer in vivacity, and everything that the heart has to offer in delights. Nothing disturbed their repose; everything contributed to their pleasures. They were never sick. They were never troubled by the slightest inconvenience.

Their youthfulness was not changed by the passing of the years, for in this delightful asylum everyone drank long draughts from the Fountain of Youth. Neither the anguishes of love, nor jealous suspicions, not even the petty quarrels that sometimes disturb the happy tranquility of lovers until they make sweet amends, nothing of this kind happened to them. They were intoxicated with pleasure, and up to that time there had never been a mortal who had enjoyed such good luck as constant as that of the prince. However, the condition of mortality carries with it sad consequences. Their good fortune could not last forever.

One day, when Adolph was with the princess, it occurred to him to ask her how long he had been enjoying the pleasure of being with her. "The moments pass so quickly where you are," he continued, "that I haven't paid any attention to time since my arrival."

"I'll tell you," she said, "after you reveal to me how long you think you've been here."

He pondered this and said, "If I consult my heart and the gratification I've experienced, I'd believe that I've only spent a week here. But, my dear princess, according to certain things that I can recall to mind, it's been approximately three months."

"Adolph," she said more seriously, "it's been three hundred years."

Ah, if she had only known what those words would cost her, she would have never uttered them.

"Three hundred years!" cried the prince. "What's going on in the world? Who's

governing it right now? What are the people doing there? When I return, who will recognize me, and whom will I be able to recognize? My dominions have undoubtedly fallen into somebody else's hands rather than those close to me. I cannot dare hope that there's anything left for me. I'm going to be a prince stripped of his robe. People will regard me like a ghost. I'll no longer know the manners and customs that I'll need to live."

Becoming impatient, the princess interrupted him. "What do you regret, Adolph? Isn't this price worth all the love and kindness I've shown you? I received you in my palace where you are the master. I've preserved your life for three centuries. You haven't aged at all and apparently, until now, you haven't been bored. You wouldn't have had any of this if it weren't for me."

"I'm not ungrateful, beautiful princess," he replied, somewhat confused. "I know all that I owe you. But ultimately, if I were dead at this moment, I would have perhaps performed such great deeds that my name would be eternally engraved in stone. As it is, I see with shame that there has been nothing virtuous about my actions, and my name is not famous. The brave Reginald may have ended in the arms of his Armida, but it was honor that tore him away from her."

"You barbarian!" the princess screamed as a flood of tears streamed from her eyes. "It will be honor that tears you away from me. You want to leave me, and you minimize the pain that it will cause me."

Upon saying this, she collapsed in a dead faint. The prince was greatly moved. He dearly loved her, but he reproached himself for having spent so much time with a mistress without having done anything that would place his name among the ranks of heroes. He tried in vain to restrain himself and conceal his misgivings. However, he fell into an apathy that soon rendered him unrecognizable.

Now the prince, who had mistaken centuries for months, mistook months for centuries. The princess saw this and suffered greatly because of it. Not wanting him to remain out of a sense of obligation, she declared, "You are master of your destiny and can depart whenever you wish. All the same, I fear something terrible will happen to you."

Her last words caused him less pain than her first, which were not very pleasing themselves. Although he grew tender and melancholy when he thought about separating, his sense of his destiny was stronger, and at last he said farewell to the woman whom he had adored, and whom he still loved with a great deal of tenderness. He assured her that as soon as he had achieved a measure of glory and made himself more worthy of her magnanimity, he would return and acknowledge her as his sole sovereign and the only treasure of his life. However, the princess was too

intelligent to be misled, and she had sad forebodings that told her she was going to lose the person she would cherish forever.

Despite the fact that she was terribly upset, she did not express her pain. She gave the indifferent Adolph magnificent weapons and the most magnificent horse in the world. "Bichar (that was the name of the horse) will conduct you," she said, "and he will take you wherever you must go to do battle and triumph. But don't place your foot on the ground no matter what happens in your country, for the fairy spirit that the gods have given me enable me to prophesy that, if you neglect my advice, Bichar will not be able to extricate you from your trouble."

Promising her that he would obey her wishes, the prince kissed her beautiful hands a thousand times, and he was so eager to leave that delightful place that he even forgot to take his green cloak with him.

Once they reached the border of the island, the vigorous horse threw himself into the water with his master on top of him. After swimming across it, he galloped over hill and dale. He passed through fields and forests with such great speed that it seemed he had wings. However, one evening, in a narrow, rutted path, filled with rocks and pebbles and bordered by thorn bushes, they encountered a wagon blocking the path. Loaded with different kinds of old wings, it had turned over on an old man who had been driving the wagon. His head was gray, his voice trembled, and the prince felt pity for the old man's distress because he was bearing the weight of the wagon. Bichar wanted to jump over the wagon blocking the way and was about ready to soar over it, when the good man cried, "Sir, have some compassion for my predicament. If you don't deign to help me, I'll soon be dead."

Adolph could not resist helping the old man. He put his feet on the ground, approached the man, and gave him his hand. But alas! He was tremendously surprised to see the man get up quickly and seize him before he could get ready to defend himself.

"Finally, the Prince of Russia," the old man said in a terrible, menacing voice, "I've found you. I'm called Father Time, and I've been looking for you for three centuries. I've used all the wings this wagon is carrying to go around the universe in order to find you. But no matter where you may have hidden yourself, nothing that lives can escape me."

Thereupon, he clapped his hand on Adolph's mouth with such force that he prevented the prince from drawing breath until he was smothered. At this sad moment, Zephir, who had witnessed everything, passed by and was greatly disturbed by the misfortune of his dear friend. When the old barbarian left Adolph, Zephir approached and tried to bring him back to life with his sweet breath. However, his efforts were in vain. He took him in his arms just as he had done the first time, and weeping bitter tears, he brought him back to the gardens of Princess Felicity. He set him down in a grotto on a rock that was flat across the top. Then he covered him and surrounded him with flowers. After taking off his weapons, he formed a trophy with them and engraved an epitaph on a column of jasper that he placed near the unfortunate prince.

The sorrowful princess had been going every day to this grotto since the departure of her lover, adding a flood of tears to the flow of the stream. But then, what unexpected joy to find him again at the very moment when she believed him to be so far away! She imagined that he had just arrived and that, exhausted from the trip, he had fallen asleep. She contemplated whether she should wake him, and finally giving way to her tender feelings, she opened her loving arms to embrace him. As she approached, however, she began to realize her extreme misfortune, and she uttered such bitter cries that they could have moved the most insensitive heart.

She ordered the doors of her palace to be closed forever, and ever since that fatal day, nobody has seen her. Her suffering is the reason why she rarely shows herself, and one never finds this princess without her being preceded by some anguish accompanied by sorrow or followed by disturbances. This is the company that is usually with her most of the time. Human beings can certainly bear witness to this, and ever since that deplorable adventure, everyone keeps saying that there is no avoiding Father Time. Nor is there perfect happiness.

The Tale of Mira

I **DEPARTED** somewhat late from Victoria because I had stopped at the home of the governor of this region, whom I mentioned before, and we slept at Miranda. The country is very pleasant until you reach Arigny. Afterward, we took a difficult road to the banks of the Urola River, whose noise is made greater by numerous rocks against which the water smashes, soars, and then falls down, forming natural cascades in several places. Then, we continued to mount the high mountains of the Pyrenees, where we ran into a thousand different dangers. At one point, we saw the ancient ruins of an old castle where sprites have their dwellings just like we have in Guevara. It is near Garganson, and we had to stop there because one has to pay a certain customs fee to the king.

I learned from the magistrate of the town, who came up to my carriage to converse with me, that there is a tale that circulates in this region about a king and queen who had once upon a time lived here. They had a daughter so beautiful and charming that people took her for a goddess rather than a mortal creature. She was called Mira, and it is a name that comes from the Spanish expression *Mira*. It means "Look," because as soon as she appeared anywhere, people gazed at her and cried out "Mira, Mira" to draw attention to her. There you have it, the etymology of a word drawn from long ago.

Anyone who saw her fell desperately in love with her. However, her pride and indifference made all of her lovers die.

The notorious Basilisk had never killed as many people as the beautiful and very dangerous Mira. Consequently, she depopulated her father's kingdom. Moreover, the surrounding countries were full of dying and dead lovers. After the people had vainly appealed to her to stop, they finally called upon Heaven to demand due justice.

Eventually, the gods grew irritated, and even the goddesses soon expressed their anger. The result was that the scourges of Heaven ravaged her father's kingdom to punish her. In the midst of this general calamity, the king consulted the Oracle, which told him that all these misfortunes would not end until Mira had made amends for all the sorrow caused by her eyes and that she must leave the kingdom. The fates were to conduct her to the fatal place where she was to lose her tranquility and liberty.

The princess obeyed, believing that it was impossible for her to be touched by tender feelings. She took only her nurse with her, and she dressed like a simple shepherdess, fearing that someone might notice her. She did this at sea and on land. She traveled through two-thirds of the world, committing three or four dozens of murders every day because her beauty did not decrease from all the arduous journeys she took.

After some time had passed, she arrived near an old castle that, at that time, belonged to a young count named Nios, endowed with many talents and exceedingly shy. He spent his days in the forest, and as soon as he saw a woman, he fled from her. Of all the things that he had ever encountered on earth, he detested women. Now one time, when the beautiful Mira was resting herself under the shade of trees, Nios passed by, dressed in a lion's skin, a bow attached to a belt, and

a mace on his shoulder. His hair was all a mess, and his face was besmeared like a chimneysweeper's. (That detail was part of the story.) Yet, the princess thought him the most handsome and charming man in the world. She ran after him as if she were mad, and he ran from her as if he were suffering from the same madness. Then, she lost sight of him and did not know where to look for him. As a result, she became distraught and wept day and night with her nurse next to her.

Some time later, Nios returned to the hunt, and as soon as Mira saw him again, she wanted to pursue him. However, when he perceived her, he did exactly what he had done before. Once again, Mira wept bitter tears, but her passion was so strong that she eventually outran him and stopped him. Then she grabbed hold of his locks and pleaded with him to gaze upon her, thinking that this would be enough to win his heart. Yet, he cast his eyes on her with as much indifference as if she had been made of wood. Mira was astonished, but she would not leave him. Despite his indifference, she went with him to his castle where, as soon as he entered, he left her and was never seen again. Poor Mira could not be consoled, and she died from grief.

From that time on, people heard deep sighs and groans coming from the Castle of Nios. The young country girls of this region are accustomed to going there and to carrying her little presents of fruit, milk, and eggs that they set down at the mouth of a cave that nobody dares enter. They say that this was to comfort her. However, it was abolished as superstition. Though I did not believe a single word of this tale told to me at Garganson, I was nevertheless pleased to listen to this story of which I omit a thousand particulars for fear of exhausting you because of its length.

My waiting woman was so delighted by this tale that she wanted us to return to the mouth of the cave and to set down some red partridges that my people had just bought. She thought that the princess's ghost would be mightily consoled by receiving this testimony of our good will, but for my part, I thought I would be more content than her in having those partridges prepared for my supper.

Finette Cendron

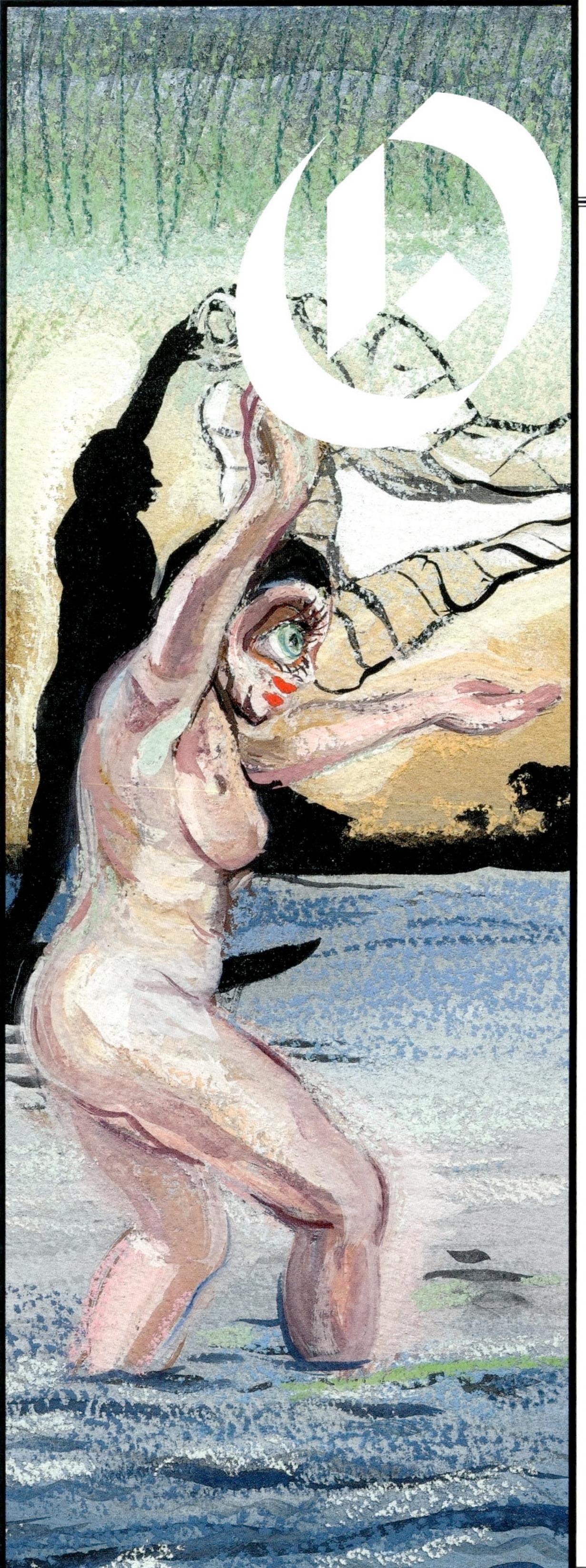

ONCE upon a time, there lived a king and a queen who managed the affairs of their realm very badly. Consequently, they were driven out of their kingdom and had to sell their crowns to support themselves. Afterward, they had to part with their wardrobes, their linen, lace, and all their furniture, piece by piece. Soon the brokers tired of purchasing their goods because something else was sent for sale almost every day. When they had disposed of nearly everything, the king said to the queen, "We're exiled from our own country and no longer have any possessions. We must do something to earn a living for our poor children and ourselves. Give some thought as to what we can do. Up to now, the only profession I've known is the very pleasant one of a king."

The queen, who was endowed with an abundance of good sense, asked for a week to think the matter over. At the end of that time, she announced, "Sire, there's no need for us to be unhappy. You need only to make nets, with which you can catch both fowl and fish. As the lines wear out, I'll spin new ones. With regard to our three daughters, they're downright idle girls who still think of themselves as fine ladies and would like to continue living in that style without sullying their hands. Since we cannot support them as they would like, we must take them so far away that they'll never be able to find their way back home again."

The king began to weep when he found he had to separate himself from his children, for he was a kind father. However, the queen was the mistress of the family, and he agreed to whatever she proposed.

"Get up early tomorrow morning," he said to her, "and take your three daughters wherever you think fit."

While they were thus plotting together, the Princess Finette, who was the youngest daughter, listened at the keyhole, and when she discovered the plans of her mother and father, she set off as fast as she could in the direction of a large grotto, a considerable distance away, which was the abode of her godmother, the fairy Merluche.

Finette took two pounds of fresh butter, some eggs, milk, and flour to make a nice cake for her godmother and to ensure she would be given a warm reception. She began her journey in good spirits, but the farther she went, the wearier she became. The soles of her shoes were worn completely through, and her pretty little feet became so sore that they were a sad sight to see. Indeed, she became so exhausted that she sat on the grass and cried. Just then a beautiful Spanish horse came by, already saddled and bridled. He had more than enough diamonds on his saddle-cloth to purchase three cities. When he saw the princess, he stopped and began to graze quietly beside her. Bending his knees, he appeared to pay homage to her. Thereupon, she took him by the bridle and said, "Gentle hobby, would you kindly carry me to my fairy godmother's dwelling? You would do me great service. I'm so weary that I am ready to expire. If you help me on this occasion, I'll give you good oats and hay and a litter of fresh straw to lie upon."

The horse bent himself almost to the ground, and when young Finette jumped upon him, he galloped off with her as lightly as a bird until he came to a halt at the entrance of the grotto, as if he had known where to land. In fact, he knew well enough, for Merluche herself had foreseen her goddaughter's visit and had sent the fine horse for her.

As soon as Finette entered the grotto, she made three respectful curtsies to her godmother. Then she took the hem of her gown, kissed it, and said to her, "Good day, godmother, how are you doing? I've brought you some butter, milk, flour, and eggs to make you a cake according to the custom of our country."

"You're welcome, Finette," the fairy said. "Come here, so I may embrace you."

She kissed her twice and this delighted Finette a great deal, for Madame Merluche was not one of those fairies one finds by the dozen.

"Come, goddaughter," she said, "you'll be my lady's maid. Take down my hair and comb it."

The princess took down her hair and adroitly combed it.

"I know full well why you've come. You overheard the king and queen discussing how they might lose you, and you want to avoid such a calamity," Merluche said. "Here, you have only to take this skein of

unbreakable thread. Fasten one end to the door of your house and keep the other in your hand. When the queen abandons you, you'll easily find your way back by following the thread."

The princess thanked her godmother, who gave her a bag filled with fine dresses made of gold and silver. She embraced her, placed her again on the pretty horse, and in two or three minutes, he had carried Finette to the door of her parents' cottage.

"My friend," Finette said to the horse, "you're very handsome and clever, and your speed is as great as the sun's. I thank you for your service. You may now return to your stable."

She entered the house quietly and hid her bag under her pillow. Then she went to bed appearing to know nothing that had taken place. At daybreak, the king woke his wife.

"Come, come, madame," he said. "Get ready for your journey."

The queen got up immediately, took some sturdy shoes, a short petticoat, a white jacket, and a stick. Then she summoned her eldest daughter, who was named Fleur d'Amour; her second, who was named Belle-de-Nuit; and her third, named Fine-Oreille, whom they familiarly called Finette.

"I've been thinking all last night that we ought to go and see my sister," the queen said. "She'll entertain us in splendid fashion. We can feast and laugh as much as we like there."

Fleur d'Amour, who despaired of living in such a desert, said to her mother, "Let us go, madame, wherever you please. Just as long as I can stroll somewhere, anywhere."

The two others agreed and took their leave of the king. They set off all four together and walked so very far that Fine-Oreille was terrified her thread would not be long enough, for they walked nearly a thousand miles. She always kept behind the others, drawing the thread skillfully through the thickets.

When the queen thought her daughters would be unable to find their way back, she entered a dense forest and told them, "Sleep, my little lambs. I'll be like the shepherdess who watches over her flock for fear the wolf will devour them."

Once they had lain down on the grass and fallen asleep, the queen left them there, believing she would never see them again. Finette had shut her eyes but not gone to sleep. "If I were an evil-natured girl," she said to herself, "I'd go straight home and leave my sisters to die here." (The fact is, they beat her and scratched her until they drew blood.) Yet, despite their malice, she did not abandon them. She roused her sisters and told them the whole story. They began to cry and begged her to take them with

her, promising that they would give her beautiful dolls, a child's set of silver plates, and all their other toys and candy.

"I'm quite sure you'll do nothing of the kind," Finette said. "Nevertheless, I'll behave as a good sister should."

Upon saying this, she rose and followed the thread with the two princesses, and thus they reached home almost as soon as the queen did. While they were at the door, they heard the king say, "It troubles my heart to see you come back alone."

"Pshaw," said the queen. "Our daughters were much too great a burden for us."

"If you had brought back my Finette," the king said, "I might have felt consoled about the loss of the others because they love nothing and nobody."

At that moment, they knocked at the door—rap, rap. "Who's there?" the king asked.

"Your three daughters," they replied, "Fleur d'Amour, Belle-de-Nuit, and Fine-Oreille."

The queen began to tremble. "Don't open the door!" she exclaimed. "It must be their ghosts, for they could not possibly have found their way back alive."

The king, who was as great a coward as was his wife, called out, "You're lying! You're not my daughters!"

But shrewd Fine-Oreille said, "Papa, I'll stoop down so that you can look at me through the hole made for the cat to come through. If I'm not Finette, I agree to be whipped."

The king did as he was told, and as

soon as he recognized her, he flung open the door. Pretending to be delighted to see them again, the queen said that she had forgotten something and had come home to fetch it, but that she would surely have returned to them. They pretended to believe her and went upstairs to a snug hayloft in which they always slept.

"Now, sisters," Finette said, "you promised me the doll. Give it to me."

"Don't hold your breath, you little scamp," they said. "You're the reason why they care so little about us."

Thereupon, they grabbed their distaffs and beat her terribly. After they had abused her as much as they desired, they let her go to bed. However, since she was covered with wounds and bruises, she could not sleep, and consequently, she heard the queen say to the king, "I'll take them much

farther in another direction, until I'm positive they'll never return."

When Finette heard this plan, she rose quietly and went to see her godmother again. First, she entered the chicken yard, where she wrung the necks of two hens, a cock, and two little rabbits that the queen was fattening on cabbages for the next festive event. She put them all into a basket and set off, but she had not gone a mile, groping her way and quaking with fear, when the Spanish horse approached at a gallop, snorting and neighing. Thinking that some soldiers were about to seize her, she cried, "Alas, it's all over for me!"

When she saw the beautiful horse all alone, however, she jumped upon his back, delighted to travel so comfortably, especially since she arrived almost immediately at her godmother's dwelling. After the usual greetings, she presented her with the hens, cock, and rabbits, and asked for her sage advice, especially because the queen had sworn that she would lead them to the end of the world. Merluche told her goddaughter not to worry and gave her a sack full of ashes. "Carry this sack in front of you and shake it as you go along. You'll walk on the ashes, and when you wish to return, you'll only have to follow your footsteps," she said. "Don't bring your sisters back with you. They're too malicious. If you do bring them back, I'll never see you again."

Finette bid farewell to her and was given thirty or forty millions of diamonds in a little box, which she put in her pocket to take with her. The horse was ready and waiting and carried her home just as he had done before.

At daybreak, the queen called the princesses and said, "The king isn't well, and I dreamed last night that I must go and gather some flowers and herbs that'll help him recuperate. There's a particular country where they grow to perfection. Therefore, let us be off right away."

Fleur d'Amour and Belle-de-Nuit, who never imagined that their mother intended to lose them again, were quite grieved at hearing that they had to make another long trip. Yet, they had to go, and their journey was farther than any that had ever been made. Finette, who never said a word, kept behind them and shook her sack of ashes with such superb skill that neither wind nor rain spoiled them.

The queen was perfectly convinced that they would not find their way back again, and one evening, when she observed her three daughters fast asleep, she used the opportunity to leave them and returned home. As soon as it was light and Finette found her mother gone, she woke her sisters. "We're alone," she said. "The queen has left us."

Fleur d'Amour and Belle-de-Nuit began to weep. They tore their hair and beat their own faces with their fists. "Alas, what will become of us?" they exclaimed.

Finette was the most generous and sympathetic girl in the world, and therefore she took pity on her sisters once again. "See how vulnerable I'm leaving myself," she told them. "When my godmother furnished me with the means to return, she forbade me to show you the way and told me that if I disobeyed her, she'd never see me again."

Fleur d'Amour and Belle-de-Nuit embraced Finette, kissing her so affectionately that it required nothing more to bring all three back together to the king and the queen. Their majesties were greatly surprised at the return of the princesses, and they conversed long into the night. Meanwhile, their youngest daughter, who was not called Fine-Oreille for nothing, heard them concoct a new plan that involved the queen taking them on another journey the next morning. Once more, Fine-Oreille ran to wake her sisters.

"Alas," she said to them, "we're lost! The queen is determined to lead us into some wilderness and leave us there. I offended my godmother for your sakes. Therefore, I don't dare to go to her for advice as I did before."

Faced with such a terrible prospect, they asked each other, "What shall we do, sister? What shall we do?"

At last, Belle-de-Nuit said to the two others, "Why should we worry ourselves? Old Merluche doesn't possess all the brains in the world. There are other folks who possess just as much. We need only take plenty of peas and drop them all along the road as we go. Then we'll be sure to trace our way back home."

Fleur d'Amour thought this was a remarkable idea, and they loaded all their pockets with peas. But instead of peas, Fine-Oreille packed her bag filled with fine clothes and the little box of diamonds, sensing that they might be gone a long

time. As soon as the queen called them, they were ready to go.

"I dreamed last night," she said, "that in some country, which is unnecessary to name, there are three handsome princes

who are waiting to marry you. I'm going to take you there to see if my dream was true."

The queen went first, and her daughters followed her, confidently dropping their peas, for they were sure of finding their way home. This time, the queen went farther than she had ever gone before, and during one dark night she left the princesses. When she reached home, she was very weary but delighted for having gotten rid of the great burden of her three daughters.

After sleeping until eleven, the three princesses awoke, and Finette was the first to discover the queen's absence. Although she was perfectly prepared for it, she could not help crying, especially because she trusted the power of her fairy godmother much more than the cleverness of her sisters. Frightened, she went to them and said, "The queen's gone. We must follow her as soon as possible."

"Hold your tongue, you little hussy," replied Fleur d'Amour. "We can find our way well enough when we choose. There's no need in making such a fuss."

Finette did not dare to answer, but when they did try to retrace their steps, there were no signs or paths to be found. Since immense flocks of pigeons inhabited that country, they had eaten up all the peas. The princesses began to scream with grief and terror. After spending two days without eating, Fleur d'Amour said to Belle-de-Nuit, "Sister, don't you have anything to eat?"

"Nothing."

She put the same question to Finette.

"Nor do I," she answered, "but I've just found an acorn."

"Ah! Give it to me," one sister said.

"Give it to me," said the other.

Each insisted on having it.

"An acorn will not go far among the three of us," Finette said. "Let us plant it, and maybe a tree will spring from that which will be useful to us."

Although there was scant chance of a tree growing in a country where none were to be seen, they agreed. The only things they could find to eat were cabbages and lettuces, and this was what the princesses

lived on. If their constitutions had been delicate, they would have starved a hundred times. They slept usually in the open air, and every morning and evening they took turns watering the acorn and saying, "Grow, grow, beautiful acorn!"

Indeed, it began to grow so fast that they could watch it grow. When it had reached a certain height, Fleur d'Amour tried to climb it, but it was not strong enough to bear her. Feeling it bend under her weight, she came back down again. Belle-de-Nuit was no more successful. Since Finette was lighter, she managed to climb up and remain there a long time.

Her sisters called to her, "Can you see anything, sister?"

"No, I can't see a thing," she answered.

"Ah, then, the oak is not tall enough," said Fleur d'Amour.

Therefore, they continued to water it and say, "Grow, grow, beautiful acorn!"

Finette kept climbing it twice a day, and one morning, when she was up in the tree, Belle-de-Nuit said to Fleur d'Amour, "I've found a bag that our sister has hidden from us. What can be in it?"

Fleur d'Amour replied, "She told me it contained some old lace she had brought along to mend."

"I believe it's full of candy," Belle-de-Nuit said. Since she had a sweet tooth, she decided to look. When she opened the bag, she found a good deal of old lace belonging to the king and queen, but hidden beneath it were the fine clothes and the box of diamonds the fairy had given to Finette.

"Well, now! Was there ever such a sly little scamp?" exclaimed Belle-de-Nuit. "We'll take out all the things and put some stones in their place."

This they did hastily, and when Finette rejoined them, she did not notice what they had done, for she never dreamed of decking herself out in a desert. She thought only about the oak, which quickly became the finest that the world has ever seen. One day when she had climbed it and her sisters as usual had asked if she could see anything, she exclaimed, "I can see a large mansion so very beautiful that I can't find the words to describe it. The walls are composed of emeralds and rubies, the roof of diamonds. It's covered all over with golden bells and weathercocks that whirl about as the wind blows."

"You're lying," they said. "It can't be as beautiful as you say."

"Believe me," Finette replied, "I'm not a liar. Come and see for yourselves. My eyes are quite dazzled by it."

Fleur d'Amour climbed up the tree. When she saw the chateau, she could talk about nothing else. Belle-de-Nuit became extremely curious and climbed the tree in her turn. As soon as she caught sight of the chateau, she was just as enchanted as her sisters were.

"We must certainly go to this palace," they said. "Perhaps we'll find those handsome princes who'll be happy to marry us."

They spent the entire evening discussing the subject before they lay down to sleep on the grass. But when Finette seemed to be fast asleep, Fleur d'Amour said to Belle-de-Nuit, "I'll tell you what we should do, sister. Let's get up and dress ourselves in the fine clothes Finette has brought with her."

"That's a splendid idea," Belle-de-Nuit responded.

Therefore, now they curled their hair, powdered it, put patches on their cheeks, and dressed themselves in the beautiful gold and silver gowns arrayed with diamonds. What a magnificent sight they made!

The next morning, unaware of her wicked sisters' theft, Finette took her bag with the intention of dressing herself and was greatly distressed to find nothing in it but flint stones. At that moment, she turned and saw her sisters shining like suns. She wept and complained about their treachery, but they only laughed and joked about it.

"I can't believe," Finette said, "that you have the effrontery to take me to the chateau without dressing and making me as beautiful as you are."

"We have barely enough for ourselves," Fleur d'Amour replied, "and you'll get nothing but a good beating if you pester us."

"But the clothes you have on are mine. My godmother gave them to me. They don't belong to you."

"If you say one more word about it," they responded, "we'll clobber your head and bury you without anyone being the wiser!"

Poor Finette did not dare to provoke them, but followed them slowly, walking a short distance behind them, as if she were merely their servant.

The nearer they approached the mansion, the more wonderful it appeared. "Oh," Fleur d'Amour and Belle-de-Nuit said, "we'll certainly amuse ourselves! What splendid dinners we'll have! We'll dine at the king's table. But Finette will have to wash the dishes in the kitchen, for she looks like a scullion. If anybody asks who she is, we must take care not to call her 'sister.' We must say that she is the little cowherd from the village."

When they reached the castle gate, they knocked, and a terrifying old hag opened it immediately. She had just one eye in the middle of her forehead, but it was bigger than five or six ordinary ones. Her nose was flat, her complexion swarthy, and her mouth so horrible that it was frightening to behold. She was fifteen feet tall and had a waist thirty feet wide.

"Unfortunate wretches," she said to them, "what's brought you here? Don't you know that this is the ogre's castle, and that all three of you would hardly make do for his breakfast? However, I'm more good-natured than my husband is.

Come in. I won't eat you all at once. You'll have the consolation of living two or three days longer."

Upon hearing the words of the ogress, they began to flee, but one of her strides was equal to fifty of theirs. Consequently, she pursued and caught them, one by the hair and the others by the nape of their necks. Then she tucked them under her arm, took them into the castle, and threw all three into the cellar, which was filled with toads and adders and strewn with the bones of those the ogres had eaten. Because she desired to eat Finette right away, the ogress went to fetch some vinegar, oil, and salt to make her into a salad. At that moment, however, she heard the ogre approaching and thought, "The princesses are so white and delicate that I want to eat them all myself." Quickly, therefore, she popped them under a large tub, and now they could only look through a hole.

The ogre was six times as tall as his wife. When he spoke, the building shook, and when he coughed repeatedly, his coughs resembled peals of thunder. He had just one huge, filthy eye, and his hair stood all on end. Using a log of wood for a cane, he entered with a covered basket in his hand, from which he pulled fifteen children he had stolen on the road and swallowed them like fifteen freshly laid eggs. When the princesses saw him, they trembled under the tub. They were afraid to cry, lest they be heard, but they whispered to each other, "He'll eat us alive. How can we possibly save ourselves?"

The ogre said to his wife, "You know, I smell fresh meat. Give it to me."

"That's a good one," the ogress said. "You always think you smell fresh meat. It's your sheep that have just passed by."

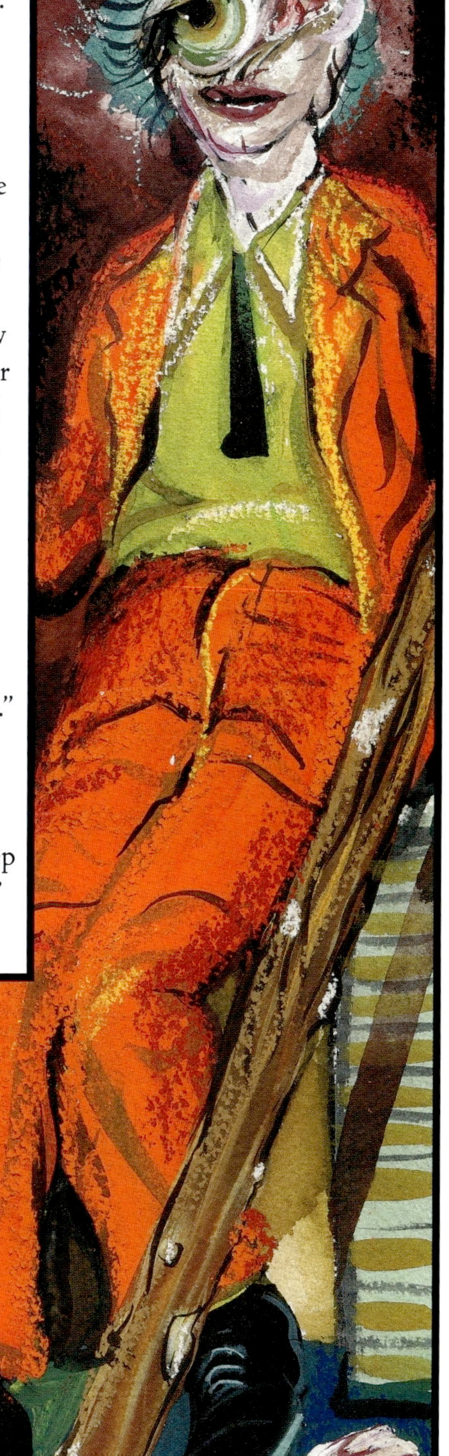

"You can't fool me. I smell fresh meat for certain, and I'll search everywhere until I find it."

"Search," she said. "You won't find anything."

"If I do find something, and you've hidden it from me, I'll cut your head off and make a ball out of it."

She was frightened by this threat and said, "Don't be angry, my dear ogre. I'll tell you the truth. Three young girls came here today, and I hid them away. It would be a pity to eat them right away because they know how to do everything. I'm old and need some rest. You can see that our fine house is very dirty; our bread is badly made; and your soup rarely pleases you. Moreover, I myself no longer appear so beautiful in your eyes ever since I began working so hard. These girls will be my servants. I beg you not to eat them just now. If you should desire one of them some other day, they'll always be within your reach."

The ogre was loath to promise that he would not eat them immediately. "Let me do as I please," he said. "I'll only eat two of them."

"No, you won't eat them."

"Well, then, I'll only eat the smallest."

"No, you won't touch a single one of them."

After a great deal of bickering, he at last promised he would not eat them, but she thought to herself, "When he goes hunting, I'll eat them and tell him they managed to escape."

The ogre emerged from the cellar and told his wife to bring the girls to him. The poor princesses were nearly paralyzed with fright, and the ogress had to coax them to come forward. When they were brought before the ogre, he asked them what they could do. They answered, "We can sweep, sew, and spin exceedingly well."

"We can make ragouts so delicious that people are tempted to eat even the plates. As for bread, cakes, and patties, people have been known to order them from a thousand miles around."

Since the ogre was fond of good cooking, he said, "Aha! Set these good housewives to work immediately." Then he asked them as a test, "After you light the fire, how do you know when the oven is hot enough?"

"I throw some butter into it, my lord," Finette replied, "and then I taste it with my tongue."

"Very well," he said, "light the oven fire!"

The oven was as big as a stable because the ogre and ogress ate more bread than two armies could eat. The princess built a terrific fire, until the oven was as hot as a furnace. In the meantime, the ogre became impatient waiting for his new bread. Therefore, he ate a hundred lambs and a hundred suckling pigs, while Fleur d'Amour and Belle-de-Nuit made the dough. "Well," the mammoth ogre asked, "is the oven hot?"

"You shall see, my lord," said Finette. She threw in a thousand pounds of butter and then said, "It should be tasted with the tongue, but I'm too short to reach it."

"I'm tall enough," the ogre said as he stooped. Then he thrust his body so far into the oven that he could not keep his balance, and all his flesh was burned off his bones. When the ogress approached the oven, she was astounded to find her husband a mountain of cinders!

Fleur d'Amour and Belle-de-Nuit saw how distressed she was and consoled her as best as they could. However, they feared her grief would subside all too soon, and once her appetite returned, she would make a salad out of them, as she had been about to do before.

"Don't be discouraged, madame," they said to her, "you'll find some king or some marquis who'll be delighted to marry you."

She smiled slightly, showing teeth that were longer than most people's fingers. When they saw her in such a good mood, Finette said, "If you would only take off these horrible bearskins that you wrap yourself in and follow the fashion, we'll dress your hair to perfection. Then you'll resemble a star."

"Come," the ogress said, "let's see what you can do. But rest assured that, if I find any ladies lovelier than me, I'll make mincemeat out of you."

Soon thereafter, the three princesses took off her cap and began combing and curling her hair. While they entertained her with their chatter, Finette took a hatchet and struck her from behind with such a blow that her head was sliced clean off her shoulders. Never was there such rejoicing! The three princesses climbing to the roof of the mansion and amused themselves by ringing the golden bells. Then they ran through all the apartments, which were made of pearls and diamonds and filled with costly furniture. They nearly fainted with pleasure. They laughed, they sang, they had all they wanted: corn, marmalade, fruit, and dolls in abundance. When they went to sleep in beds of brocade and velvet, Fleur d'Amour and Belle-de-Nuit said to each other, "Look at us, we're richer than our father was when he still had his kingdom."

"On the other hand, though, we want to

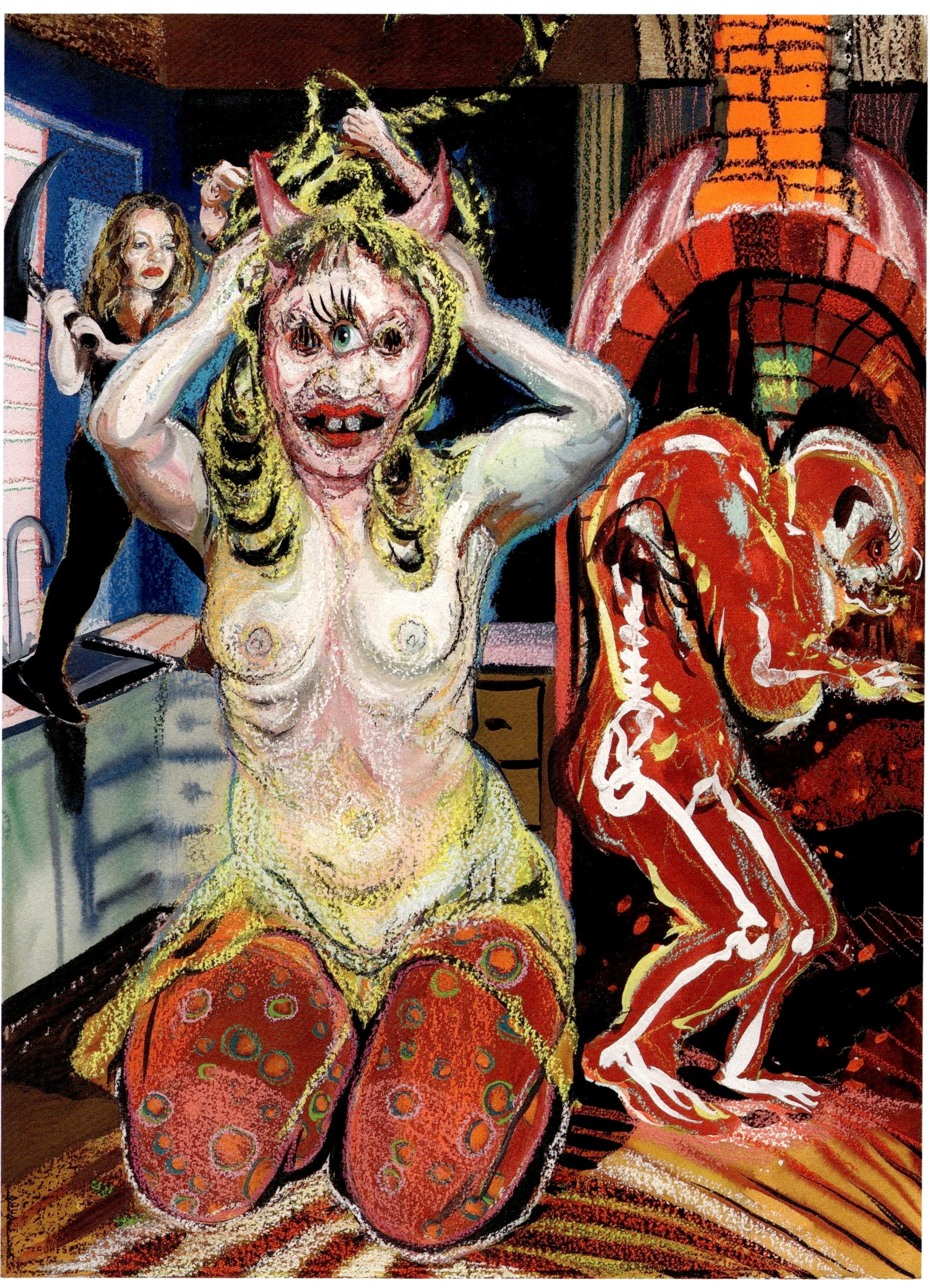

be married, and nobody will dare to come here. People assume that this mansion remains a cutthroat den because they don't know that the ogre and the ogress are dead. We must go to the nearest city and show ourselves in our fine dresses. Then we're bound to find some honest bankers who'll be quite glad to marry princesses."

As soon as they were dressed, they told Finette they were going to take a stroll. "But you must stay home and cook and wash and clean the house. We had better find everything as it should be on our return. If not, you'll be beaten within an inch of your life!"

Poor Finette, whose heart was full of grief, remained alone in the house, sweeping, cleaning, washing, and crying incessantly. "How unfortunate," she lamented, "that I disobeyed my godmother! All sorts of awful things have happened to me. My sisters have stolen my precious dresses and adorned themselves with my jewels. If it weren't for me, the ogre and his wife would be alive and well at this moment. What have I gained from killing them?"

Upon saying this, she broke into sobs until she almost choked. Shortly afterward, her sisters returned loaded with Portuguese oranges, preserves, and sugar. "Ah," they announced, "what a splendid ball we attended! How crowded it was! The king's son was among the dancers, and we received a thousand compliments. Come take off our shoes and clean them. It's one of your tasks."

Finette obeyed them, and if by accident she uttered a single word of complaint, they jumped on her and beat her savagely. The next day and the day after, they went out and returned with accounts of new wonders.

One evening, Finette was sitting in the chimney corner on a heap of cinders, idly examining the cracks in the chimney, when she discovered a little key lodged in one of them. It was so old and so dirty that she had the greatest trouble cleaning it, but after she had done so, she found it was made of gold. Assuming that a golden key ought to open some beautiful little casket, she ran all over the mansion, trying it in all the locks. Eventually, she found it fit the lock of a casket that was a masterpiece of art. When she opened it, she found it filled with clothes, diamonds, lace, linen, and ribbons worth immense sums. She didn't say a word to her sisters about her good fortune, but waited impatiently for their departure the next day. As soon as they were out of sight, she adorned herself until she looked more beautiful than the sun and the moon together.

It was in this altered condition that she went to the ball where her sisters were dancing, and though she was not wearing a mask, she had changed so much for the better that they did not recognize her. As soon as she appeared, a murmur arose throughout the gathering. Some were filled with admiration, others with jealousy. When she was asked to dance, she soon showed that she surpassed all the other ladies in grace as well as beauty. The mistress of the mansion came to her, and after making a respectful curtsy, she asked her name so that she would always have the pleasure of remembering such a marvelous person. Finette replied civilly that her name was Cendron. Now, there was not a lover who did not leave his mistress for Cendron, not a poet who did not write verses about Cendron. Never did such a shabby name cause so much commotion in so short a time. Every echo repeated the praises of Cendron. People did not have eyes enough to gaze at her, nor tongues enough to extol her.

Fleur d'Amour and Belle-de-Nuit, who had previously created a sensation wherever they appeared, were ready to burst with spite as they observed the reception accorded to this newcomer. However, Finette extricated herself from all such rivalry with the best grace in the world. Her manners seemed to be those of one born to command. Fleur d'Amour and Belle-de-Nuit, who never saw their sister except with her face covered with chimney soot and looking as dirty as a dog, had completely forgotten how beautiful she was. Consequently, they did not have the slightest inkling who she was. Like all the rest, they paid their respects to Cendron.

As soon as she saw the ball was nearly over, she hurried home, undressed herself quickly, and put on her old rags. When her sisters arrived, they said to her, "Ah,

Finette, we've just seen a perfectly charming young princess! She's not a baboon like you. She's as white as snow with a richer complexion than the roses. Her teeth are pearls and her lips are coral. She was wearing a gown so decked with gold and diamonds it must have weighed more than a thousand pounds. How beautiful, how charming she was!"

Finette murmured, "So was I, so was I."

"What are you muttering there?" her sisters asked.

She repeated even more softly, "So was I, so was I."

This little game was played for some time. Hardly a day passed that Finette did not appear in a new dress, for the casket was a fairy one. The more she took out, the more it was filled, and every item was so fashionable that all the ladies dressed themselves in imitation of Finette.

One evening when Finette had danced more than usual and had delayed her departure to a later hour, she was so anxious to get home before her sisters that she walked too hurriedly and lost one of her slippers, made of red velvet and embroidered with pearls. She tried to find it on the road, but the night was so dark that she searched in vain. Thus, she entered the house with one foot shod and the other foot not.

The next day, Prince Chéri, the king's eldest son, went out hunting and found Finette's slipper. He picked it up and examined it, admiring its diminutive size and elegance. After turning it over and over, he kissed it and carried it home with him. From that day on, he refused to eat, and his looks underwent a great change: he became as yellow as a quince, thin, melancholy, and depressed. The king and queen, who were devoted to him, had the choicest game and best comfiture brought in from everywhere, but they meant nothing to him. He gazed blankly at everything and did not respond when his mother spoke to him. They summoned the best physicians from all around even as far as Paris and Montpellier. After observing him continually for three days and three nights, they concluded that he was in love and that he would die if they did not find the sole remedy for him.

The queen, who doted on her son, burst into tears because she did not know the object of his love and could not help him

marry her. She had the most beautiful women she could find brought into his chamber, but he refused to glance at them. Finally, the queen said, "My dear son, you're going to be the cause of our death. We know you're in love, and you're hiding it from us. Tell us whom you love and we'll give her to you, even if she's just a simple shepherdess."

Taking courage from the queen's promise, the prince drew the slipper from under his pillow. Showing it to her, he said, "Look, madame, this is the cause of my malady. I found this petite, delicate slipper when I went out hunting, and I refuse to marry anyone but the woman who can wear it."

"Very well, my son," said the queen, "there's no need to trouble yourself. We'll organize a search for her."

She rushed to the king with this news. He was very surprised and immediately ordered a proclamation to be announced with drum and trumpet: all single women were to come and try on the slipper, and she whose foot fit the slipper would marry the prince.

Upon hearing this, every woman washed her feet with all sorts of waters, pastes, and pomades. Some women actually had them peeled, while others starved themselves in order to make their feet smaller and prettier. They converged in hordes to try on the slipper, but no one could fit her foot into it, and the more they came and failed, the more the prince's suffering increased.

One day, Fleur d'Amour and Belle-de-Nuit dressed themselves so superbly that they looked astonishingly beautiful.

"Where are you going?" Finette inquired.

"We're going to the capital city where the king and queen reside," they replied. "We're going to try on the slipper the king's son has found. If it fits one of us, the prince will marry her, and then one of us will become queen. "

"And why can't I go?" Finette responded.

"Really! You're awfully stupid!" they said. "Go and water our cabbages. That's all you're fit for."

Without a second's thought, Finette decided she should put on her finest clothes and take her chance with the rest, for she had a vague suspicion that she would be successful. However, she was troubled because she did not know her way. The ball she had attended had not been held in the capital. Nevertheless, she dressed herself magnificently. Her gown was made of blue satin and covered with diamond stars. She had a corona of them in her hair and a full

moon on her back, and all these jewels glistened so brightly that no one could look at her without blinking. Upon opening the door to depart, she was quite surprised to find the pretty Spanish horse that had carried her to her godmother's dwelling. He was covered all over with golden bells and ribbons, and his saddlecloth and bridle were incomparable. She patted him and said, "You're a most welcome sight, my little hobby. I'm much obliged to my godmother, Merluche."

When he knelt down and she gracefully climbed upon him like a nymph, she was thirty times more beautiful than fair Helen of Troy. Then the Spanish horse galloped off sprightly, his bells ringing ting-a-ling. When Fleur d'Amour and Belle-de-Nuit heard these sounds, they turned around and saw her coming. They were completely taken by surprise, for they now recognized her as both Finette and Cendron.

"Sister!" Fleur d'Amour cried to Belle-de-Nuit, "Look, that's Finette Cendron!"

As the other echoed the cry, Finette passed so close to them that her horse splashed them all over and left their fine dresses dripping with mud. Finette laughed at them and called, "Your highnesses, Cendrillon despises you as you deserve."

Then she passed them like a shot and disappeared. Belle-de-Nuit and Fleur d'Amour looked at each other. "Are we dreaming?" they asked. "Who could have supplied Finette with clothes and a horse? It's a miracle! She's got luck on her side. Her foot will fit the slipper, and we'll have made a long journey in vain."

While they were bemoaning their situation, Finette arrived at the palace. The moment she appeared, everybody thought she was a queen. Guards presented arms, drums rolled, and trumpets sounded a flourish. All the gates were flung open, and those people who had seen her at the ball preceded her and cried, "Make room! Make room for the beautiful Cendron, the wonder of the world!"

Such was the state that she entered the room of the dying prince. Casting his eyes on her, he was enraptured by the sight of her and prayed fervently that her foot would be small enough to fit into the slipper. Immediately, she slipped it on and produced its fellow, which she had brought with her for this purpose. All at once, the people began shouting, "Long live the Princess Chérie! Long live the princess who will be our queen!"

The prince rose from his couch and advanced to kiss her hand, and she was struck by how handsome and intelligent he was. While he paid her a thousand courteous attentions, the king and queen were informed of the event. Consequently, they came as quickly as they could. The queen took Finette in her arms, called her daughter, her darling, her little queen! She gave her several magnificent presents, and the generous king added many more. They ordered the guns to be fired, and violins, bagpipes, and every sort of musical instrument began to play. No one talked of anything but dancing and rejoicing. The king, queen, and prince begged Cendron to consent to let the marriage take place immediately.

"No," she said, "I must first tell you my story," which she did in a few words.

When they found that she was born a princess, they again were so filled with joy that they thought they would burst. In addition, when she told them the names of her father and mother, they recognized them as sovereigns of dominions that they had conquered. When they informed Finette of this fact, she immediately vowed that she would not consent to marry the prince until they had restored the estates of her father. Of course, they promised to do so, for they had upward of a hundred

kingdoms, and one more or less was not worth haggling over.

In the meantime, Belle-de-Nuit and Fleur d'Amour had arrived at the palace, and the first news that greeted them was that Cendron had put on the slipper. They did not know what to do or say. They decided to return again without seeing her, but when Finette heard they had arrived, she insisted that they come to her. Instead of berating and punishing them, as they deserved, Finette advanced to embrace them tenderly and then presented them to the queen. "Madame, these are my sisters. They are very charming, and I ask you to love them."

So confused were they by Finette's kindness that they were rendered speechless. She promised them they could return to their own kingdom, which the king was restoring to their family. Upon hearing these words, they threw themselves on their knees before her and wept for joy.

The wedding was the most splendid that has ever been seen. Finette wrote to her godmother and put the letter along with valuable presents on the back of the pretty Spanish horse. The letter requested that she visit the king and queen, tell them of their good fortune, and inform them they could now return to their kingdom, arranged most graciously by the fairy Merluche. Consequently, Finette's father and mother regained their estates, and her sisters later become queens just like her.

If it's revenge on the ungrateful you want to see,
Then follow Finette's wise policy.
Do favors for the undeserving until they weep.
Each gift inflicts a wound most deep,
Cutting the haughty bosom to the core.
Finette's proud, selfish sisters suffered more,
Thanks to her kindness and generosity
Than what the ogres might have done:
She overcame her sisters with kindness and pity.
So from her example, this lesson learn,
And give good for evil in your turn.
No matter what wrong may ignite your wrath,
There is no greater vengeance than this kind path.

Belle-Belle,
or
The Chevalier
Fortuné

ONCE upona time, there was a very good, gentle king. He was a powerful monarch, but his neighbor, the Emperor Matapa, was even more powerful. In the last of the great wars they had waged against each other, the emperor had won a tremendous battle. After killing or taking prisoner most of the king's officers and soldiers, Matapa besieged and conquered the king's capital city. Afterward, he took possession of all its treasures. The king had just enough time to save himself and his sister, the queen dowager, who had become a widow at a very early age. Though intelligent and beautiful, she was, to tell the truth, also proud, violent, and difficult to approach.

The Emperor Matapa transported all the king's jewels and furniture to his own palace, and he carried away an extraordinary number of soldiers, women, horses, and anything else that he found useful or pleasurable. After he had ravaged the greater part of the kingdom, he returned triumphant to his own realm, where he was joyously received by the empress and his daughter.

In the meantime, the defeated king was not inclined to accept his misfortune lightly. He gathered the remnants of his troops around him and formed a small army. To increase their numbers as quickly as possible, he issued a proclamation requiring all the nobles of his kingdom to come and serve him in person, or to send one of their children, well armed with a horse and disposed to support all his ventures.

Now, there was an old nobleman, eighty years of age, who lived on the frontier of the kingdom. He was a wise and prudent man, but fortune had not been kind to him. After having been quite wealthy at one time, he found himself reduced almost to poverty. He would have endured such straits if his three beautiful daughters had not been compelled to share his fate. Nevertheless, they were understanding and never grumbled at their misfortunes. If by chance they discussed them at all with their father, they did so more to console him than to add to his disquiet. Without the least desire to seek a better life, they lived with him in their rustic setting.

When the king's proclamation reached the ears of the old man, he called his daughters to him, looked at them sorrowfully, and said, "What can we do? The king has ordered all the nobles of his kingdom to join him to fight against the emperor, and if they refuse, he intends to levy a heavy tax. I am not in a position to pay the tax, and therefore I am in a terrible dilemma. This will be either my ruin or my death."

His three daughters were just as distressed as he himself was. Despite this, they implored him to have courage, for they were convinced that they would find some way out of this predicament. The next morning, the eldest daughter went looking for her father, who was walking sadly in an orchard that he tended by himself.

"Sire," she said, "I've come to ask your permission to join the army. I am tall and strong enough. Let me dress myself in male attire and pass for your son. Even if I don't perform a single heroic deed, I'll at least save you the journey or the tax, and given our situation, that is a great deal."

Embracing her affectionately, the count at first objected to such an extraordinary proposition, but she argued so convincingly that he finally had no choice but to consent. All he had to do now was to provide her with the clothes suitable to the person she was to represent. Therefore, he furnished her with arms and gave her the best of his four plough horses. Then they bade their tender farewells to each other.

After traveling for several days, she passed through a meadow bordered by a quickset hedge. There she saw a shepherdess who was trying with the greatest difficulty to drag one of her sheep out of a ditch into which it had fallen.

"What's the matter, good shepherdess?" she asked.

"Alas," replied the shepherdess, "I'm trying to save my sheep. It's drowning, and I don't have the strength to drag it out."

"I'm sorry about your plight," she said, riding off without offering her any help.

The shepherdess immediately cried out, "Good-bye, disguised beauty!"

Our lovely damsel was bewildered when she heard that. "How is it possible," she remarked, "that I could be so easily detected? That old shepherdess only saw me for a moment, and yet she knew that I was disguised! What am I to do now? Everyone will know who I am, and if the king finds out, my shame will be great, and so will his anger. He'll think my father's a coward, who shrinks from danger."

After much reflection, she decided to return home. The count and his daughters had been talking about her, counting the days she had been gone, when they saw her enter. She told them about the incident with the shepherdess. In turn, the good man responded that he had warned her about this, and if she had listened to him, she would never have set out because it is impossible not to detect a maiden disguised as a man.

Once again, this little family was in a predicament and did not know what to do. Then the second daughter went to the count in her turn and said, "My sister had never been on horseback, so it's not surprising that she was discovered. If you'll allow me to go in her place, I dare promise that you'll be satisfied with me."

Nothing the old man said in opposing her intention had the slightest effect on her. Consequently, he was forced to let her depart. Therefore, she put on different clothes and took some other arms and another horse. After she had equipped herself, she embraced her father and sisters a thousand times, determined to serve the king well. However, as she passed through the same meadow where her sister had seen the shepherdess and her sheep, she encountered her at the bottom of the ditch trying to drag the sheep out of the hole.

"Unfortunate creature that I am!" cried the old woman, "half my flock has perished this way. If someone would assist me, I could save this animal, but nobody wants to stop and help me."

"If you took better care of your sheep, shepherdess, they wouldn't fall into the water," the maiden responded as she spurred her horse and rode on without giving her any relief.

The old woman bellowed after her, "Good-bye, disguised beauty!"

These few words upset our brave amazon a great deal. "What bad luck? She has recognized me too! Now I've experienced the same fate as my sister. I'm not any luckier than she was, and it would be ridiculous for someone with my effeminate appearance to join the army. Everybody would recognize me!"

She returned at once to her father's

house, very sad that she had not succeeded to carry out her mission. Though her father received her affectionately and praised her for having had the good sense to return, he fell into a depression even deeper than before because he had spent money on two useless suits of clothes and the other accoutrements. The good old man, however, kept his sorrow to himself, not wishing to add to that of his daughters.

After some time had passed, the youngest girl came to him and begged him most urgently to grant her the same permission he had granted her sisters. "Perhaps," she said, "it's presumptuous of me to hope I'll succeed where they haven't. Nevertheless, I'd like to try. I'm taller than they are, and as you know, I go hunting every day. This exercise has prepared me in some degree for war, and my great desire to relieve you in your distress has inspired me with extraordinary courage."

The count loved her more than either of her sisters, for she cared for him so tenderly that he regarded her as his chief consolation. She read pleasant stories to amuse him, nursed him in his illness, and gave him all the game she killed. Consequently, he argued against her plan much more than he had with her sisters, doing all he could to change her mind. "Do you want to leave me, my dear child?" he asked. "Your absence will be the death of me. If fortune should really smile on you and you should return covered with laurels, I won't have the pleasure of witnessing them. My old age and your absence will bring about my demise."

"No, my dear father," said Bellebelle (for this was her name). "Don't think for a minute that I'll be away that long. The war will soon be over, and if I find any other way of fulfilling the king's orders, I won't hesitate to take advantage of them. I dare say that, though my absence will be upsetting to you, it will be even more distressing to me."

Finally, he granted her request, and she made a plain suit of clothes for herself because her sisters' clothes had cost so much that the poor old count's finances would not bear any more expenses. She was also compelled to take a very bad horse since her two sisters had nearly crippled the other two. Not all this, however, discouraged her. She embraced her father, received his blessing with respect, and as her tears flowed with his and those of her sisters, she departed.

In passing through the meadow that I have already mentioned, she met the old shepherdess, who was trying to pull yet another sheep out of the deep ditch.

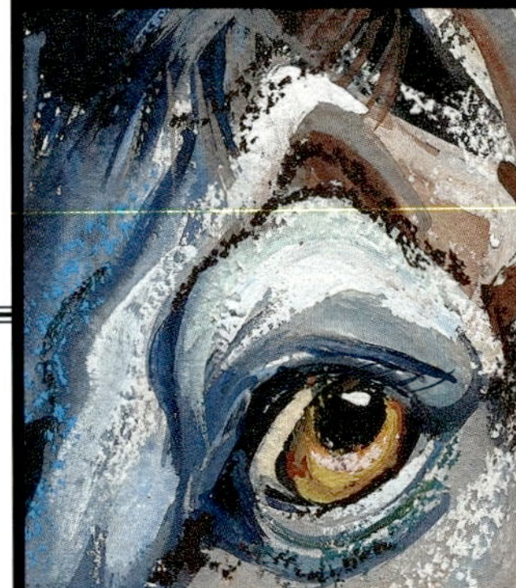

"What are you doing there, shepherdess?" Belle-belle stopped and asked.

"I can't do anything more, my lord," the shepherdess replied. "Ever since daylight I've been trying to save this sheep in vain. I'm so weary that I can scarcely breathe. There's hardly a day that passes when some new misfortune doesn't befall me, and I have nobody to help me."

"I'm truly sorry for you," Belle-belle said, "and to show it, I'll help you."

She instantly dismounted from her horse, which was so calm that she did not bother tying it to prevent its running away. Though she suffered a few scratches as she jumped over the hedge, she plunged into the ditch and worked so diligently that she succeeded in dragging out the beloved sheep. "Don't cry anymore, my good mother," she said. "Here's your sheep. Despite the fact that it's been in the water a long time, it seems quite lively."

"You won't find me ungrateful," the shepherdess said. "I know you, charming Belle-belle. I know where you're going and what your intentions are. When your sisters passed through this meadow, I recognized them as well and knew their every thought. But they were so heartless and ungracious toward me that I managed to prevent their journey. Things will be different in your case. Let me prove it to you, Belle-belle, for I'm a fairy and take pleasure in rewarding those who deserve it. Just watch. You have a miserable scraggy horse, and now I'll give you a real one."

As she spoke she struck the ground with her crook, and instantly Belle-belle heard a neighing behind a bush. As she whirled around, she saw the most handsome horse in the world prancing in the meadow. Since Belle-belle was fond of horses, she was delighted to see one so perfect. The fairy called this fine stallion to her and, touching it with her crook, she said, "Faithful Comrade, I wish you better harnessed than the Emperor Matapa's best horse."

Within seconds, Comrade wore a green velvet saddlecloth embroidered with pearls

and rubies, a saddle to match, and a bridle of pearls with a gold bit and gold studs. In short, there was not a horse in the world as magnificent as this one.

"You've seen only the least remarkable thing about this horse," the fairy remarked. "Pray, let me enumerate his many other qualities. In the first place, he eats only once a week, and it's not necessary to look after him, for he knows the present, past,

and future. I've had him a long time, and I've trained him as I'd train my own horse. Whatever you wish to know, or whenever you need advice, you need only consult him. He'll give you such good advice that most sovereigns would be blessed to have ministers like him. Consider him more as your friend than your horse. Last, your attire is not to my liking. Let me give you something more becoming."

She struck the ground with her crook, and a large trunk appeared. It was sheathed with Morocco leather, was studded with gold nails, and bore Belle-belle's initials. Then the fairy plucked a gold key made in England from the grass, and she opened the trunk, revealing an interior lined with Spanish leather and profusely embroidered. Everything inside the trunk came in dozens: twelve suits, twelve cravats, twelve swords, twelve feathers, and so forth. The coats were woven with so much embroidery and so many diamonds that Belle-belle could barely lift them. "Choose the suit that pleases you most," the fairy said, "and the others will follow you everywhere. You need only to stamp your foot and say, 'Morocco-leather trunk, come to me brimming with linen and lace,' or 'Morocco-leather trunk, come to me brimming with jewels and coins,' and it will instantly appear before you, whether you are outdoors or inside. You must also assume an alias, for Belle-belle will not suit the profession you're about to enter. It occurs to me that you might call yourself the Chevalier Fortuné. Of course, you ought to know who I am. Therefore, let me appear in my natural form."

All of a sudden, the old woman's skin was shed, and the fairy became so astonishingly beautiful that Belle-belle was dazzled. Her dress was made of blue velvet trimmed with ermine, and her hair was entwined with pearls and adorned by a superb crown. Enraptured, Belle-belle threw herself at the fairy's feet as a show of her admiration and inexpressible gratitude. The fairy raised her and embraced her

affectionately. She told her to don a suit of green and gold brocade, and Belle-belle quickly obeyed. Afterward, she mounted her horse and continued her journey so overwhelmed by all the extraordinary things that had just taken place that she could think about nothing else. Indeed, she began to ponder the unexpected good fortune that had helped her attract the kindness of such a powerful fairy.

"To be sure," she said to herself, "she didn't need me to save the sheep. A simple stroke of her wand would have brought an entire flock back from the antipodes if it had wandered off there. I was certainly lucky to have been in a position to oblige her. The trifling service I performed on her behalf is the cause of all she's done for me. She knew my heart and approved of my sentiments. Ah, if my father could see me now, so magnificent and so rich, how delighted he would be! But in any case, I'll have the pleasure of sharing the wealth she has bestowed upon me with my family."

As she finished making these different observations, she arrived in a beautiful city teeming with people. She attracted a great deal of attention, and the people followed and gathered around her.

"Have you ever seen a chevalier more handsome or strapping, or more handsomely dressed?" they cried. "Look how gracefully he manages that superb horse!"

They saluted him most respectfully, and he returned their greetings with a kindly, courteous air. Soon after he had stopped at an inn, the governor, who had been out walking and had admired him in passing, sent a gentleman to say that he hoped he would come and take his lodgings in his castle. The Chevalier Fortuné (we will now use this name when discussing Belle-belle) replied that since he had not yet had the honor of making his acquaintance, he would not take that liberty. However, he would come to pay his respects. In addition, Fortuné asked the governor to provide him with a man whom he could trust with something important that he wanted to send to his father. The governor responded immediately and sent him a very trustworthy messenger.

Soon after this man arrived, Fortuné told him to wait because his letters were not ready yet. Therefore, he shut himself in his room, stamped his foot, and said, "Morocco-leather trunk, come to me brimming with diamonds and coins!"

Within seconds, the trunk appeared but without its key. Where was he to find it? What a pity to break a golden lock enameled with so many different colors! Then again, he didn't dare trust the locksmith. Were the locksmith to mention the chevalier's treasures, thieves would descend upon him to rob or even kill him. He looked for the key everywhere, but the more he looked, the more hopeless his search appeared.

"How disturbing!" he cried. "I can't make use of the fairy's generosity, nor send my father any of the treasures she's given to me."

In the midst of his musing, it occurred to him that his best course of action would be to consult his horse. So, he went to the stable and whispered, "I beg of you, Comrade, tell me where I can find the key to the Morocco-leather trunk."

"In my ear," the horse replied.

Fortuné peered into the horse's ear and noticed a green ribbon. Once he pulled it out, he found the key he needed. He opened the Morocco-leather trunk, which

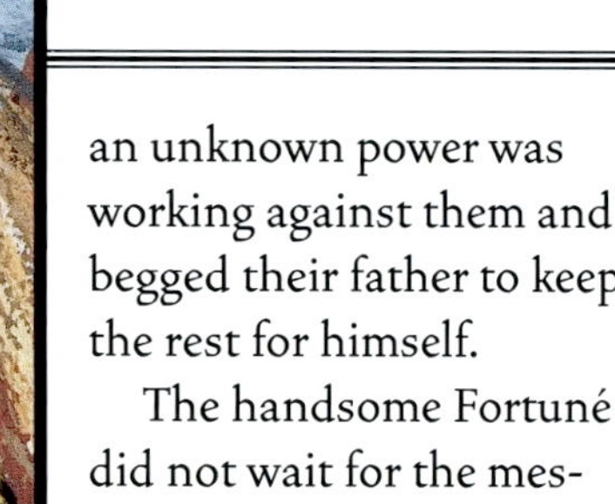

contained more than a bushel of diamonds and coins. Quickly, the chevalier filled three caskets, one for his father and two others for his sisters. Then he gave them to the governor's man and told him not to stop night or day until he arrived at the house of the count.

This messenger made a swift journey, and when he told the old man that he had brought him a very heavy casket from his son, the chevalier, the count wondered what it might contain.

"Belle-belle set out with so little money that she had no means to buy anything or even to pay the journey of the man in charge of this present."

But after reading the letter that his beloved daughter had written, he thought he would die from joy. Moreover, the sight of the jewels and gold confirmed the truth of her story. The most extraordinary thing was that, when Belle-belle's two sisters opened their caskets, they found only false coins and bits of glass instead of diamonds because the fairy did not want them to benefit from her kindness. Consequently, they thought their sister was laughing at them and became extremely angry with her. When the count noticed this, he gave them the greater part of the jewels he had just received. However, as soon as they touched them, they changed like the others. Therefore, they concluded that an unknown power was working against them and begged their father to keep the rest for himself.

The handsome Fortuné did not wait for the messenger to return to leave the city. His business was too urgent; he was bound to obey the king's orders. After he paid his visit to the governor's house, he discovered that many people had gathered to see him. His personality and manners revealed such an air of honesty that they could not help but admire and even adore him. He said nothing except what was pleasant to hear, and when so many people crowded around him, he did not know how to account for such an unusual circumstance, especially because he had spent his entire life in the country.

He continued his journey on his excellent horse, which entertained him by telling him a thousand stories about the most remarkable events in ancient and recent history. "My dear master," he said, "I'm delighted to have you as my owner. I know you possess an abundance of frankness and honor. Certain people with whom I lived a long time made me weary of life because their circle of friends was so unbearable. Among them was a man who pretended to be my friend. When he spoke in my presence, he placed me above Pegasus and Bucephalus. But as soon as I was out of sight, he treated me like a pitiful nag. He pretended to admire my faults in order to induce me to commit greater ones. One day, when I became tired of his caresses, which properly speaking were treacherous, I gave him such a severe kick that I had the pleasure of knocking out nearly all his teeth. Whenever I've seen him since then, I've told him with the utmost sincerity that it's not right for his mouth to be as handsome as others because he opens it too often to abuse those who do him no harm."

"Ho, ho," the chevalier cried, "you're full of spirit. Aren't you afraid that someday this man will become so enraged he will pass his sword through you?"

"It wouldn't matter, my lord," Comrade replied. "In any case, I'd be aware of his intention before he knew it himself."

As they continued this conversation, they approached a vast forest, and Comrade said to the chevalier, "Master, a woodcutter who lives here may possibly be of great service to us. He has been endowed with special gifts."

"What do you mean by that term?" Fortuné interrupted.

"I mean that he's received one or more gifts from fairies," the horse replied. "You must recruit him to join our company."

Just as they were talking, they reached the spot where the woodcutter was working, and the young chevalier approached him with a gentle, winning air. He asked him several questions about the forest, whether there were many wild beasts there, and whether he was allowed to hunt them. The woodcutter responded to all of the questions like an intelligent man. Fortuné then inquired what had happened to the men who had been helping him chop down so many trees. The woodcutter replied that he had cut them down all by himself. "It took only a few hours, and I have many others yet to chop down to make a load for myself."

"What? Do you mean to say you'll take away all this wood today?" the chevalier asked.

"Ah, my lord," replied Strongback (for this is what people called him), "my strength is quite extraordinary."

"So you make a great deal of money, I suppose?" Fortuné said.

"Very little," the woodcutter replied. "The people hereabouts are poor. Everyone works for himself without asking for his neighbor's help."

"Since you live in such a poor region," the chevalier remarked, "you have only to decide to leave it and travel to another. Come with me, and you will have everything you desire. Whenever you believe it's time to return, I'll give you money for your return journey."

Thinking he would never get a better offer than this, the woodcutter laid his ax aside and followed his new master.

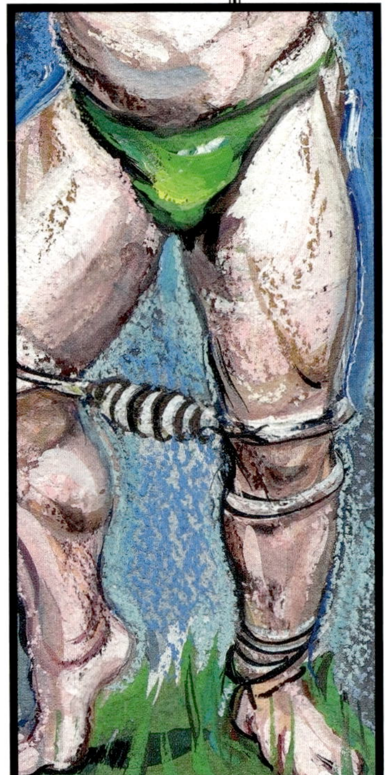

As they passed through the forest, they came upon a man in a glade who was tying his legs with a rope so tightly together that it seemed he could do nothing but hobble. Upon seeing him, Comrade stopped and said to his master, "My lord, here's another gifted man you'll need. You must recruit him as well."

Fortuné approached this man, and with his usual grace, he asked him, "Why are you tying your legs like that?"

"I'm going hunting," he said.

"What?" the chevalier smiled. "Do you mean to say you can run better when your legs are bound like that?"

"No, my lord," he replied. "I'm aware that I won't be move very fast, but that's my goal. There's not a stag, deer, or hare I can't outrun when my legs are free. As a result, I always run right by them so that they escape, and I rarely have the pleasure of catching them!"

"You seem to be an extraordinary fellow," Fortuné said. "What's your name?"

"They've given me the name of Swift," the hunter replied, "for I'm well-known in this region."

"If you'd like to see another region," the chevalier responded, "I'd be happy to take you with me. You won't have difficult tasks, and I'll treat you well."

Swift was not particularly well off, and he gladly accepted the offer.

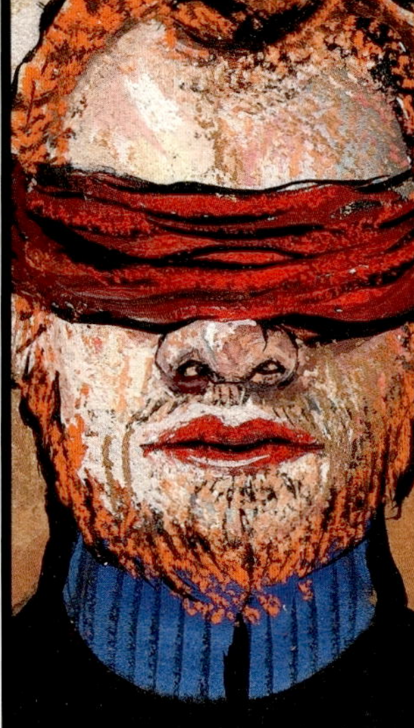

Now Fortuné continued his journey, followed by his new servants, and the next morning he noticed a man binding his eyes on the border of a marsh. Once again, the horse stopped and said to his master, "My lord, I advise you to recruit this man as well."

Fortuné immediately asked him why he was binding his eyes.

"I see too clearly," he said. "I can spot game more than four miles away, and I always kill more than I wish when I shoot. Therefore, I'm obliged to bind my eyes, for I wouldn't have any game left once I caught sight of all the animals around me."

"You're a very talented fellow," replied Fortuné.

"They call me Sharpshooter," the man said, "and I wouldn't abandon this occupation for anything in the world."

"Well, despite what you've just said, I'd

like to invite you to travel with me," the chevalier said. "You won't be prevented from exercising your talent."

The Sharpshooter hesitated somewhat, and Fortuné had more difficulty in persuading him than the others, since sportsmen as a lot are fond of their freedom. However, Fortuné eventually succeeded and left the marsh with his new servant. A few days later, he passed by a meadow in which he saw a man lying on his side, and Comrade said, "Master, this man is most gifted. I can see that you'll need him very much."

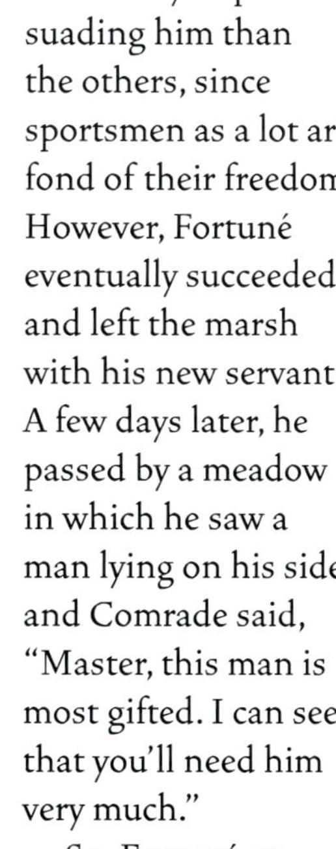

So, Fortuné entered the meadow and asked the man what he was doing. "I want some herbs," he replied, "and I'm listening to the grass as it grows to find out which ones I'll need."

"What?" the chevalier remarked. "Are your ears so sharp that you can hear the grass grow and know what's about to sprout?"

"That's why they call me Hear-all," said the man.

"Very well, Hear-all," Fortuné continued, "would you like to join me? I'll give you such high wages that you won't have any regrets."

The man was delighted by such a generous proposition and joined the others without hesitation.

Continuing his journey, the chevalier saw a man standing on the side of the road. His cheeks were so inflated that he looked rather droll. His back was turned away from Fortuné and he faced a lofty mountain two miles away where fifty or sixty windmills were standing. When the horse saw him, he said to his master, "Here's another of our gifted ones. Do all you can to make him come with you."

Fortuné, who had the power of fascinating everyone he encountered, approached this man and asked him what he was doing.

"I'm blowing a little, my lord," he said. "I want to get all those mills turning."

"It appears to me that you're rather far off," the chevalier replied.

"On the contrary," the blower remarked, "I'm afraid I'm too near. If I weren't holding back half of my breath, I'd upset the mills and perhaps the mountains they stand on. I do a great deal of harm this way without intending to, and I can tell you, my lord, that once, when my mistress had treated me badly, I went into the woods to indulge my sorrow, and my sighs tore the trees up by their roots and created a great deal of chaos. So in these parts, they now call me Boisterous."

"If they're tired of you," Fortuné said, "and you'd like to come with me, I have some men who'd keep you company. They too possess unusual talents."

"I have a natural curiosity for anything out of the ordinary," Boisterous replied, "and so I accept."

Immensely pleased, Fortuné proceeded on his way with his talented recruits. After passing through a densely wooded countryside, they came to a large lake that was fed by several springs. On its shore was a man who was staring at it attentively.

"My lord," Comrade said to his master, "this man will nearly complete your entourage. You'd do well to induce him to join you."

The chevalier promptly approached him and asked, "Tell me, sir, what are you doing?"

"My lord," the man replied, "you'll see as soon as this lake is full. I intend to drink it in one swig, for I'm still thirsty, although I've already emptied it twice."

Accordingly, he stooped down to drink, and in a few minutes he had hardly left enough water for the smallest minnow to swim in. Just as surprised as his followers, Fortuné asked, "Are you always so thirsty?"

"No," the man said. "I only drink like this for a wager, or when I've eaten something too salty. I'm known in these parts as Tippler."

"Come with me, Tippler," said the chevalier. "I'll give you wine to tipple, which you'll find much better than spring water."

This promise pleased the man very much, and he decided on the spot to join the others.

When Fortuné was within sight of the general meeting place set for the king's forces, he noticed a man eating so greedily that, although he had more than sixty thousand loaves of the superb Gonesse bread before him, he seemed determined to eat every last crumb. Comrade said to his master, "My lord, this is the final man you need. Please persuade him come with you."

The chevalier approached him and smiled, "Do you really intend to eat all this bread for your breakfast?"

"Yes," he replied. "My only regret is that there's so little, but the bakers are lazy fellows and refuse to exert themselves whether you're hungry or not."

"If you require so much every day," Fortuné remarked, "there is hardly a country you wouldn't bring to the brink of starvation."

"Oh, my lord," replied Gorger (as people called him), "I'd feel badly if I always had such a huge appetite. Neither my possessions nor those of my neighbors would be enough to support it. To tell the truth, I only feast in this fashion every now and then."

"My friend Gorger," Fortuné said, "join me, and I'll show you good cheer. You won't regret choosing me for a master."

Then Comrade, who had a good deal of

sense and forethought, warned the chevalier to forbid his men from boasting about the extraordinary gifts they possessed. Therefore, Fortuné lost no time in gathering them around him and said, "Listen to me, Strongback, Swift, Sharpshooter, Hear-all, Boisterous, Tippler, and Gorger. If you want to please me, you'll keep your talents an inviolable secret. In return, I guarantee that I'll try my utmost to keep you satisfied."

Each one of them took an oath to obey Fortuné's orders, and soon after, the chevalier, who stood out more because of his good looks and graceful demeanor than his magnificent attire, entered the ravaged capital city on his excellent horse, and he was followed by the finest companions in the world. He lost no time in procuring uniforms laced with silver and gold for them. He also provided horses for each of them. After taking lodgings in the best inn, he waited for the day set for the royal review. At the same time, he became the talk of the city, and the king, who became aware of his reputation, was eager to meet him.

On the day of the review, all the troops assembled on a vast plain, and there the king arrived with his sister and the entire court. Because the dowager queen had not forsworn pomp despite the misfortunes of the kingdom, Fortuné was dazzled by so much splendor. However, if the king and his sister attracted his attention, they were just as much struck by his incomparable beauty. Everyone asked who that handsome, graceful young gentleman was, and the king passed close by him and gave him a signal to approach. Fortuné dismounted immediately to make a low bow, and Fortuné and was unable to stop blushing when the king gazed at him so earnestly. Indeed, this additional color heightened the radiance of his complexion.

"I'd like to hear from your own lips," the king said, "who you are and what your name is."

"Sire," he replied, "I'm called Fortuné, without having any reason for bearing this name up to now, for my father, who's a count on the frontier, has been living in great poverty, although he was born of a rich and noble family."

"Fortuné, whoever has served as your godmother has done well to bring you here," the king replied. "I feel a particular affection for you, for I remember your father. He once rendered me a great service. Let me reward him by favoring his son."

"That's quite just of you, brother," said the queen, who had not spoken yet. "And since I'm older than you and am more familiar with the service this count rendered the state, I request that you to let me take charge of rewarding this young chevalier."

Enchanted by his reception, Fortuné could not sufficiently thank the king and queen. He did not, however, venture to express his deep feeling of gratitude because he believed silence more respectful than talking too much. The little he did say was so correct and to the point that everyone applauded him. Afterward, he remounted his horse and mixed among the nobles

who accompanied the king, even though the queen called him away every minute to ask him a thousand questions. Turning toward Floride, her favorite confidante, she whispered, "What do you think of this chevalier? Have you ever seen anyone with a nobler demeanor or features that are more regular? I confess to you, I've never laid eyes on anyone more charming."

Floride agreed with the queen wholeheartedly and lavished praise on the chevalier, for he seemed just as charming to her as to her mistress. For his part, Fortuné could not help gazing at the king from time to time. He was the handsomest prince in the world, and his manners were most engaging. Belle-belle, who had not renounced her sex with her dress, felt fervently drawn to him.

After the review, the king told Fortuné, "I fear this war will be a bloody one, and I've decided to keep you near me."

The queen, who was present, exclaimed that she had also been thinking the same thing. He ought not to be exposed to a long campaign, and since the place of premier *maître d'hôtel* was vacant in her household, she would give it to him.

"No," the king said. "I intend to make him my squire."

Thereupon, they argued with each other as to who would have the pleasure of promoting Fortuné. Since the queen feared revealing the secret emotions already exciting her heart, she eventually yielded to the king's wish.

Hardly a day passed that Fortuné did not call for his Morocco-leather trunk and take out a new garment. He was certainly the most magnificent prince at the court. Sometimes, the queen asked him how his father could afford to give him such clothes. Other times, she would jest with him: "Tell the truth," she said, "you have a mistress, and she's the one who sends you all these beautiful things."

Though Fortuné blushed, he replied respectfully to the various questions the queen put to him. He also performed his duties remarkably well. He had come to appreciate the king's merits and became more attached to him than he had wanted. "What will be my fate?" he said. "I love a great king without any hope of his loving me. Nor will he ever know what I'm suffering."

In sum, the king overwhelmed him with favors, and he found nothing to his liking unless the handsome chevalier did it. Meanwhile, the queen, deceived by his dress, seriously contemplated arranging a secret marriage with him, and the inequality of their birth was the only issue that troubled her. However, she was not the only one who entertained such feelings for Fortuné. The most beautiful women at the court were taken with him. He was swamped with tender letters, assignations, presents, and a thousand gallantries, but he replied to all of them with so much indifference that they were certain he had a mistress in his province. No matter how much he tried to be modest at the great entertainments of the court, he always distinguished himself. He won the prize at all the tournaments. He killed the most game when he went hunting. He danced at all the balls with more grace and skill than any other courtier did. In short, it was delightful to watch him and hear him speak.

Anxious to be spared the shame of declaring her feelings for him, the queen asked Floride to make him understand that a young and beautiful queen's many signs of kindness ought not to be a matter of indifference to him. Floride was taken aback by this request, for she herself had been unable to avoid the fate of all those who had seen the chevalier, and she thought it would be too nice on her part to give her mistress's interests precedence over her own. Therefore, whenever the queen gave her an opportunity of talking to him, she told him only about the queen's bad temperament and what injustices her attendants suffered from her instead of speaking about her beauty and noble qualities. Floride also told him how badly she abused the power she had usurped in the kingdom. Finally, she drew a comparison between their feelings and said, "I wasn't born a queen, but really I ought to have been one. I have so much generosity in my nature that I'm eager to do good for everybody. Ah, if I were in that high station," she continued, "how happy I'd make the handsome Fortuné. He'd love me out of gratitude even if he could not love me from inclination."

Quite dismayed by this conversation, the young chevalier did not know what to say. Therefore, he vowed to avoid any future tête-a-têtes with her.

When Floride returned, the impatient queen constantly inquired, "What impression did you make for me on Fortuné?"

"He esteems himself so little," she said, "and he's so bashful that he won't believe anything I tell him about you. Or he pretends not to believe it because he's absorbed by some other matter."

"I think so, too," said the distressed

queen. "But I can't imagine that he'd curb his ambition to advance himself."

"And I can't imagine," Floride replied, "that you'd use your crown to capture his heart. You're so young and beautiful and possess thousands of charms. Is it necessary for you to take recourse in the splendor of a diadem?"

"One may have to take recourse in anything possible," the queen replied, "if it becomes necessary to subdue a rebellious heart."

Floride saw clearly that she could not possibly put an end to her mistress's infatuation. Every day, the queen expected some positive result from her confidante's work, but she made such little headway with Fortuné that the queen was eventually compelled to seek some means of speaking to him herself. She knew that he was accustomed to take a walk early every morning in some small woods in front of the windows of her apartment. Therefore, she arose at daybreak, and as she watched his customary path, she saw him approaching with a melancholy and distracted air. She called Floride immediately.

"You've spoken the truth," she said. "Fortuné is without a doubt in love with some lady at this court or in his province. Look how sad he looks."

"I've noticed this sadness in all his conversations," Floride replied. "You'd do well to forget all about him."

"It's too late," the queen exclaimed, sighing deeply. "Since he's already entered that green arbor, let's go there. I want you alone to come with me."

The girl did not dare to stop the queen no matter how much she wanted to. Indeed, she feared the queen would induce Fortuné to fall in love with her, and a rival of such exalted rank is always dangerous. As soon as the queen had taken a few steps into the wood, she heard the chevalier singing. His voice was very sweet, and he sang these words to a melody then current:

"How rare a thing it is for love and peace
To dwell together in the same heart!
When my joys begin to surge, my fears increase,
That they, like a morning dream, will soon
depart!
Dread of the future robs my soul of rest,
Most unhappy I am when most blessed!"

Fortuné had composed these verses, stirred by his feelings for the king as well as by the favor the king had shown him, and his fear of being found out and forced to leave a court that he preferred above any other in the world.

Stopping to listen, the queen was distraught. "What shall I do?" she whispered softly to Floride. "This ungrateful young man doesn't want to honor or please me. He believes himself content with this conquest of his. He sacrifices me to another."

"He's at that age," Floride replied, "when reason has yet to establish its rights. If I may venture to give some advice to your majesty, forget such a giddy fellow so incapable of appreciating his good fortune."

The queen would have preferred a different answer from her confidante. Casting an angry look at her, she hastened onward and entered the arbor where the knight was standing. She pretended to be surprised to find him there and to be upset at his seeing her in such disarray, although she had taken great pains to make herself magnificently attractive. As soon as she appeared, he took a step to withdraw out of respect for her, but she asked him to remain so that he might aid her in walking.

"I was wakened this morning most pleasantly by the singing of the birds. The fine weather and pure air induced me to come outside and listen more closely to their warbling. How happy they are! Alas, all they know is pleasure. Grief does not trouble them!"

"It appears to me, madame," Fortuné replied, "that they're not entirely exempt from pain and sorrow. They're always in danger of a murderous shot or deceitful snares of sportsmen. Moreover, birds of prey make war against these little innocents. When a hard winter freezes the ground and covers it with snow, they die for want of hemp or millet seed, and every year they have difficulty finding a new mistress."

"So you think, then, chevalier," the queen said, smiling, "that this is a difficulty? Some men have a fresh one every month, but you appear surprised by this, as if your heart were not of the same stamp. Can you not change your heart like this?"

"I'm unable to predict how I'd act," the chevalier said, "for I've never been in love. I do believe, however, that if I formed an attachment, it would end only when I breathed my last."

"You've never been in love?" cried the queen, looking so earnestly at him that the poor chevalier changed color several times. "Fortuné, how can you possibly declare this to a queen who reads in your face and your eyes the passion that occupies your heart? Just now, I heard the words you sang to that new melody that's just become so popular."

"It's true, madame," the chevalier replied, "that those lines are my own. My friends ask me every day to write drinking songs for them, although I never drink anything but water. There are others who prefer love songs. So I sing about love and Bacchus without being a lover or a drinker."

As the queen listened to him, she trembled so with emotion that she could scarcely keep standing. All that he told her had rekindled the hope in her bosom that Floride had sought to extinguish. "I'd think you were sincere," she said, "but I'd indeed be surprised if you hadn't found one lady at this court sufficiently lovely to attract your attention."

"Madame," Fortuné replied, "I try so hard to carry out the duties of my office that I have no time for sighing."

"You love nothing, then?" she responded vehemently.

"No, madame," he said, "my heart is not so gallant. I'm a kind of misanthrope who loves his liberty and doesn't want to lose it for anything in the world."

Sitting down, the queen gave him the kindest of looks. "There are some chains so beautiful and glorious," she replied, "that anyone might feel happy to wear them. If fortune has made this your destiny, I'd advise you to renounce your liberty."

As she spoke, her eyes revealed her meaning too clearly for the chevalier to mistake what she meant. He already had strong suspicions and was now convinced they were correct. Fearing the conversation might lead even further, he looked at his watch and held up his hand. "I must beg your majesty to permit me to go to the palace," he said. "It's time for the king to get up, and he asked me to be at his side."

"Go, callous youth," she said, sighing profoundly. "You're doing the right thing by paying court to my brother, but remember, it's not wrong to pay some attention to me."

The queen followed him with her eyes, and then let them fall. After reflecting on what had just transpired, she blushed with shame and rage. Her grief was further augmented by the fact that Floride had witnessed everything, and she noticed a smirk of satisfaction on her face that implied: "You would have done better had you taken my advice instead of speaking to Fortuné." She pondered all this for some time. Then she took up her tablet and wrote these lines, which she later had set to music by a celebrated court composer:

"Behold! Behold! The torment I endure!
My victor knows, but covers the clue.
My heart shows, but it can't have a cure,
Still stung by the shaft he's shot so true.

"He's not concealed his coldness or disdain,
He hates me, and his hate I should return;
But ah, my foolish heart tries in vain,
For it only has love for him to burn!"

Floride played her part cleverly: she consoled the queen as much as she could and gave her some hope to keep her going. "Fortuné thinks himself so beneath you, madame," she said, "that perhaps he failed to understand what you meant. It seems to me that he's already said a good deal by assuring you that he doesn't love anyone."

It is so natural for us to expect our hopes will be fulfilled that the queen was eventually encouraged to believe she had a chance with Fortuné. She was unaware that the malicious Floride, who knew all too well the chevalier's indifference toward her, wanted to induce him to speak even more forthrightly and offend the queen by his coolness.

As for Fortuné, he was most confused, for he was caught in a cruel dilemma. He would not have hesitated to leave the court if his love for the king had not detained him despite himself. As for the queen, he never went near her except when she held her court, and then always in the king's entourage. She noticed this change in his conduct instantly and responded by giving him the opportunity of paying her attention several times. But he steadfastly refused to do so. One day, however, when she descended into her gardens, she saw him cross one of the grand avenues and about to enter some small woods. Therefore, she called to him, and he was afraid of displeasing her by pretending not to hear and approached her respectfully.

"Do you remember, chevalier," she said, "the conversation we had together some time ago in the green arbor?"

"I'd never forget that honor," he answered.

"No doubt the questions I put to you then were distressing," she said. "Ever since that day you've continually avoided me so that I haven't been able to quiz you further."

"Your majesty, it was by chance alone that gave me that opportunity," he said. "So, I thought it would be presumptuous of me to seek another one."

"Why don't you say instead that you've been avoiding my presence, you ungrateful man?" she demanded, blushing. "You know quite well how I feel about you."

Fortuné cast down his eyes in an embarrassed and modest manner, and since he hesitated to reply, she continued, "You seem dismayed. Go! Don't try to answer me. Your silence speaks louder than words."

She would have continued scolding him, but she noticed the king coming their way. She advanced toward him, and upon seeing how melancholy he was, she asked him to tell her the reason.

"You know," the king said, "that about a month ago I received news that an enormous dragon was ravaging the country. I thought my soldiers could kill him and issued the necessary orders for that purpose. But they've tried everything in vain. He devours my subjects, their flocks, and anything he encounters. He poisons all the rivers and springs wherever he quenches his thirst, and ruins the grass and the herbs wherever he lies."

While the king was talking to her, it occurred to the irritated queen that this would be an opportune way to take out her resentment on the chevalier. "I'm aware of the bad news you received. As you saw, Fortuné was just with me and told me all about it. But, brother, you'll be surprised at what I have to tell you. He's implored me most insistently to ask you for permission to go and fight this terrible dragon. Indeed, he's so skilled in the use of arms that I'm not surprised he's willing to be so daring.

Besides, he's told me he has some secret power that he can use to put the most dangerous dragon to sleep, but that must never be mentioned because it doesn't show much courage on his part."

"No matter how he does it," the king replied, "it will bring him great glory and be of great service to us if he succeeds. But I fear he's overzealous, and it may well cost him his life."

"No, brother," the queen added, "there's no need to fear. You know that he's naturally sincere and thus has no intention in dying so rashly. In short, I've promised to obtain what he wants, and if you refuse him, it will kill him."

"I'll grant your wish," the king said, "but I confess, I do so with a great deal of reluctance. Come, let us call him." He then made a signal for Fortuné to approach and said kindly, "I've just learned from the queen that you want to fight the dragon that is devastating our country. It's such a

bold decision that I scarcely believe you've considered the danger involved."

"I've depicted all this to him," the queen said. "But he's so eager to serve you and to distinguish himself that nothing can dissuade him, and I predict he'll succeed."

Fortuné was taken aback by what the king and queen said. Though he quickly grasped the queen's wicked intentions, his natural deference would not permit him to expose them. Therefore, he did not respond and simply let her continue. He contented himself by making low bows so that the

king thought he was now pleading with him directly to grant him what he desired.

"Go, then," the king said, sighing. "Go where glory calls you. I know you're skillful in everything you do, especially in the use of weapons. Perhaps this monster won't be able to avoid your blows."

"Sire," the chevalier replied, "no matter what the outcome of this combat, I'll be satisfied. Either I'll rescue you from a terrible scourge, or I'll die for you. But grant me one favor dear to my heart."

"Ask for whatever you wish," said the king.

"May I be bold enough to ask for your portrait?" Fortuné said.

The king was very pleased that he had thought of obtaining his portrait at a time when he should have been occupied with far more weighty matters, and the queen resented once again that he did not request her portrait as well. However, he would have had to possess a superabundance of goodness to desire the portrait of such a wicked woman.

Once the king had returned to his palace and the queen to hers, Fortuné mulled over the consequences of the pledge he had made. Going to his horse, he said, "My dear Comrade, I have a good deal of news to tell you."

"I know it already, my lord," he replied.

"What shall we do, then?"

"We must set out right away," the horse said. "Go and get the king's order commanding you to fight the dragon, and then we'll do our duty."

These words comforted our young chevalier, and the next morning he awaited the king in a riding dress just as handsome as all the others that he had taken from the Morocco-leather trunk. As soon as the king saw him, he exclaimed, "What? You're ready to go?"

"Your commands cannot be executed too quickly, sire," he replied. "I've come to take my leave of your majesty." The king could not help feeling pity for Fortuné, seeing that such a young, handsome, and accomplished gentleman was about to expose himself to the greatest danger a man could ever face. He embraced him and gave him a portrait framed by large diamonds. Fortuné accepted it joyfully, for the king's noble qualities had made such an impression on him that he could not imagine anyone in the world more charming. If Fortuné was upset at leaving him, it was much less from the fear of being devoured by the dragon than from being deprived of the presence of one so dear.

The king added a general order to Fortuné's commission, calling upon all his subjects to aid and assist Fortuné whenever he might be in need. Taking leave of the king, Fortuné went to the queen so that nothing might be taken amiss. She was sitting at her dressing table, surrounded by several of her ladies. She changed color when he appeared, and she began reproaching herself for what she had done. He saluted her respectfully and asked her if she would honor him with her commands since he was on the point of departure.

These last words completely disconcerted her, and Floride, who did not know that the queen had plotted against the chevalier, was thunderstruck. She would have liked a private chat with him, but he carefully avoided such an embarrassing situation.

"I pray to the gods," the queen said, "that you may conquer the dragon and return triumphant."

"Madame," the chevalier replied, "your majesty does me too much of an honor. You're sufficiently aware of the danger to which I shall be exposed. However, I'm full of confidence. Perhaps, on this occasion, I'm the only one who has hope."

The queen understood very well what he meant. No doubt she would have replied to this reproach if fewer persons had been present. The chevalier returned to his lodgings and ordered his seven excellent servants to get their horses and follow him.

"The time has arrived to prove what you can do."

None of them failed to rejoice at having a chance to serve him. In less than an hour, everything was ready, and they set out with him and assured him they would do their utmost to carry out his commands. Soon thereafter, when they had reached the open country and had no fear of being seen, each one gave proof of his talent. Tippler drank the water from the lakes and caught the finest fish for his master's dinner. Swift hunted some stags and caught a hare by its ears, despite the tricks it made. Sharpshooter gave no quarter to partridges and pheasants, and when the game was killed by the one, the venison by another, and the fish plucked from the water, Strongback carried everything cheerfully. Even Hear-all made himself useful: he found truffles, morels, mushrooms, salads, and fine herbs by listening to where they grew in the ground. Therefore, Fortuné rarely had to pay anything to cover the expenses of his journey. He would have been greatly amused at the sight of so many extraordinary events if he had not been so troubled by all that he had just left. Even though the king's qualities continued to impress him, the queen's malice seemed so great that he could not help hating her.

As he was riding along lost in thought, he was aroused from his reverie by the shrieks of a host of poor peasants whom the dragon was devouring. When he caught sight of some who had escaped and were running away as fast as they could, he called to them, but they would not stop. So, he followed and spoke to them, and he learned that the monster was not far away. When he asked them how they had managed to escape, they told him that since water was scarce in this region, they had only rainwater to drink and had made a pond to conserve it.

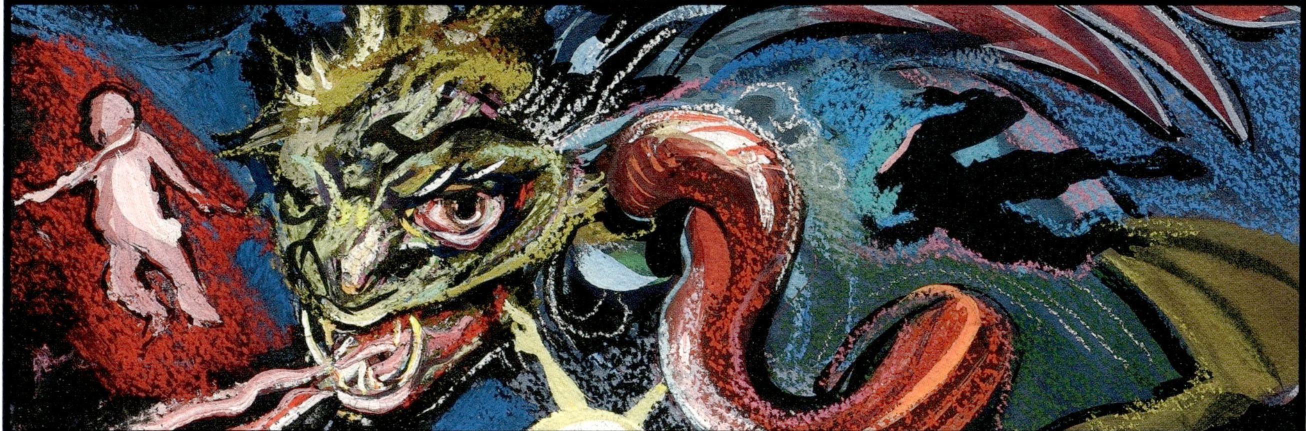

After making his rounds, the dragon went to drink there and uttered such tremendous roars when he arrived there that he could be heard a mile away. So alarmed did everybody become that they hid themselves and locked their doors and windows.

The chevalier stopped at an inn, not so much to rest as to seek some sound advice from his handsome horse. After everyone had retired, he went into the stable and asked, "Comrade, how are we going to conquer this dragon?"

"My lord," he said, "let me dream about it tonight. Then I'll tell you what I think tomorrow morning."

Accordingly, the next morning, when the chevalier came again, the horse said, "Let Hear-all listen to discover if the dragon is near here."

Hear-all lay on the ground and heard the rumble of the dragon some seven miles away. When the horse was informed of this, he said to Fortuné, "Tell Tippler to drink up all the water in the pond and have Strongback carry enough wine there to fill it. Then you must scatter dried raisins, pepper, and other herbs around the pond that will make the dragon thirsty. Order all the villagers to lock themselves up in their houses. And you, my lord, must stay there and lay in wait with your companions. The dragon won't fail to drink at the pond. He'll relish the wine, and then you'll see how it will all end."

As soon as Comrade had indicated what was to be done, they all set off to fulfill their tasks. The chevalier himself went into a house that overlooked the pond, and no sooner had he done so than the frightful dragon arrived at the pond and drank several times. Next, he gobbled up the breakfast they had prepared for him, and then he drank more and more, until he became intoxicated. Unable to move, he lay on his side, his head hung down, his eyes closed. When Fortuné saw him like this, he knew he did not have a moment to lose. Emerging from the house, sword in hand, he courageously attacked the dragon. Though wounded on all sides, the dragon tried to stand so that he could fall on the chevalier, but he lacked the strength because he had lost too much blood. The chevalier was overjoyed that he had reduced him to this sorry state and called his companions to bind the monster with cords and chains so that the king would have the pleasure and glory of putting an end to his life. Once they had nothing more to fear from the beast, they dragged him to the city, with Fortuné at the head. On approaching the palace, he sent Swift to

the king with the news of his great success. Such tidings seemed incredible to everyone until they actually saw the monster tied on a machine constructed for the beheading.

The king descended and embraced Fortuné. "The gods have reserved this victory for you," he said. "I feel more joy at your safe return than at the sight of this horrible dragon reduced to this condition, my dear chevalier."

"Sire," he replied, "it would please me if your majesty would give the monster his death blow. I brought him here expressly so you could do this."

The king drew his sword and terminated the existence of one of his most cruel enemies. Everybody uttered shouts of joy at such unexpected success. Floride, who had been fretting unceasingly, soon heard about the return of her handsome chevalier and ran to tell the queen. She, in turn, was so astonished and confounded by her love and her hatred that she could not respond to her confidante's news. She had reproached herself hundreds of times for the malicious trick she had played, but she preferred to see him dead than so indifferent to her. Consequently, she did not know whether she should be pleased or sorry that he had returned to disturb her peace.

Eager to tell his sister of this extraordinary event, the king entered her chamber, leaning on the chevalier's arm. "Here's the dragon slayer," he said. "This faithful subject has performed for me the greatest service that I could have ever demanded. Since you were the one, madame, to whom he first expressed his desire to fight this monster, I hope you appreciate the courage with which he exposed himself to utter peril."

Composing herself, the queen honored Fortuné with a gracious reception and a thousand praises. She thought him handsomer than when he went away, and the way she gazed at him indicated that her heart was not cured of its wound. However, she did not want to leave it up to looks alone to explain how she felt. So, later when she went hunting with the king, she stopped following the hounds and felt suddenly indisposed. Turning to the young chevalier nearby, she said, "Do me the pleasure of remaining with me. I want to get down and rest a little.—Go," she continued, speaking to those who accompanied her, "don't leave my brother!"

She dismounted from her horse with Floride and sat by the side of a stream. There she remained for some time in deep silence, trying to think of the best way to start the conversation. Finally, she raised her eyes and gazed at the chevalier.

"Since good intentions are not always obvious," she said, "I fear you haven't grasped the motives that induced me to urge the king to send you to fight the dragon. I have presentiments that never mislead me, and I felt certain that you'd prove yourself brave. Your rivals have not thought highly of your courage because you didn't join the army. That's why I felt you needed to perform some act of valor that would stop their tongues from wagging. Perhaps I ought to have told you what they had been saying about you, but I feared there might be consequences resulting from your resentment. So, I thought it better for you to silence such evil-minded people by demonstrating your valiant behavior in action rather than by exerting influence that would mark you as a favorite, not a soldier. Thus, you see, chevalier, that I longed to do something that might contribute to your glory, and you'd be very wrong if you were to judge otherwise."

"The distance is so great between us, madame," he replied modestly, "that I'm not worthy of the explanation you've been so kind to give me, or the care you took to imperil my life for the sake of my honor. The gods protected me with more beneficence than my enemies had hoped, and I'll always esteem myself lucky to serve the king or you and to risk my life, the loss of which is a matter of more indifference to me than one might imagine."

This respectful reproach from Fortuné nettled the queen, for she wholly comprehended his meaning, but he was still too pleasing for her to feel alienated by such a sharp reply. On the contrary, she pretended to sympathize with his sentiments and asked him, "Tell me again how skillfully you conquered the dragon."

Fortuné had carefully avoided telling anyone how his men had helped him defeat the dragon. He boasted of having faced this redoubtable enemy alone, and that his own skill and courage, even to the point of rashness, had enabled him to triumph. The queen, who scarcely paid attention to what he was saying, interrupted to ask whether he was now convinced of her sincere concern in his affairs. She would have pressed the matter further, but he interrupted her by saying, "Madame, I hear the blast of the horn. The king approaches. Does your majesty want your horse to go and meet him?"

"No," she said spitefully. "It's sufficient for you to do so."

"The king would blame me, madame," he added, "if I were to leave you by yourself in such a dangerous place."

"I can dispense with your attention," she replied imperatively. "Be gone! Your presence annoys me!"

At this command, the chevalier made a dignified bow, mounted his horse, and disappeared from her sight. Concerned by how she would react to this fresh offense, he consulted his fine horse. "Let me know, Comrade," he said, "if this queen, who's much too passionate and angry, is going to find another monster for me."

"No, she won't find another one," the handsome horse replied. "But she herself

is more of a dragon than the one you've killed, and she'll certainly put your patience and virtue to the test."

"Will she cause me to fall out of favor with the king?" he cried. "That's all I fear."

"I won't reveal the future to you," Comrade said. "Just know that I'm always on the alert."

The horse stopped talking, for the king had appeared at the end of an avenue. Fortuné joined him and reported that the queen had not felt well and had commanded him to remain at her side.

"It seems to me," the king said, smiling, "you're very much in her good graces, and you speak your mind to her rather than to me. I've not forgotten that you asked her to procure the illustrious opportunity of fighting the dragon."

"I won't dare to contradict you, sire," the chevalier replied, "but I can assure your majesty I make a great distinction between your favors and those of the queen, and if a subject were permitted to make his sovereign a confidant, I'd be most delighted to declare my feelings to you."

At that point, the king interrupted him abruptly by asking him where he had left the queen, who meanwhile was complaining to Floride about Fortuné's indifference to her.

"I'm finding the sight of him more and more hateful," she cried. "Either he leaves the court, or I must withdraw from it. I can no longer tolerate the presence of an ungrateful youth who dares show me so much contempt. Any other mortal would be enraptured to know he pleased a queen who's so powerful in this kingdom! He is the only one in the world who doesn't. Ah, the gods have selected him to disturb my tranquility!"

Floride was not at all sorry that her mistress was so displeased with Fortuné, and far from endeavoring to oppose her displeasure, she augmented it by recalling a thousand other disturbing signs that the queen had perhaps not wanted to notice. Thus, her rage increased, and she began devising some new way to destroy the poor chevalier.

When the king rejoined her and expressed his concern about her health, she said, "I confess I was very ill, but it's difficult to remain so with Fortuné near. He's so cheerful, and his ideas are quite amusing. So, I must tell you, he's implored me to obtain another favor from your majesty. He's asked, with the greatest confidence of success, to be allowed to undertake the most rash enterprise in the world. "

"What now, sister?" cried the king.

"Does he want to fight another dragon?"

"Several all at once," she said, "and he's certain he will triumph. Do you want me to tell you? Indeed, he boasts he'll compel the emperor to restore all our treasures, and he doesn't even need an army to achieve this."

"What a pity," the king replied, "that this poor young man has to exaggerate so much."

"His fight with the dragon has made him think of nothing but great adventures," the queen remarked. "But what risk do you run if you permit him to serve you like this?"

"I risk his life, which is dear to me," the king replied. "I'd be extremely sorry to see him throw it away so recklessly."

"No matter what you decide, he's bound to die," she said. "I assure you that his desire to recover your treasures is so strong that he'll pine away if you refuse him permission."

The king felt deeply distressed. "I can't imagine," he said, "how these notions get into his head. I'm extremely disturbed to find him so foolhardy."

"The fact remains," the queen replied, "he's fought the dragon and conquered him. Perhaps he'll succeed equally well in this adventure. I'm seldom deceived by my presentiments, and my heart tells me that he'll also accomplish this mission. Please, brother, don't oppose his zeal."

"Let him be called," the king said. "In any case, I must inform him of the risk he runs."

"That's just the way to exasperate him," the queen replied. "He'll think you won't let him go, and I assure you he won't be deterred by any consideration for himself, for I've already said all that can be thought about the subject."

"Very well," the king cried, "let him go. I consent."

Delighted with this permission, the queen sent for Fortuné.

"Chevalier," she said, "be grateful to the king. He's granted you the permission you desired so much—to seek out the Emperor Matapa and by guile or by force, recover the treasures he's taken from us. Prepare to depart as soon as possible just like you did when you fought the dragon."

Fortuné was shocked. Was this the extreme to which the queen's malice and fury had driven her? On the other hand, he was pleased by the prospect of laying down his life for a king so dear to him. Therefore, without objecting to this monstrous task, he knelt and kissed the king's hand. For his part, he was very much moved, and even the queen felt a degree of shame in witnessing the respect with which he received this order to charge toward certain death.

"Can it be possible," she said, "that he has some affection for me? Rather than disavow what I've supposedly done on his behalf, he prefers to suffer without a complaint. Ah, if this were true, I'd wish a good deal of harm to myself for having caused him so much!"

The king said little to the chevalier before he remounted his horse, and the queen entered her chariot again, feigning a return of her indisposition. Fortuné accompanied the king to the end of the forest and then reentered it to converse with his horse.

"My faithful Comrade," he said, "it's all up with me. I must die. The queen has plotted a course I'd never have expected."

"My charming master," the horse replied, "don't alarm yourself. Although I wasn't present when all of this occurred, I've known about it for some time. The mission isn't as terrible as you imagine."

"You don't realize that this emperor is the most wrathful man in the world," the chevalier said. "If I suggest to him that he restore all that he has taken from the king, he'll answer by having me strangled and thrown into a river."

"I've heard of his violent ways," Comrade said, "but don't let that prevent you from taking your companions with you. If you perish there, we'll all perish together. However, I trust we'll have better luck than that."

Somewhat consoled by this, the chevalier returned home, issued the necessary orders, and then received the king's commands along with his credentials. "You'll tell the emperor for me," he said, "that I demand that he return my subjects whom he holds in bondage, my soldiers who are prisoners, my horses that he rides, and all my goods and treasures."

"What shall I offer him in exchange for all these things?" Fortuné asked.

"Nothing," replied the king, "but my friendship."

The young ambassador's memory was not overburdened by these instructions. He departed without seeing the queen, and though she was offended, he had no reason to treat her with any respect. Besides, what worse could she do to him in a fit of rage that she had not already done in the throes of love? Passions of this kind seemed to him to be the most dreadful thing in the world. Even her wily confidante was exasperated with her mistress for wanting to sacrifice the flower of chivalry.

Taking all he needed for his journey in the Morocco-leather trunk, Fortuné was not satisfied simply with dressing himself magnificently, but wanted his seven companions to make just as fine an appearance. They all rode on their excellent horses. Indeed, Comrade seemed to fly through the air rather than gallop over ground, and soon they arrived at Emperor Matapa's capital city. Larger than Paris, Constantinople, and Rome put together, it had so many people that all the cellars, garrets, and lofts were inhabited.

Fortuné was surprised to see such a tremendous city. He demanded an audience with the emperor, and when he announced the purpose of his mission, the emperor could not help smiling even though his ample grace made his speech more effective.

"If you were at the head of five hundred thousand men," he said, "one might listen to you, but they tell me you have but seven."

"I've not undertaken this task, my lord," Fortuné said, "to make you restore what my master wishes by force but by my very earnest objections to your previous actions."

"It doesn't matter which way you choose," the emperor responded. "You'll never succeed unless you can accomplish a task that's just come to my mind: find a man who has such an appetite that he can eat all the hot bread baked at breakfast for the inhabitants of this great city."

The chevalier was most pleasantly surprised by this proposal, but since he did not answer right away, the emperor burst into a fit of laughter. "It's perfectly natural to respond to a ridiculous request with a ridiculous answer."

"Sire," Fortuné said, "I accept your offer. Tomorrow I'll bring a man who will eat all the fresh bread and likewise all the stale bread in this city. Just order it to be brought to the great square, and you'll have the pleasure of seeing him devour it down to the very last crumb."

The emperor agreed, swearing he would put him to death if he did not keep his word, and people talked of nothing but the madness of the new ambassador for the rest of the day.

Fortuné returned to the tavern where he had taken up residence and called for Gorger to come to him. "Now's the time for you to prepare yourself to eat bread," he said. "Everything depends on it." Thereupon, he told him what he had promised the emperor.

"Don't worry, master," Gorger said. "I'll eat until they're exhausted by feeding me."

Since Fortuné was afraid of any exertion on Gorger's part, he forbade him to have supper so he would be better able to eat his breakfast, but this precaution was not really necessary. The next morning, the emperor, empress, and princess took seats on a balcony so that they would have a better view. When Fortuné arrived with his small retinue, he saw six mountains of bread higher than the Pyrenees rising in the great square. This sight made him turn pale, but it had the opposite effect on Gorger. Delighted by the prospect of eating so much good bread, he asked them not to keep the smallest morsel from him and declared, "Nothing will be left even for a mouse."

The emperor and the entire court amused themselves at the expense of Fortuné and his companions, but Gorger became impatient and demanded the signal to begin. At a flourish of drums and trumpets, he immediately threw himself on one of the mountains of bread and devoured it in less than a quarter hour. All the rest he gulped down at the same rate. Everyone was astonished and, wondering if their eyes had deceived them, they had to satisfy themselves by touching where they had placed the bread. That day everyone, from the emperor to the cat, was compelled to dine without bread.

Delighted by his great success, Fortuné approached the emperor and asked respectfully if he were pleased by the way he had kept his word with him. The emperor, who was rather irritated at being duped this way, said, "Monsieur Ambassador, it won't do to satisfy such hunger without also slaking thirst. Therefore you, or one of your men, must drink all the water in the fountains, aqueducts, and reservoirs in the city, and all the wine in the cellars."

"Sire," Fortuné said, "you're trying to make it impossible for me to obey your orders. However, I don't mind endeavoring to fulfill this task if I can expect that you'll restore what I've requested for my master."

"I'll do so if you succeed in your undertaking," the emperor stated.

When the chevalier inquired if the emperor would like to be present, he replied that he would certainly attend such an extraordinary event. Thereupon, he got into a magnificent chariot and drove to the fountain of lions, where seven marble lions spouted torrents of water that formed such a mighty river that the inhabitants of the city usually crossed in gondolas.

Tippler approached the great basin, and without taking a breath, he drained it so dry that the bewildered fish cried out for vengeance. Then Tippler turned to all the other fountains, aqueducts, and reservoirs and did the same. In fact, he could have drunk the sea, he was so thirsty. After seeing such an example, the emperor was convinced Tippler could drink the wine as easily as the water, and he watched his disturbed subjects refuse to give up their wine to him. However, Tippler complained that they were being unfair, for he needed the wine to settle his stomach. Not only did he expect all the wine, but also the spirits. Fearing to appear miserly, Matapa consented to Tippler's request.

Once this feat was accomplished, Fortuné reminded the emperor of his promise. At these words, the emperor looked very stern and told him he would consider it. Thereupon, he convoked his council and expressed his extreme annoyance at what he had promised the young ambassador. Indeed, he had thought the conditions he had set for Fortuné were so impossible to fulfill that he would not have to comply with them. After he had spoken, his daughter, one of the loveliest creatures in the world, remarked, "You're aware, sire, that until now I've beaten all those who have dared to race against me. You must tell the ambassador that if he can reach a certain designated spot before me, you'll stop procrastinating and keep your word."

The emperor thought her advice was excellent and embraced his child. The next morning, he received Fortuné graciously and said, "I have one more condition; which is that you or one of your men must run a race with my daughter. I swear by all

the elements that, if she's beaten, I'll satisfy your master in every respect."

Since Fortuné did not refuse this challenge, Matapa added that the race would take place in two hours and immediately informed his daughter that she should get ready. She did so with alacrity, for she had raced since childhood and soon appeared in an avenue of orange trees three miles long and so beautifully graveled that not a stone the size of a pin's head could be seen in it. She wore a light rose-colored taffeta dress embroidered down the seams with gold and silver spangles; her beautiful hair was tied by a ribbon in back and fell carelessly on her shoulders; she wore extremely pretty slippers and a belt of jewels that displayed her figure sufficiently to prove that none had ever been as lithe. Even that of the young Atalanta could never have matched hers.

Fortuné arrived, followed by the faithful Swift and his other companions. The emperor took his seat with his entire court. The ambassador announced that Swift would have the honor of running against the princess. The Morocco-leather trunk had furnished him with a Dutch suit trimmed with English lace, scarlet silk stockings, feathers to match, and exquisite linen. He looked very handsome in this garb, and the princess accepted him as her competitor. But before they started, she had a liqueur brought to her that she used to strengthen her and give her additional speed. Swift said he ought to have some as well, and that the advantages ought to be equal. "Gladly," she said, "I'm too just to refuse you."

She immediately poured some out for him, but since he was not accustomed to such potent liquid, it went quickly to his head. Turning around two or three times, he· collapsed at the foot of an orange tree and fell fast asleep. Meanwhile, the signal for starting had already been given three times, and the princess had kindly waited for Swift to wake up. Finally, feeling the grave importance of freeing her father from his predicament, she set off with wonderful grace and speed. Since Fortuné was at the other end of the avenue with his men, he was unaware of what was happening until he saw the princess a half mile from the finish line running all alone. "Ye gods!" he cried, speaking to his horse. "We're lost. I see nothing of Swift. "

"My lord," Comrade said, "Hear-all must listen. Perhaps he'll be able to tell us what's going on." So, Hear-all threw himself onto the ground, and although he was two miles from Swift, he could hear him snoring.

"Truly," he said, "he has no intention of coming. He's sleeping as though he were in bed."

"Ah, what shall we do?" Fortuné cried again.

"Master," Comrade said, "Sharpshooter must shoot an arrow at the tip of his ear to wake him."

So, Sharpshooter took his bow and aimed so well that he indeed pierced Swift's ear. Woken by the pain, he opened his eyes to see the princess near the finish, and he heard shouts of joy and mounting applause. At first astonished, he soon regained the ground he had lost in slumber. The very winds seemed to bear him, and nobody could follow him with their eyes. In short, he arrived first with the arrow still in his ear, for he hadn't had the time to extract it.

So astonished was the emperor by the three events that had occurred since the ambassador had arrived that he believed the gods favored him, and that he better not defer keeping his word.

"Approach," he said to Fortuné, "I want you to hear from my own lips that I consent to your taking as much of your master's treasures from here as you or one of your men can carry. Indeed, you couldn't have expected that I'd ever do more than that or that I'd let either his soldiers, his subjects, or his horses go."

Making a profound bow, the ambassador said that he was very much obliged to him. "Pray give your orders to execute your will."

Deeply mortified, Matapa spoke to his treasurer and then rode to a palace just outside the city walls. Fortuné and his companions immediately asked for permission to enter all those rooms where the king's furniture, rarities, money, and jewels were deposited. The emperor's servants hid nothing from him, but reminded him of the condition that only one man carry them. Strongback made his appearance and carted off all the furniture in the emperor's palace, five hundred statues of gold taller than giants, coaches, chariots, and countless other articles. Everything was taken, and Strongback walked so jauntily, it seemed as though his back bore not a pound.

When the emperor's ministers saw the dismantled palace without chairs, chests, saucepans, or even a bed to lie on, they rushed to warn him. You can imagine how astonished he was when he learned that one man carried everything.

"I shall not stand for this!" he exclaimed and commanded his guards and musketeers to mount and quickly follow the robbers.

Although Fortuné was more than ten miles away, Hear-all told him that he heard a large body of cavalry galloping toward them, and the Sharpshooter with his excellent vision spotted them at a distance. Having just arrived on the banks of a river with his men, Fortuné said to Tippler, "We don't have any boats. If you could drink some of this water, we might be able to ford the river."

Tippler instantly performed this task. The ambassador was anxious to make the best use of his head start and get away, but his horse said, "Don't worry. Let our enemies approach."

They appeared on the opposite bank, and since they knew where the fishermen moored their boats, they speedily embarked in them and rowed with all their might. Then Boisterous inflated his cheeks and began blowing. Immediately, the river became so tumultuous that the boats were upset, and the emperor's troops perished without a single soldier escaping to tell the news.

Fortuné's men rejoiced at this event, and each one's thoughts turned to what reward he might demand as his just deserts. They wanted to make themselves masters of all the treasures they had carried away, and a great dispute arose among them about how to divide everything.

"If I had not won the race," the runner said, "you'd have had nothing."

"And if I hadn't heard you snoring," Hear-all said, "where would we have been then?"

"Who would have wakened you if it weren't for me?" Sharpshooter responded.

"In truth," Strongback added, "I admire your arguments. But it's clear to me that I should have first choice since I've been carrying it all. Without my help, you wouldn't have the opportunity of sharing it."

"You really mean without mine," Tippler responded. "The river that I drank like a glass of lemonade would have defeated you."

"You would have been much more defeated if I hadn't upset the boats," Boisterous said.

"I've been silent up till now," interrupted Gorger, "but I must remark that it was I who started this chain of events. If I had left just a crust of bread, everything would have been lost."

"My friends," Fortuné said commandingly, "you've all done wonders, but we ought to leave it to the king to acknowledge our services. I'd very much regret it if we were to be rewarded by some other hand than his. Believe me, it's best to leave everything to his will. He sent us to recover his treasures, not to steal them. Just the thought of it is so shameful that I beg you never to mention it again. I assure you, I shall do everything I can to guarantee that you'll be rewarded even if the king neglects you."

Deeply moved by their master's remonstrance, the seven gifted men fell at his feet and promised him that his will would be theirs. So, onward they went and soon completed their journey. However, when they approached the city, the charming Fortuné became worried because he had a thousand different concerns. On the one hand, he was overjoyed at having performed such a great service to the king whom he loved so tenderly, and the hope of his favorable reception made him eager to return. On the other hand, he feared irritating the queen again and suffering torments from her and Floride.

When he finally arrived at the city gates, everyone was overwhelmed by the immense quantity of valuables he had brought back with him, and they followed him with a thousand acclamations. The sounds of the people soon reached the palace, and the king could not believe the extraordinary event taking place. He ran to the queen to tell her about it, and at first, she was thunderstruck, but quickly regained her composure.

"You see," she said, "the gods protect him, and he's fortunately succeeded. I'm not surprised that he's always ready to undertake what appears impossible to others."

As she uttered these words, she saw Fortuné enter. He informed their majesties of the success of his journey, adding that the treasures were in the park. Since there was so much gold, jewels, and furniture, there was no place large enough to put them. You can easily imagine that the king demonstrated a good deal of affection for such a faithful, zealous, and charming subject.

The presence of the chevalier and all the successes he had achieved reopened the wound in the queen's heart that had never fully healed. She thought him more charming than ever, and as soon as she was at liberty to speak to Floride, she began complaining again.

"You've seen what I've done to destroy him," she said. "I thought it the only way of forgetting him. Yet, some sort of irrefutable fate keeps bringing him back to me again. Whatever reasons I had to despise a man so much my inferior, and who's returned my affections with the meanest ingratitude, I can't help but love him still, and I've determined to marry him privately."

"To marry him?" Floride cried. "I can't believe this! Have I heard you rightly?"

"Yes," the queen replied. "you've heard my intentions, and you must help me. Bring Fortuné to my room this evening. I myself shall declare to him how far I'm willing to go because of my love for him."

In despair at being chosen to assist the queen in her plans to marry Fortuné, she tried every possible argument to dissuade the queen from seeing him. She maintained that the king would be so angry if he discovered this intrigue that perhaps he would order the chevalier to be executed. At the very least, he might condemn him to life in imprisonment, and she would never see him again. However, all her, eloquence was in vain. Seeing that the queen was beginning to get angry, she decided that there was nothing to be done but obey her.

She found Fortuné in the palace gallery, where he was having the golden statues arranged that he had brought from Matapa, and she told him to come to the queen's room that evening. This order made him tremble, and Floride noticed his distress.

"Oh," she said, "how I pity you! What unlucky fate has caused the queen to lose her heart to you? Alas! I know one less dangerous than hers, but it's afraid to reveal itself."

The chevalier was not eager for further explanation, for he had endured too much already. Since he didn't care the least bit for pleasing the queen, he dressed himself so plainly that she could not possibly think him distinguished. Yet, even though he dispensed with his diamonds and embroidery, he could not efface the qualities of his person. He was charming and remarkable no matter what he wore. In a word, he was incomparable.

On the contrary, the queen went to great pains to heighten the luster of her appearance by an extraordinary display, and she was quite pleased to see how tongue-tied Fortuné was.

"Appearances," she said, "are sometimes so deceptive that I'm delighted to have the chance to defend myself against the charges you no doubt have brought against me in your heart. When I convinced the king to send you to the emperor, my object may have seemed to destroy you. Nevertheless, believe me, handsome chevalier, I knew how everything would turn out. I had no other object than to provide immortal glory for you."

"Madame," he said, "you're too far above me to condescend to any explanation. I would never presume to inquire into your motives. The king's commands are sufficient justification for me."

"You're making light of the explanation I want to give you," she remarked. "But the time has come to demonstrate how much I care for you. Approach, Fortuné, approach. Receive my hand as a pledge of my faith."

The poor chevalier was utterly thunderstruck. Twenty times he was on the verge of declaring his sex to the queen, but he did not dare to do so and could only respond to her show of love by an excessive coldness. He tried to explain to her the innumerable reasons why the king would be angry if he were to hear that a subject in his own court had ventured to contract such an important marriage without his sanction. After the queen vainly endeavored to remove the obstacles that alarmed him, she suddenly assumed the voice and countenance of a Fury. Flying into the most violent rage, she threatened him with a thousand punishments, heaped abuse on him, fought and scratched him. Then she turned her rage on herself. She tore her hair, scratched her face and throat until they bled, ripped her veil and lace. Finally, she cried out, "Help, guards! Help!" As they rushed into her room, she bellowed at them, "Fling that wretch of a chevalier into a dungeon!"

Running to the king to demand justice for the way that young monster had violated her, she told her brother that Fortuné had had the audacity some time ago to declare his feelings for her. She had hoped that by being severe and sending him away, she could cure him. As the king might have observed, she had used every opportunity to have him removed from the court. However, he was such a villain that nothing could change him. The king could see for himself to what extremes he had gone to possess her. She insisted on his being brought to justice, and that if she were denied such satisfaction, she wanted to know why.

The manner in which she spoke to the king alarmed him, for he knew that she was one of the most violent women in the world. She had a great deal of power and could cause turmoil in the kingdom. Therefore, Fortuné's rash actions demanded an exemplary punishment. Everyone already knew what had happened, and his own feelings should have prompted him to avenge his sister. But, alas, who was to be the target of his vengeance? It was a gentleman who had exposed himself to numerous perils in his service. Indeed, the king was indebted to him for the peace and all his treasures, and he had a particular affection for him. He would have given half his life to have saved his beloved favorite. So, he explained to the queen how useful Fortuné had been to him, the services he had rendered the kingdom, his youth, and everything else that might induce her to pardon him. Yet, she would not listen and demanded his execution.

The king, realizing that he could not avoid having him tried, appointed the mildest and most tender-hearted judges in the hope they would weigh the offense as lightly as possible. His assumption, though, was mistaken. The judges wanted to establish their reputation at the expense of this unfortunate prisoner. Since it was an affair of great notoriety, they were extremely severe and condemned Fortuné without deigning to hear his side: he was sentenced to be stabbed three times in the heart with a dagger because it was his heart that was guilty.

The king trembled at this sentence as though it had been passed on himself. He banished all the judges who had pronounced it, but could not save his beloved Fortuné. The queen exulted because of the punishment the chevalier was to suffer, and her eyes thirsted for the blood of her illustrious victim. The king made various attempts to intercede, but they served only to exasperate her.

Finally, the day set for the terrible execution arrived. Off they went to lead the chevalier from his prison. Meanwhile, he was unaware of the crime that he had allegedly committed because he had been placed in isolation, and he merely imagined that he was to be persecuted once again because of his indifference to the queen. What distressed him most was his belief that the king was just as enraged as the queen was.

At the same time, Floride was inconsolable at seeing the predicament in which her lover was placed and made a most drastic decision: she was prepared to poison the queen and herself if Fortuné was doomed to die a cruel death. From the moment she knew the sentence, she was overcome with despair and thought about nothing but how to execute her plan. The poison she procured, however, was not as powerful as she desired. After she had given it to the queen, her majesty seemed not to feel the slightest effects. Instead, she ordered the charming chevalier to be brought into the palace square so that the execution could take place in her presence. The executioners brought him from his dungeon according to custom and led him like a tender lamb to the slaughter. The first person who caught his eye was the queen in her chariot, who wanted to be as close as possible in the hope that his blood might splatter her. The king meanwhile had locked himself up in his chamber so that he might freely lament the fate of his beloved favorite.

After they tied Fortuné to the stake, they tore off his robe and vest to pierce his heart. Imagine everyone's astonishment when they uncovered the ivory bosom of Belle-belle! Immediately, the crowd of people realized Fortuné was an innocent girl unjustly accused. So upset and confused was the queen by this sight that the poison began to roar through her veins. After a series of long convulsions, she recovered only to utter lamentations in agony. The people, who loved Fortuné, had already freed her and ran to announce the wonderful news to the king. He, who had succumbed to the deepest grief, now felt joy replace his sorrow. Racing into the square, he was delighted to see Fortuné's transformation.

The last sighs of the queen subdued his rapture somewhat, but when he thought about her malice he could not feel sorry for her. Indeed, he decided to marry Belle-belle in order to repay her for the great debt he owed her, and he declared his intentions to her. You can easily imagine that his wish had been the goal of all that she had ever desired, and it was not the crown she had wanted but the worthy monarch for whom she had long cherished the greatest affection.

The day was set for celebrating the king's marriage, and when Belle-belle reassumed her female attire, she appeared a thousand

times more charming than in the garb of the chevalier. Consulting her horse with regard to her future adventures, she was assured that she would have nothing but pleasant ones. In gratitude for all the good services he had rendered, she had a stable built of ebony and ivory, and she installed the best satin mattress on which he could take his repose. As for her seven followers, they were rewarded in proportion to their services. Comrade, however, disappeared, and when they came and told Belle-belle, the new queen was distressed, for she adored him and ordered her attendants to look for her horse everywhere they could. They did this for three whole days, but it was all in vain. On the fourth day, she was so worried that she got up before sunrise and descended into the garden. Then she crossed the wood and entered a large meadow, calling from time to time, "Comrade, my dear Comrade! Where are you? Have you deserted me? I still need your wise advice. Come back, come back, and give it to me!"

While calling out like this, she suddenly noticed a second sun rising in the west. As she stopped to gaze at this miracle, she was immensely astonished as she watched it advance toward her by degrees. Within moments she recognized her horse, whose trappings were set with jewels and led a chariot of pearls and topazes drawn by twenty-four sheep. Their wool was of gold thread and purl and extremely radiant. Their traces were made of crimson satin and covered with emeralds, and their horns and ears were ornamented with carbuncles. Belle-belle recognized her fairy protectress in the chariot, and she was accompanied by the count, her father, and her two sisters, who called out to her. They clapped their hands and made affectionate signs to her, intimating that they had come to her wedding. Thinking she would die from joy, she did not know what to do or say to show her delight. She got into the chariot, and this splendid equipage entered the palace, where everything had already been prepared to celebrate the finest wedding ceremony that had ever taken place in the kingdom. Thus, the enamored king bound his destiny to that of his beloved Fortuné, and the story about this charming adventure has circulated for centuries and been passed down to our own.

The lion roaming Libya's burning plain,
Pursued by the hunter, galled by countless
darts,
Is less to be dreaded than that woman vain,
Whose charms are disdained and foiled by arts.

Poison and steel are trifles in her eyes,
As agents of her vengeance and her hate;
The dire effects that from such passions arise
You've now seen in Fortuné's very strange fate.

Belle-belle was saved by her innocent soul,
That caused the perfidious queen to be struck
down.
Heaven protects the innocent and plays its role
By rewarding virtue with a radiant crow.

The Blue Bird

ONCE upon a time, there was a king who was extremely rich. Despite the fact that he had a great deal of property and money, he was inconsolable when his wife suddenly fell ill and died. He shut himself up for a week in a small room and beat his head against the walls in his distress. Since his servants were afraid that he would kill himself, they put some mattresses between the tapestries and the walls so that he would not harm himself no matter how much he threw himself about. Moreover, his subjects all agreed that they had better speak to him to alleviate his grief as best they could. Some prepared grave and serious speeches; others, charming and even lively talks. But none made the least impression on him, for he barely heard a word they said.

At last, a lady covered by black crepe, veils, mantles, and other long mourning garments came before him. She wept so much and sobbed so loudly that he was quite astonished. She told him she would not attempt, as others had done, to mitigate his sorrow. Rather, she came to augment it because nothing could be more just than to lament the loss of a good wife. "As for myself, I have lost the best of husbands and have made up my mind to weep as long as I have eyes in my head." Thereupon, she redoubled her groans, and the king, following her example, began to howl as well.

He paid more attention to this visitor than all the others paid and talked to her about the excellent qualities of his dear departed wife. In turn, she recapitulated all those of her beloved dead husband. They talked so much about their sorrow that they were eventually at a loss for words. When the cunning widow saw the subject was nearly exhausted, she raised her veil a little so that the grieving king could get a peek. Indeed, this poor mourner knew how to roll her large blue eyes and flutter her long black lashes in a most effective manner. Her complexion was still blooming, and the king examined her with a great deal of attention. Gradually, he spoke less and less about his wife, until he stopped discussing her altogether. The widow declared, however, that she would never stop mourning for her husband.

In response, the king implored her not to make her sorrow eternal, and soon, to everyone's astonishment, he declared that he would marry her. His mourning garments were exchanged for those with green and rose. Apparently, one needs only to determine a person's weakness in order to gain his trust and do just what one wishes with him.

The king had just one daughter by his first wife. Considered an eighth wonder of the world, she was named Florine because she was so sweet, young, and beautiful. Seldom was this artless maiden seen in splendid attire. She preferred light morning dresses of taffeta fastened with a few jewels and the finest flowers, which produced an admirable effect when twined with her beautiful hair. She was only fifteen when the king married the widow.

The new queen sent for her own daughter, who had been brought up by her godmother, the fairy Soussio, but she was not particularly more graceful or beautiful because of this upbringing. Since Soussio loved her dearly, she had worked hard to make something out of her goddaughter, but her efforts were in vain. The girl's name was Truitonne, and her face was covered with reddish spots like those on the back of a trout. Her black hair was so greasy and dirty that no one would venture to touch it, and oil oozed out of her yellow skin. Her mother doted on her and talked about nothing but her charming Truitonne.

In contrast, she had nothing good to say about Florine, who possessed many advantages over her daughter. Eventually, the queen was aroused to use every possible means to belittle the unfortunate princess in the eyes of her father. Not a day passed that the queen and Truitonne did not play some mischievous trick on Florine. The princess, who was as mild as she was sensible, merely endeavored to keep herself beyond the reach of their malice.

One day, the king remarked to the queen that Florine and Truitonne were of an age

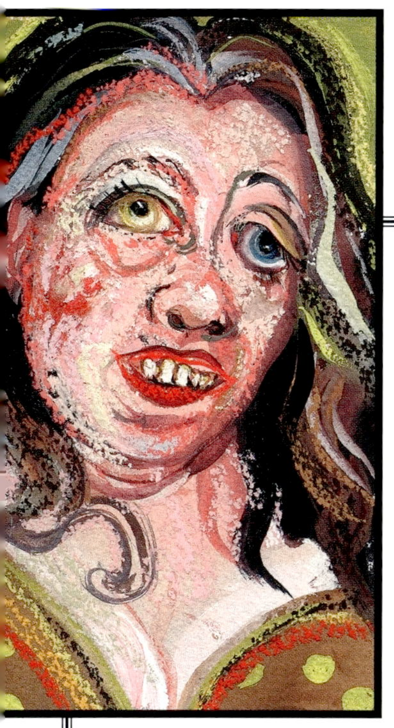

to be married, and that they should bestow the hand of one of them on the first prince who visited their court.

"I want my daughter married first," said the queen. "She's older than yours, and since she's a thousand times more charming, there should be no hesitation about the matter."

The king, who disliked arguments, replied that he was quite willing to do it her way, and she was to arrange everything as she desired. A short time afterward, it came to everyone's attention that King Charmant was soon to arrive. No prince was more celebrated for gallantry and magnificence than he was. In mind and appearance, he was just as charming as his name implied. When the queen heard this news, she employed all the embroiderers, all the tailors, and all the artisans to make dresses for Truitonne. On the other hand, she not only requested that the king give nothing new to Florine, but she also bribed the princess's ladies-in-waiting to steal all her clothes, headdresses, and jewels on the very day King Charmant arrived so that, when she went to dress herself, she could not find even a ribbon. Florine knew full well who had done her this turn, and she sent her servants to purchase materials for a new dress. However, all the tradesmen responded that the queen had forbidden them to furnish her with a single thing. Therefore, she was left only with the gown she had on her back, and this was very soiled. She became so ashamed of her appearance that when King Charmant arrived, she hid herself in a comer of the hall.

The queen received the royal visitor with great pomp and presented her daughter in a blaze of such magnificence that she looked even more ugly than usual. When King Charmant averted his eyes, the queen tried to convince herself that he was so stunned by her that he had to keep turning away to control his emotions. Thus, she continually pushed Truitonne before him, but he responded by inquiring, "Isn't there another princess, named Florine?"

"Yes," said Truitonne, pointing with her finger, "there she is, hiding herself because she's not dressed properly."

Upon being discovered, Florine blushed. However, she looked so exceedingly beautiful in her confusion that King Charmant was dazzled. He rose immediately and made a deep bow to the princess. "Madame," he said, "your incomparable beauty makes the artificial aid of ornaments quite unnecessary."

"Sir," she replied, "I confess I'm not accustomed to wearing such a disgraceful dress as this one, and I would have preferred to have escaped your notice."

"It would be impossible for such a marvelous princess like yourself to go anywhere and not have all eyes focused on you!" he exclaimed.

"Ah," said the queen, greatly irritated, "it's nice listening to you pay these compliments. However, believe me, sir, Florine is already enough of a flirt. She doesn't need such excessive flattery."

King Charmant quickly perceived the queen's motives for speaking this way, but since he was not accustomed to suppressing his inclinations, he continued to manifest his admiration for Florine. Indeed, he conversed with her for three whole hours.

The queen was in despair, and Truitonne, inconsolable, because the princess had received such preference. Complaining bitterly to the king, they compelled him to consent to imprisoning Florine in a tower during King Charmant's stay so that they could not see each other.

No sooner had Florine returned to her room than four masked men seized and carried her to a room at the top of the tower, where they left her greatly distressed, for she saw clearly that she was being treated this way to prevent her from pleasing King Charmant. He had already gained her affections, and she would willingly have accepted him for her husband. Yet, Charmant was not aware of Florine's violent abduction, and he looked forward with the greatest impatience to the hour when he would meet her again. He talked about her to the gentlemen the king had placed in his company to do him honor, but they had been ordered by the queen to say the worst possible things about Florine they could imagine:

"She is coquettish, inconstant, and ill-tempered."

"She torments her friends and her servants."

"It is impossible to imagine anyone more slovenly."

"She is so niggardly that she prefers to dress like a poor shepherdess than spend the money allowed her by her father to purchase rich garments befitting her rank."

As each detail was mentioned, Charmant smarted, scarcely able to restrain his anger. "No," he said to himself, "it's impossible that Heaven would permit so worthless a soul to inhabit this masterpiece of nature. I admit she was badly dressed when I first saw her, but the shame she expressed proves that she was not accustomed to dressing in that way. How can she be ill-tempered and coquettish with such an enchanting air of gentleness and modesty? It makes no sense! I can much more easily imagine that it's the queen who's slandering her. She's not her stepmother for nothing, and the Princess Truitonne, her own daughter, is such an ugly beast that it wouldn't be unusual for her to envy the most perfect of beings."

While he was pondering all of this in his mind, the courtiers suspected from his manner that he was displeased by their abuse of Florine. One courtier more astute than the rest changed his tune and began extolling the princess's virtues in order to discover the prince's true sentiments. Upon

hearing this praise, Charmant awoke as from a deep sleep. He participated eagerly in the conversation, and his features lit up with joy. Oh love, how hard you are to hide! You are visible everywhere on a lover's lips, in his eyes, in the tone of his voice. When we truly love, both silence and speech, happiness and misery, equally express the passion we feel.

Impatient to learn if King Charmant was in love, the queen sent for the courtiers who had won the king's trust and spent the rest of the night interrogating them. Everything they reported served only to confirm the opinion she had already formed—the king was in love with Florine.

But how can I describe the melancholy state of that poor princess? She lay stretched on the floor in the prison of that terrible tower. "I wouldn't have to be pitied so much," she said, "if I had been locked up here before I had seen that charming monarch. My recollection of him only serves to increase my distress. I'm positive that the queen treated me this cruelly only to prevent my seeing him again. Alas, the little beauty that Heaven has bestowed on me has cost me a great deal of tranquility." She then began to weep so bitterly that her worst enemies would have pitied her if they had witnessed her torment. And so, the night passed.

The queen was anxious to win over King Charmant by showing him all the attention she could. She sent him the most costly and magnificent garments made in the newest fashion of that country, and also the Order of the Knights of Cupid, which she had compelled the king to institute the day they themselves had married in honor of their wedding. This badge was a golden heart enameled and colored like fire. It was surrounded by several arrows and pierced with one that bore the words, "One alone wounds me." For Charmant, however, the queen had a heart cut from a ruby as large as an ostrich's egg; each arrow was made of a single diamond the length of a finger, and the chain of the badge was composed of pearls, the smallest of which weighed a whole pound. In short, nothing like it had ever been seen in the world. Charmant was so astonished when he saw it that it was some time before he could speak. At the same time, they gave him a beautifully illustrated book with pages of the finest vellum and a binding encrusted with gold and jewels. In it were written the statutes of the Order of the Knights of Cupid in a gallant, refined style. They told him that the princess he had seen requested that he be her knight and had sent him this present. Upon hearing this, he imagined that they had come from his beloved. "My goodness," he cried, "does the beautiful Princess Florine think of me in this splendid and flattering way?"

"Sire," they replied, "you've confused the names. We come from the charming Truitonne."

"Truitonne! Is she the one who wants me to be her champion?" the king asked coldly. "I regret that I cannot accept this honor. A sovereign is not wholly his own master and cannot accept just any engagement that pleases him. I know the duties of a knight and would like to be able to fulfill them all. But I'd prefer not receiving the honor she has offered me rather than proving myself unworthy of it."

So saying, he put the heart, chain, and book back into the basket and sent them all back to the queen, who, along with her daughter, almost choked with rage at the contemptuous manner in which the illustrious foreigner had declined such a signal honor.

King Charmant visited the king and queen as often as he was permitted in the hope of meeting Florine in the royal apartments. His eyes searched everywhere for her. The moment he heard anyone enter the room, he turned sharply toward the door and seemed always restless and unhappy when Florine did not appear. The malicious queen easily guessed what was on his mind, but she appeared to take no notice of it. She talked to him only about pleasure parties, and he replied with the most incongruous answers. At last, he asked her plainly, "Where is Princess Florine?"

"Sir," the queen replied haughtily, "her father has forbidden her to leave her apartment until my daughter is married."

"And what motive," inquired King Charmant, "can there be for making that beautiful princess a prisoner?"

"I don't know," the queen said, "and even if I did, I don't feel obligated to inform you."

Enraged, Charmant cast an angry glance at Truitonne. He thought to himself, "This little monster is the cause of my being deprived of the pleasure of seeing Florine." So, he abruptly left the queen's presence, which gave him too much pain.

On returning to his room, he told a young prince, a cherished companion of his, to do his utmost to win the confidence of one of the princess's attendants so that he could speak to Florine for even one moment. This prince easily found some ladies of the palace, and one of them, whom he thought he could trust, guaranteed him that Florine would be at a small lower window that very evening. This window overlooked the garden, and she could converse with Charmant from it, provided he was extremely careful and made sure that no one knew. "The king and queen are so severe," she added, "that they'll put me to death if they discover I've sided with Charmant's feelings."

Delighted that he had succeeded in his mission, the prince promised her anything she desired. Then he returned to his royal master and told him the appointed time of meeting. Meanwhile the confidante, who had deceived him, went and told the queen what had happened and waited for further instructions. The queen immediately decided to place her daughter at the little window and gave Truitonne special instructions. Despite the fact that she was naturally stupid, Truitonne was to carry them out without a mistake.

The night was so dark that King Charmant could not have possibly noticed the trickery, even if he had been suspicious. When he drew near the window, he was overflowing with joy and expressed a wealth of tender thoughts to the supposed Florine to convince her of his affection. Taking advantage of the situation, Truitonne told him that she felt like the most unfortunate person in the world in having such a cruel stepmother, and that she would continue to suffer until the queen's daughter was married. Charmant assured her that if she would accept him for her husband, he would be delighted to share his heart and crown with her. Thereupon, he drew his ring from his finger and, placing it on one of Truitonne's, begged her to receive it as a token of eternal fidelity and added, "You need only fix the hour for our flight."

Truitonne made the best possible answers she could to his ardent appeals. He noticed they were not very sensible, and they normally would have made him uneasy, but he thought they arose from the terror she felt at possibly being surprised by the queen. He left her only on condition that she would meet him again the next night at the same hour, which she promised faithfully to do.

Upon hearing of the good success of this meeting, the queen felt sure of everything. When the day was fixed for the elopement, King Charmant prepared to carry off his beloved in a flying chariot drawn by winged frogs, a present to him by a friend who was an enchanter. The night was pitch black, and Truitonne snuck out mysteriously through a little door. The king, who was waiting for her, received

her in his arms with a hundred vows of everlasting affection. But since he was not eager to be flying about in his chariot for a long time before marrying his beloved princess, he asked her to tell him where she wanted their wedding to be held. She answered that she had a godmother named Soussio who was a celebrated fairy, and she felt they should go at once to Soussio's castle. Although the king did not know the way, he only had to mention to his great frogs where he wished to go. They were perfectly acquainted with the whole map of the world, and in no time, they brought Charmant and Truitonne to Soussio's abode.

The castle was so brilliantly illuminated that Charmant would have discovered his mistake the moment he entered if the princess had not carefully covered herself with her veil. She asked for her godmother and contrived to see her alone. Telling her how she had ensnared Charmant, she begged her to pacify him.

"Ah, my child," the fairy said, "the task won't be an easy one because he is too fond of Florine. I feel certain he'll give us a great deal of trouble."

Meanwhile, the king was awaiting them in a salon that had walls made of diamonds so pure and transparent that he saw Soussio and Truitonne conversing together through them. He thought he must be dreaming. "What?" he said. "Have I been betrayed? Have some demons brought this enemy of our peace to this place? Has she come to disturb our wedding? Where's my dear Florine? Perhaps her father has done something to her!"

A thousand thoughts ran through his mind, all of them disconcerting. But matters looked even worse when he entered the salon and Soussio addressed him in an authoritative tone, "King Charmant, here is the Princess Truitonne, whom you have pledged to marry. She is my goddaughter, and it's my desire that you marry her immediately."

"Me?" he exclaimed. "You want me to marry that little monster? You must think me a docile babe to propose such a thing. I've made no promise to her whatsoever, and if she's told you otherwise, then she has—"

"Hold your tongue," interrupted Soussio. "Don't you dare forget to show me the proper respect."

"I agree to respect you as much as a fairy can be respected," the king replied, "provided that you restore my princess to me."

"Aren't I your princess, faithless one?" Truitonne said, showing him his ring. "To whom did you give this ring as a pledge of your troth? With whom did you converse at the little window if not with me?"

"How's this possible?" he cried. "Have I been deceived? No! No, I'll not be your dupe! Come, my frogs, come! I want to leave here immediately!"

"Oho, it's not in your power to leave without my consent," exclaimed Soussio. At her touch, his feet were fastened to the floor as if they had been nailed to it.

"You may stone me to death, you may flay me alive!" cried the king. "I'll marry no one but Florine. My mind is made up. So you can do with me as you please."

Soussio tried sweet talk, threats, promises, and prayers. Truitonne wept, shrieked, groaned, stomped, and became sullen again. The king merely surveyed them both with an air of the greatest indignation, not giving the slightest response to anything they said.

Twenty days and twenty nights passed without their ceasing to talk and without eating, sleeping, or sitting down. Finally,

Soussio became exhausted and lost her patience. "Well, since you so obstinately refuse to listen to reason," she said to the king, "choose right now whether you'll marry my goddaughter, or do penance for seven years as a punishment for breaking your word."

All of a sudden, the king, who up to this time had been perfectly silent, exclaimed, "Do what you want with me, just so that I'm freed from this wretch!"

"You're a wretch yourself!" Truitonne said angrily. "A petty king like you, with your marsh-bred postures. You come to my country, break your word to me, and insult me. Had you a penny's worth of honor in you, you'd behave differently!"

"How touching," said the king in an ironical tone. "I must be making a mistake not to take such a lovely person for my wife."

"No, no, she won't be your wife!" screamed Soussio in a rage. "You may now fly out of that window if you like because you're going to be a blue bird for the next seven years!"

At that very moment, the king underwent a complete transformation: his arms grew feathers and formed wings; his legs and feet became black and scrawny and furnished with crooked talons; his body shrank. He was entirely covered with long, fine, thin feathers of celestial blue; his eyes became round and as bright as two stars; his nose was but an ivory beak; a white crest rose on his head in the form of a crown. He was able to sing and talk in a remarkable fashion, but all he uttered was a cry of anguish at seeing himself transformed into this condition. Finally, he flew from Soussio's fatal palace as fast as his wings could carry him.

Overwhelmed with grief, Charmant flitted from branch to branch, selecting only those trees dedicated to love or sorrow. Sometimes he landed on myrtles, other times on cypresses, and sang the most lamentable tunes, deploring his sad fate and that of Florine. "Where have her enemies hidden her?" he asked. "What has become of that beautiful victim? Has the queen's barbarity permitted her to remain alive? Where should I search? Am I condemned to spend seven years without her? Perhaps during that period they'll compel her to marry, and I'll never regain the hope that sustains me." This whirl of thoughts tormented the blue bird to such a degree that he would have welcomed death.

Meanwhile, the fairy Soussio sent Truitonne back to the queen, who was anxiously waiting to learn all about the nuptials. When she heard from her daughter's lips all that had transpired, she became terribly enraged, and poor Florine was to feel her backlash. "She will repent more than once for having captivated Charmant," the queen said.

To the tower she went with Truitonne, whom she had dressed in her richest clothes with a crown of diamonds on her head and a royal mantle whose train was carried by three daughters of the richest barons in the realm. On her thumb was

King Charmant's ring, which Florine had noticed the day she had conversed with him. Florine was greatly surprised to see Truitonne in such splendid apparel.

"My daughter's come to bring you a wedding present," she said. "King Charmant was so madly in love with her that he's married her. Oh, you've never seen such a happy couple."

Thereupon, they showed the princess heaps of gold and silver tissues, jewels, lace and ribbons, all contained in large baskets worked in gold filigree. While presenting these objects, Truitonne made sure that Florine noticed King Charmant's sparkling ring, and the latter became convinced of her misfortune. With an air of desperation, she told them to remove the base gifts from her sight. "I wish to wear nothing but black, and, indeed, I shall soon be dead." Upon saying this, she fainted.

The cruel queen was delighted to have succeeded so well. She did not permit anyone to assist her, but left her alone in the most wretched state imaginable. Then she maliciously reported to the king that his daughter was so carried away by her emotions that she had lost control of her wits, and great care should be taken to prevent her leaving the tower. The king told her to manage the matter as she thought best, and that he would be satisfied as always.

When the princess recovered from her swoon and began to consider how they had behaved toward her, how her wicked stepmother had mistreated her, and how her hope of becoming King Charmant's wife had been destroyed, her anguish became so keen that she wept the entire night. In this wretched condition, she went to an open window, where she uttered the most tender and touching lamentations. When day began to break, she shut the window, but continued to weep. The following night she again opened the window, sobbing and sighing and shedding a torrent of tears. Morning dawned, and she hid herself in the recesses of her chamber.

In the meantime, King Charmant—or, to speak more correctly, the beautiful blue bird, kept flying around the palace, for he believed his dear princess was confined somewhere in it. If her lamentations were distressing, his were no less so. He approached the windows as near as he could in order to look into the rooms, but the fear of being noticed and recognized by Truitonne prevented his examining the rooms as closely as he wished. "It would cost me my life," he said to himself. "If these wicked princesses were to discover where I am, they'd take their revenge on me. I must keep my distance, or else I'll be exposed to extreme danger." For these reasons, he took the greatest precautions and rarely sang except at night.

Now, there happened to be a towering cypress right in front of the window at

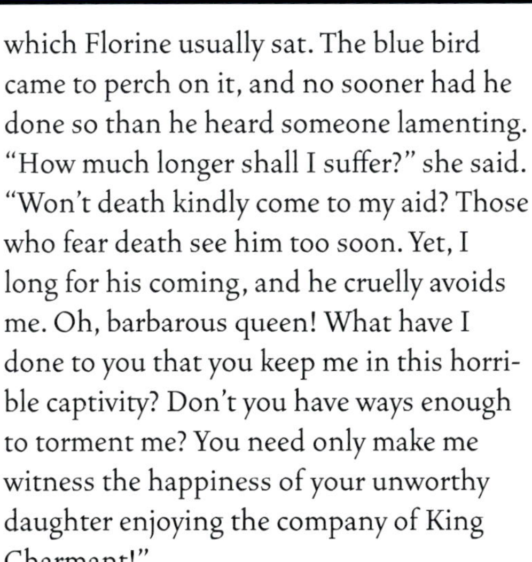

which Florine usually sat. The blue bird came to perch on it, and no sooner had he done so than he heard someone lamenting. "How much longer shall I suffer?" she said. "Won't death kindly come to my aid? Those who fear death see him too soon. Yet, I long for his coming, and he cruelly avoids me. Oh, barbarous queen! What have I done to you that you keep me in this horrible captivity? Don't you have ways enough to torment me? You need only make me witness the happiness of your unworthy daughter enjoying the company of King Charmant!"

The blue bird heard every syllable of this lament in astonishment. He could hardly wait for daylight to arrive in order to catch a glimpse of the distressed lady, but just before morning dawned, she closed her window and retired. The bird, whose curiosity was wakened, did not fail to return the following night, and in the moonlight, he saw a girl begin to sigh at the tower window.

"Oh, fortune," she exclaimed, "you who flattered me with the prospect of reigning, you who had kept my father's love alive, what have I done to deserve being plunged so suddenly into such bitter grief? Is it at such a tender young age as mine that one must begin to experience your inconstancy? Return, you cruel thing! Return, if you can. The only favor I ask of you is to end my unhappy fate."

The blue bird listened attentively, and the more he did, the more convinced he became that it was his charming princess who was doing the lamenting.

"Adorable Florine," he cried, "wonder of our days, why do you desire to terminate your life so hastily? Your misfortunes can still be remedied."

"Ah! Who's that speaking in such a consoling way?" she asked.

"An unfortunate king," replied the bird, "who loves you and will never love any other than you:"

"A king who loves me!" replied Florine. "Is this a trap set for me by my enemy? But what would she gain by it? If she seeks to discover my sentiments, I'm ready frankly to own up to them."

"No, my princess," replied the bird. "The lover who's speaking to you is incapable of betraying you"—and as he uttered these words he flew to the window.

At first, Florine was alarmed at the appearance of such an extraordinary bird, who spoke with as much sense as a man and yet had the small, sweet voice of a nightingale. The beauty of his plumage, however, and the words he uttered soon reassured her.

"May I be permitted once more to behold you, my princess?" he exclaimed. "Can I taste such perfect happiness and not die with joy? But, alas, how this happiness is troubled by your captivity, and the condition that the wicked Soussio has reduced me to for seven years."

"And who are you, charming bird?" the princess inquired, caressing him.

"You've pronounced my name," said the king, "and you pretend you do not know me?"

"What? The greatest monarch in the world, King Charmant?" cried the princess. "Can the little bird I hold in my hand be you?"

"Alas, beautiful Florine, it is but too true," the bird replied. "And if anything can console me, it's the feeling that I chose this pain instead of renouncing my love for you."

"For me?" said Florine. "Ah, don't attempt to deceive me. I know that you've married Truitonne. I recognized your ring on her hand. I saw her glistening with the diamonds you had given her. She came to insult me in my sad prison, wearing the rich crown and royal mantle she had received from your hands, while I was bound in chains and fetters."

"You've seen Truitonne dressed that way?" interrupted the king. "Did she and her mother dare tell you those jewels came from me? Oh, Heaven! Is it possible that I hear such awful lies, and that I cannot gain immediate revenge on the liars? I want you to know that they tried to deceive me by basely using your name. Indeed, they succeeded in getting me to elope with the ugly Truitonne. But the instant I discovered my error, I tried to flee from her, and eventually I chose to become a blue bird for seven years rather than betray the pledge of fidelity I made to you."

Florine was so pleased by her charming lover's explanation that she forgot the misery of her prison. She told him many things to console him in his sad circumstances, and assured him that she would have done as much for him. Day had dawned and the majority of the officers of the royal household had risen before the blue bird and the princess had finished conversing. It cost them a thousand pangs to part, but they agreed they would meet every night in the same manner.

Their delight at having found each other was so great that it cannot be described. Both offered thanks to love and fortune, but Florine's happiness was tempered by her anxiety about the blue bird. "Who will protect him from the hunters?" she asked. "Or from the sharp talons of some eagle or hungry vulture? They'll eat him with relish not knowing that he's a great king. Oh, Heaven! What would become of me if some of his delicate feathers were blown to my window and announced to me the dreaded disaster?" This thought prevented the poor princess from closing her eyes, for when one loves, thoughts appear like facts, and what one would at another time think impossible seems certain to occur. Therefore, she spent the day in tears until the hour arrived for her to return to the window.

Hiding in a hollow tree, the charming bird occupied himself all day by thinking of his beautiful princess. "How happy

I am to have found her," he said. "How fascinating she is! How deeply I appreciate the kindness she's extended to me." The tender lover counted every second he was condemned to spend in the shape that prevented his marrying her, and never was the termination of a sentence more ardently desired. Since he was eager to be as gallant to Florine as possible, he flew to the capital city of his own kingdom. Landing at his palace, he entered his cabinet through a broken pane of glass in one of the windows, took a pair of diamond earrings more perfect than any other in the world, and brought them that evening to Florine's cell, where he requested that she wear them.

"I'll consent," she said, "if you visit me by daylight. Since I only see you at night, I won't put them on."

The bird promised he would find a way to come to the tower whenever she wished. In response, she put on the earrings, and the night passed in tender discourse just like the night before.

The next day the blue bird returned to his palace, entered his cabinet by the broken window, and carried away the richest bracelets ever seen. Each was made of a single emerald cut in facets with a hole through the center to enable the wearer to pass her hands and arms through them. "Do you think," the princess said to him, "that my affection for you can be measured by presents? Ah, how you misjudge me!"

"No, madame," he replied, "I don't believe that the trifles I offer you are required to keep your love, but mine will not permit me to neglect the least opportunity of showing you my respect, and when I am absent, these little trinkets will bring me to mind."

Florine said a thousand kind things to him on this subject, and he replied with as many no less tender. The following night, the enamored bird brought his beautiful lady a watch. It was encased in a single pearl, and the workmanship was superior to its luster.

"It's useless to present me with a watch," said the princess sweetly. "When you are absent, the hours seem endless, and when you are with me, they pass so like a dream that I cannot keep time of them with any precision."

"Alas, my princess," exclaimed the blue bird, "I agree with you and am certain that I feel the pain of absence and the pleasure of returning even more deeply than you do."

"After what you have suffered to remain true to me," replied the princess, "I truly believe that your affection and respect cannot be carried further."

As soon as morning appeared, the bird flew back to his hollow tree, where he lived on wild fruits. Sometimes, he sang the finest tunes, to the great delight of all who passed that way. Since they could not see anything, they believed it must be the voice of a spirit. This belief became so widespread that eventually nobody dared enter the wood. A thousand fabulous adventures were told about those who had done so, and the general alarm ensured the blue bird's safety. Not a day passed without his making Florine some present, either a pearl necklace, or the most brilliant and uniquely wrought rings, diamond loops, bodkins, and bouquets of jewels in imitation of natural flowers, entertaining books, and interesting medals, until she possessed a stack of marvelous valuables. She wore her jewels only by night to please the king, and in the daytime, since she had no other place to put them in, she hid them carefully in the straw of her mattress.

Two years passed this way without Florine once complaining about her captivity. Indeed, how could she? She had the pleasure of conversing all night with the man she loved. Never were so many pretty speeches made. Though the bird spent the whole day in a hollow tree and never saw anyone, they had a thousand new things to tell each other. Their love and wit alone furnished them with an inexhaustible abundance of subject matter for their conversation.

In the meantime, the malicious queen vainly endeavored to marry off Truitonne. She sent ambassadors with proposals to every prince who had come to her attention, but these envoys were sent packing almost as soon as they arrived. "If your mission concerned Princess Florine, you would be joyously received," was the answer. "But as for Truitonne, let her remain a virgin, for nobody will object."

These tidings infuriated both mother and daughter, and they vented their anger against the innocent princess. "What? This arrogant creature continues to thwart us despite her captivity?" they cried. "We shall never be able to forgive the injuries she has caused us! She must have some secret correspondence with foreign countries and thus must be guilty of high treason at the very least. Let's act on this suspicion and use every possible means to convict her."

They finished talking about this matter so late that it was past midnight when they decided to climb the tower to interrogate Florine. At that moment, she was at the window with the blue bird and was arrayed in all her jewels. Her beautiful hair was dressed with a nicety unusual for tormented souls. Her room and bed were strewn with flowers, and some Spanish pastilles that she was burning emitted an exquisite perfume. Listening at the door, the queen thought she heard a melody sung in a duet (Florine's voice was nearly divine), and these are the tender words she heard:

"Oh, how wretched is our lot,
Nor can we forget our torment,
Loving thus while forced to part.
But even though our woes are deep,
And our cruel foes force us to weep,
Nothing will destroy our hearts."

A few deep sighs finished this little concert.

"Ah, my Truitonne, we've been betrayed," exclaimed the queen. All at once, she opened the door and rushed into the room. Imagine the alarm of Florine at this sight! She promptly pushed open the window to give the royal bird an opportunity to fly off unseen. She was much more anxious about protecting his life than her own, but he felt unable to fly away. His sharp eyes had discovered the danger that the queen and Truitonne posed to the princess. As they approached like Furies bent on devouring her, he was frustrated and troubled because he was not to be able to defend her!

"Your intrigues against the state have been detected!" cried the queen. "Do not imagine that your rank can save you from the punishment you deserve."

"Intrigues with whom, madame?" inquired the princess. "Haven't you been my jailer these two years? Have I seen any other people than those you have sent me?"

As she was speaking, the queen and her daughter examined her with great surprise. Her remarkable beauty and her extraordinary attire dazzled them.

"And where, madame, have you obtained these jewels that outshine the sun?" the queen asked. "Are we to believe there are mines in this tower?"

"I found them," answered Florine. "That's all I know about it."

The queen gazed at Florine with a penetrating look, trying to ascertain what was happening in the core of her heart. "We are not your dupes," she cried. "You think you can deceive us, Princess, but we are aware of all you do from morning till night. These jewels have been given to you with the sole object of inducing you to sell your father's kingdom."

"I'm in a good position to deliver, aren't I?" replied Florine with a disdainful smile. "An unfortunate princess who has languished in captivity so long can be of great service, certainly, in a conspiracy of such a nature."

"Well, for whom," added the queen, "are you so coquettishly dressed up? Your room is so full of perfume, and your attire so magnificent that it is as if you were at court."

"I have plenty of time on my hands," the princess responded. "It's not unusual I should strive to wile away a few moments by taking care of the way I look. I spend so many hours in weeping over my misfortunes that my innocent occupation surely cannot be a subject of reproach."

"Indeed, indeed!" said the queen. "Let

us just see if this innocent miss is not in league with our enemies."

She began to search everywhere and, after emptying the mattress, she found such an immense quantity of diamonds, pearls, rubies, emeralds, and topazes that she could not imagine where they all had come from. While searching, she hid incriminating documents in various places so that their discovery would inculpate the princess. When she thought nobody was looking, she began thrusting them into the chimney, but by good luck, the blue bird was perched there. He had eyes as sharp as a lynx and saw everything.

"Beware, Florine!" he cried. "Your enemy is trying to betray you."

This voice was so unexpected that it frightened the queen, and she became afraid to conceal the papers.

"Madame," said the princess, "you see that the spirits of the air are my friends."

"I believe," the queen exclaimed in a fit of rage, "that you are in league with demons. In spite of them, though, your father will have justice done."

"Would be to heaven," cried Florine, "if I only had to fear the fury of my father! But yours, madame, is much more terrible."

Finally, the queen left her, greatly disturbed by all she had seen and heard. She consulted her friends as to what should be done to the princess. They remarked that, if some fairy or enchanter were protecting Florine, any further persecution would only irritate her powerful friend. "It would be better first to discover the mystery."

The queen approved this idea. She sent a young girl to sleep in Florine's apartment under the pretext that she was there to wait on her. The girl pretended to be naïve, but Florine did not fall for such an obvious ruse. The princess regarded her as a spy, and she could only feel her torment more violently. "What now? Won't I ever be able to converse again with my dear bird?" she asked. "He has helped me endure my misfortunes, and I have soothed his troubles. Our affection was everything to us! What will become of him? What will become of me?" While thinking all these things, she shed rivers of tears. She no longer dared go to the little window, though she heard the bird fluttering around it. She was dying to open it, but she feared exposing the life of her dear lover.

A whole month passed without her appearing at the window. The blue bird was in despair and uttered complaint after complaint. How could he live without seeing his princess? He had never felt the pangs of solitude and the misery of his transformation so sharply. In vain, he sought a remedy for both. Nothing brought him consolation.

After watching day and night for a whole month, the spy was eventually overwhelmed by drowsiness, and at last, she sunk into a sound slumber. When Florine saw this, she opened her little window and said: "Bird as blue as cloudless sky, come to my window, quickly fly!"

Those were her exact words without the slightest alteration. The bird heard them so distinctly that he was at the window in an instant. What delight once more to behold each other! How much they had to say to each other! They renewed their vows of love and fidelity a thousand times over. Yet, as Charmant saw that the princess was unable to restrain her tears, he was tormented and did his utmost to console her. At last, the hour of parting arrived, without the spy awakening, and they said good-bye to each other in the most touching manner.

The next night, the spy fell asleep again, and the princess lost no time in going to the window and calling as before: "Bird as blue as cloudless sky, come to my window, quickly fly!"

Immediately, the bird arrived, and the night passed without discovery like the preceding one. The lovers were delighted. They hoped that the spy would find so much pleasure in sleeping that she would do so every night, and, in fact, the third did pass as happily.

On the one following, though, the sleeper was disturbed by a noise. Listening without appearing to be awake, and peeping as best she could, she saw the most beautiful bird in the world by the light of the moon. He talked to the princess, caressed her with his claw, and pecked her gently with his bill. She overheard part of their conversation and was extremely surprised, for the bird spoke like a lover, and the beautiful Florine answered him most tenderly. When day broke and they said their farewells, they parted with extreme sorrow, as though they had a presentiment of their coming misfortune. Bathed in tears, the princess threw herself on her bed, and the king returned to his hollow tree.

Now, the spy ran to the queen and told her all she had seen and heard. The queen, in turn, sent for Truitonne and her confidantes. They talked the matter over for a long time and concluded that the blue bird was King Charmant.

"What an affront!" cried the queen. "What an affront, my Truitonne! This insolent princess, whom I thought was so wretched, has been quietly enjoying the most charming conversations with that ungrateful prince. Oh, I'll take such a bloody revenge that it will be the talk of the whole world!"

Truitonne begged her not to lose a moment, and since she considered herself more interested in the matter than the queen, she was bursting with joy at the thought of all that would be done to destroy the happiness of the lover and his mistress. The queen sent the spy back to the tower, ordering her not to show any suspicion or curiosity, but to appear sleepier than ever. Consequently, she went to bed early and snored as loudly as she could. The poor, deceived princess opened the little window and called: "Bird as blue as cloudless sky, come to my window, quickly fly!"

However, she called in vain the whole night long. He did not come, for the wicked queen had ordered swords, knives, razors, and daggers to be attached to the cypress

tree so that when he darted toward the window these murderous weapons cut off his feet. In addition, some others lacerated his wings and stabbed his chest. Only with great difficulty, leaving behind him a long trail of blood, did he reach his own tree. Why weren't you there, lovely princess, to comfort that royal bird? And yet, it would have been the death of her to have seen him in such a dismal condition.

Since he was convinced that it was Florine who had been guilty of this cruel treachery, he did not care a fig about his life. "Oh, barbarous princess," he exclaimed mournfully, "is this the way you repay the most pure and tender passion that ever was or will ever be? If you had wanted me to die, why didn't you perform the deed yourself? Death would have been sweet from your hand! I looked for you with so much love and trust. I suffered for you and suffered without complaining. And now you have sacrificed me to the cruelest of women, our common enemy! You have made your peace with her at the price of my life. It is you, Florine, you who has stabbed me! You have borrowed Truitonne's hand and guided it to my bosom!"

These furious thoughts so overwhelmed him that he looked forward to his death. However, his friend, the enchanter, who had seen the flying frogs return without the king in the chariot, became so concerned ahout him that he went around the world eight times in search of him. On his ninth journey, he passed through the forest in which the poor king was lying. As was his custom, he blew a long blast on his horn and then cried five times in a loud voice, "King Charmant! King Charmant! Where are you?"

The king recognized his best friend's voice and cried, "Come over to this tree, and behold the wretched king you cherish drowning in his own blood."

Quite surprised, the enchanter looked all around without seeing anyone. "I'm a blue bird," the king exclaimed in a feeble, plaintive voice.

After hearing this, the enchanter had no trouble locating him in his nest. Another person might have been dumbfounded, but he was well-versed in every aspect of necromancy. He needed but a few words to stop the blood from flowing, and along with some herbs, which he found in the woods, he murmured a short spell and cured the king so well that it seemed he had never been wounded. Then he asked the king to tell him how he had become transformed into a bird, and who had wounded him so cruelly. The king satisfied his curiosity and informed him that it must have been Florine, who had revealed the amorous mystery of the secret visits he paid her. To make her peace with the queen, she had consented to have the cypress tree filled with the daggers and razors that had almost hacked him to pieces. He denounced the treachery of the princess a thousand times and said he would have been happier if he had died without knowing the wickedness of her heart. The magician cried shame upon her and all her sex, and he advised the king to forget her.

"What a misfortune it would be," he said, "if you were to continue loving that ungrateful lady. After what she's done to you, you have everything to fear."

The blue bird, however, could not share this view because he still loved Florine too dearly, and the enchanter, who knew his real sentiments despite the care the king took to conceal them, said to him in a friendly manner:

Crushed by Fortune's cruel blow,
Vainly Reason's voice is heard.
We but listen to our woe,
Neglecting wise and soothing words.
Leave Old Man Time his work to do.
All things have their sunny side.
But until he brings it within view,
Nothing but darkness will be spied.

The royal bird admitted the truth of these remarks and asked his friend to take him home and put him in a cage, where he would be safe from a cat's paw or murderous weapon.

However, the enchanter asked, "Do you really want to remain in such a deplorable condition for five years? It is ill-suited to your duties and your dignity. Remember, you have enemies who claim that you're dead. They want to seize your kingdom. I fear very much that you'll lose it before you regain your proper form."

"Can't I enter my palace and govern as I used to do?" asked the king.

"Oh," exclaimed his friend, "the situation has changed! Those who would obey a man will not bow to a parrot. Those who feared you when you were a king surrounded by grandeur and pomp would be the first to pluck out all your feathers now that you're a little bird."

"Alas, for human weakness," cried the king. "Although a glittering exterior is nothing compared to virtue, it still wields a power over the minds of men that is difficult to combat. Well, then, let us be philosophers, and despise that which we cannot obtain. Our lot will be none the worse for it."

"I don't give up so easily," said the magician. "I still hope to hit upon some means of restoring you to your proper form."

Meanwhile, Florine, sad Florine, was in despair at no longer seeing the king. She spent her days and nights at the window and constantly repeated: "Bird as blue as cloudless sky, come to my window, quickly fly!"

The presence of her watchful attendant did not stop her, for her despair was so great that she did not care about the consequences.

"What has happened to you, King Charmant?" she cried. "Have our mutual enemies made you feel the cruel effects of their rage? Have you fallen victim to their fury? Alas, alas! Have you perished? Shall I never see you again? Shall I never weary

of my woes? Have you abandoned me to my hard fate?"

What tears, what sobs followed these tender complaints. How did the absence of such a dear and charming lover lengthen the dreary hours of her captivity! The princess was dejected, ill, thin, and changed. So convinced that something fatal had happened to the king, she could scarcely sustain herself. The queen and Truitonne had triumphed. Their revenge gave them more pleasure than the offense that had annoyed them. And just what was this offense after all? King Charmant had refused to marry a little monster he had a thousand reasons to hate. In the meantime, Florine's father, who had reached a considerable age, fell ill and died. Now, the fortunes of the wicked queen and her daughter assumed a new aspect. They were looked upon as favorites who had abused their influence. The people rose up and ran to the palace, demanding Princess Florine and claiming that they would recognize her alone as their sovereign. In turn, the queen was affronted by this and tried to handle the affair in a haughty manner. She appeared on a balcony and threatened the insurgents. But the revolt became widespread, and the people broke into the apartments, pillaged them, and stoned the queen to death. Truitonne fled for protection to her godmother, the fairy Soussio, or she would have shared the fate of her mother. The nobles of the kingdom met immediately and climbed the tower, where the princess was lying gravely ill. She knew neither of her father's death nor of her enemy's punishment. When she heard the noise of people approaching, she was convinced they were coming to put her to death. She was not in the least alarmed, for life had become hateful since she had lost the blue bird. Consequently, when her subjects flung themselves at her feet and informed her of the happy change in her fortunes, she was quite indifferent. Still, they carried her to the palace and crowned her. Then her frail body was given great care, and her desire to search for the blue bird fortified her health. Soon, she was able to appoint a council to govern the kingdom during her absence. In preparation for her journey, she took jewels to the value of a thousand million francs with her and set out one night quite alone without anyone knowing where she was going.

The enchanter who managed the affairs of King Charmant did not have sufficient power to undo what Soussio had done. Therefore, he decided to seek her out and propose some arrangement that would convince her to restore the king to his natural form. He called for his frogs and flew to the fairy, who was at that moment conversing with Truitonne. Enchanters and fairies are on an equal footing. These two had known each other for five or six hundred years, and during that time they had quarreled and made up again at least a thousand times.

Soussio received him very politely. "What does my compeer want?" she said (this is the way they all address one another). "Is there anything I can do for you?"

"Yes, compeer," answered the magician, "you can. It concerns one of my best friends, a king whom you have made very unhappy."

"Aha! I understand you, compeer," cried Soussio. "I'm very sorry, but there's no hope for him unless he consents to marry my goddaughter. There she is in all her beauty, as you may see. Let him think it over."

The enchanter was almost struck dumb when he caught sight of Truitonne, so hideous did she appear to him. Nevertheless, he could not leave without coming to some sort of agreement with Soussio.

"The king has run a thousand risks since he has begun dwelling in a cage," he explained. "Once, the nail on which the cage had been hanging had broken, and the cage had fallen to the ground with a severe shock to his feathered majesty. Minet, the cat, who happened to be in the room when this accident occurred, gave the poor king a scratch on the eye that nearly blinded him. On another occasion, they neglected to give him any fresh water, and he barely escaped having the pip disease. A little rogue of a monkey got loose, caught hold of some of his feathers through the bars of the cage, and toyed with him as if he were a jay or a blackbird. But worst of all, he was on the verge of losing his kingdom. His heirs were trumping up new stories every day to prove he was dead."

Finally, the enchanter came to an understanding with his compeer Soussio: she would bring Truitonne to King Charmant's palace, where she would reside for some months. During that time, the king would be allowed to make up his mind to marry her. Soussio would permit him to resume his original form with the proviso that he would become a bird again if he eventually refused to marry her goddaughter.

The fairy presented Truitonne with magnificent dresses made of gold and silver, seated her on a pillion behind herself on a dragon, and proceeded directly to Charmant's kingdom, where they found him with his faithful friend the enchanter. With three taps of Soussio's wand, King Charmant was again the handsome, charming, intelligent, and magnificent sovereign he had been before. However, his reprieve was dearly bought. The mere thought of marrying Truitonne made him shudder. The enchanter reasoned with him as well as he could, but made little impression on him. The king was less occupied with the government of his dominions than with devising means to prolong the period Soussio had allowed before he had to marry Truitonne.

In the meantime, Queen Florine had disguised herself as a peasant. Her hair was disheveled and hanging about her ears to conceal her features, and she wore a straw hat on her head and a sack upon her shoulder. Sometimes, she walked, and other times, she rode. She went by sea and land as fast as she could. However, not being certain of the route, she feared that every turn she took might lead her away from her charming monarch instead of toward him.

One day, she stopped to rest beside a fountain whose silvery water flowed over little pebbles. Taking the opportunity of washing her feet, she sat on the grassy bank, tied up her fair locks with a ribbon, and put her feet into the little stream. She looked like Diana bathing on her return from the chase. A little old woman, bent over and leaning on a stout stick, happened to be passing that way and stopped. "What are you doing there so all alone, my pretty girl?"

"My good mother," the queen answered, "I have plenty of company, for I'm beset by sorrows, anxieties, and misfortunes."

And as she uttered these words, her eyes filled with tears.

"What? So young and you're crying?" asked the good woman. "Ah, my child, don't give in to sorrow. Tell me truly what's wrong, and hopefully I may be able to comfort you."

The queen willingly told her about all her misfortunes, about the conduct of the fairy Soussio, and how she was presently searching for the blue bird. Suddenly, the little old woman drew herself up as straight as possible, changing her whole appearance. She was lovely, young, and superbly attired. She smiled graciously at the queen as she said, "Incomparable Florine, the king you seek is no longer a bird. My sister Soussio has restored him to his former shape. He's in his kingdom. Don't torture yourself, for you will reach it and obtain your goal. Here are four eggs. Break one of them whenever you need help the most, and you'll find something in each that will be useful."

Upon saying this, she instantly disappeared, leaving Florine very consoled by what she had heard. Putting the eggs into her sack, she resumed her journey toward Charmant's kingdom. After walking eight days and nights without stopping, she arrived at the foot of an enormously high mountain made entirely of ivory and so steep that one could not keep one's footing on it. She made a thousand vain attempts, but slipped back each time until she became exhausted. In despair at encountering such an insurmountable obstacle, she laid down at the bottom of the mountain and decided to die right there.

Then she remembered the eggs the fairy had given her and took one out of her sack. "Let's see if the lady was merely making fun of me when she promised that the eggs would help me in my need."

When she broke open the egg, she found some small golden clamps, which she fastened on her hands and feet. With their help she climbed the ivory mountain without the least trouble because the points of the clamps penetrated the ivory and prevented her from slipping. After she reached the top, she found herself in just as much trouble with regard to the descent. The entire valley was a sheet of mirrored glass in which upward of sixty thousand women were admiring themselves, for this looking glass was two whole miles in width and six in height. Everyone appeared in it exactly as she wished to be. The carrot-haired women seemed to have locks of gold; a coarse brunette appeared to be glossy raven black. The old looked young, the young never looked older. In sum, no fault could be seen in this wonderful mirror, and consequently the fair sex from all parts of the world resorted to using it. It was enough to make you die laughing to see the airs and graces that most of these coquettes gave themselves. Nor were men less eager to consult this magical mirror, which pleased them just as well. To some it seemed to give fine, curly hair, to others taller stature or better shape, a more martial mien or a nobler deportment. The ladies laughed and laughed at them just as much in return.

The mountain was called by a thousand different names as a result. No one had ever been able to get to the top of it. Therefore, when Florine appeared on the summit, the ladies uttered shrieks of despair. "Where is that mad creature going?" they cried. "No doubt she must know how to walk on glass, or she'll break our mirror to pieces with the first step she takes!"

Immediately, there was a terrific hubbub. The queen did not know what to do, for she saw the imminent danger of descending by that road. So, she broke another egg, and two pigeons popped out, attached to a tiny chariot that grew sufficiently large for her to sit in comfortably. The pigeons then gently descended with the queen and landed at the bottom without the least accident.

"My little friends," she said to them, "if you'll carry me to the spot where King Charmant holds his court, you won't find me ungrateful."

The civil, obedient pigeons kept going night and day until they reached the

gates of the city. Florine got out and gave each of them a sweet kiss worth more than a royal diadem. Oh, how her heart beat as she entered the city! Staining her face so that she would not be recognized, she asked a group of people she passed where she might see the king. Some of them began to laugh at her. "See the king?" they said. "Ho, what do you want with him, my young slut? Go, go and clean yourself! You are not worthy enough to look at such a monarch."

The queen made no reply, but quietly moved on and asked the next group she met where the best place would be to see the king. "He'll soon be going to the temple with Princess Truitonne, for he has finally consented to marry her," was the answer.

"Heavens, what tidings! Truitonne, the worthless Truitonne, on the verge of marrying the king?"

Struck by this bad news, Florine felt like dying, and collapsed dumbfounded on a heap of rubble under a gateway, her face covered by her disheveled hair and her large straw hat. "How unfortunate I am!" she cried. "I've come here only to add to the triumph of my rival and witness her contentment. It was for her, then, that the blue bird deserted me! It was for this little monster that he was guilty of the cruelest inconstancy. While I grieved over him and trembled for his life, the traitor had already turned away and thought no more of me than if he had never seen me. Indeed, he left me to lament his absence without a sigh."

Miserable souls rarely have much appetite, so when the poor queen sought out a lodging for the night, she went to bed without any supper. Rising with the sun, she hurried to the temple. After repeated rebuffs from soldiers and attendants, she succeeded in obtaining admission. There she saw the king's throne and that of Truitonne, whom the people already looked upon as their queen. How painful it was for such a sensitive lover as Florine! She approached the throne of her rival and paused, leaning against a marble pillar. The king arrived first, looking more handsome and fascinating than ever. Truitonne followed him, richly attired and ugly enough to frighten everybody. She frowned as soon as she noticed Florine.

"Who do you think you are to dare approach our august person and our golden throne in this way?"

"I'm called Mie Souillon," replied Florine. "I've come from a distant country to sell you some rare objects."

Upon saying this, she took out of her sack the emerald bracelets that King Charmant had given to her.

"Aha," said Truitonne, "these are pretty glass ornaments. Will you take five coins for them?"

"Show them to a connoisseur, madame," Florine responded, "and then we'll make our deal."

Truitonne, who loved the king as much as such a creature could, was delighted in having a reason to speak to him. Approaching his throne, she showed him the bracelets and requested his opinion with regard to their value. As soon as he saw them, he immediately recalled those he had given to Florine. Sighing, he turned pale and could not speak for some time. At last, fearing that people might notice how upset his conflicting emotions were making him, he made an effort to compose himself and answered, "I believe these bracelets are worth almost as much as my kingdom. I had thought there was only one pair like this in the world, but these are certainly just like the pair I knew."

Truitonne returned to her throne, and once she was seated, she looked less noble than an oyster in its shell. Then she asked Florine what was the lowest price she would ask for the bracelets.

"You would find it difficult to pay, madame," she answered. "I had better propose another kind of bargain to you. If you'll obtain permission for me to sleep one night in the cabinet of echoes, I'll give you the emeralds."

"Gladly, Mie Souillon," said Truitonne, laughing like an idiot and showing teeth longer than the tusks of a wild boar.

The king did not ask where the bracelets came from, not because he did not care about the person who possessed them—in any case, her appearance was not such as to inspire much curiosity—but because he was so overwhelmingly repulsed by Truitonne. Now, it is important to know that when Charmant had been a blue bird, he had told Florine that beneath his apartments was a small room called the cabinet of echoes, so ingeniously constructed that the slightest whispers uttered there could be heard by the king while reposing in his bedroom. And since Florine's intention was to reproach him for his inconstancy, she could not have imagined a better method. After she was led to the cabinet that evening on Truitonne's orders, she immediately began her complaints and lamentations.

"The catastrophe that I never dreamed would occur has come about, cruel blue bird," she cried. "You've forgotten me! You love my unworthy rival. The bracelets I received from your disloyal hand could not make you remember me, so entirely have you banished me from your recollection."

Here, her sobs choked off her speech, and when she was able to speak again, she resumed her lamentations and continued them until daybreak. The king's servants, who had heard her moan and sigh all night long, asked Truitonne why Florine had made such a disturbance. The queen answered that, when she slept soundly, she was in the habit of dreaming and often talked aloud in her sleep. As for the king, a fatal aberration had prevented him from hearing her. Ever since he had fallen so deeply in love with Florine, he could not

sleep soundly. Therefore, whenever he went to bed, he took a dose of opium in order to gain some rest.

Florine spent part of the next day in a strange, anxious mood. "If he heard me," she thought, "he's certainly showing his cruel indifference. If he didn't hear me, how shall I get him to do so?"

Although she did not possess any more of those rare objects, she did have plenty of beautiful jewels. However, she needed something that would particularly catch Truitonne's fancy. Consequently, Florine resorted to using her eggs. She broke one, and out sprang a coach of polished steel inlaid with gold. It was drawn by six green mice and driven by a rose-colored rat, and the postilion, also of the rat species, was a grayish-violet color. In the coach sat four puppets who were more sprightly than any ever seen at the fairs of St. Germain or St. Laurent. They could do all sorts of wonderful things, particularly two little gypsies, who could dance a sarabande or a jig and hold their own with the famous Leance. Florine was enraptured at the sight of this new masterpiece of necromancy. Remaining perfectly mum until evening, the time Truitonne usually took a walk; she took up a place on one of the paths and set the mice galloping with the coach, rats, and puppets. This novelty so astonished Truitonne that she called out two or three times, "Mie Souillon, Mie Souillon! Will you take five coins for your coach and set of mice?"

"Ask the men of letters and learned scholars of this kingdom," said Florine, "what such a wonder is worth, and I'll abide by the estimation of the best judge."

Truitonne, who did everything arbitrarily, replied, "Without offending me any longer by your filthy presence, tell me the price."

"All I ask," said Florine, "is to sleep again in the cabinet of echoes."

"Go, poor idiot," answered Truitonne, "you will have your wish."

Turning to her ladies-in-waiting, she said, "What a stupid creature to reap no greater advantage from such rare objects."

Night came, and Florine uttered all the most touching reproaches she could conceive, but again it was in vain, for the king never forgot to take his opium. His servants said to one another, "That country wench must surely be mad. What is she muttering about all night?"

"Whatever the case may be," some remarked, "there is both reason and feeling in what she says."

She waited impatiently for morning to ascertain what effect her words had produced. "What?" she cried. "Has this barbarous man become deaf to my voice? Will he no longer listen to his dear Florine? Oh, how weak I am to love him still! How well do I deserve the scorn with which he treats me!"

But all her reproaches were for nothing, for she had no power over her feelings for him. There was only one more egg left in her sack that could help her. She broke it, and out came a pie composed of six birds, which were larded, dressed, and quite ready for eating. Yet, they sang admirably, told fortunes, and knew more about medicine than Sculapius himself. Florine was enchanted at the sight of such a wonderful thing and carried her talking pie into Truitonne's antechamber. While waiting for her to come, one of the king's servants came up to Florine and said, "My friend, Mie Souillon, are you aware that if the king did not take opium to make him sleep, you would be disturbing him immensely, for you chatter all night long in the most extraordinary manner."

Now Florine was no longer surprised that the king had not heard her. She took a handful of jewels out of her sack and said, "I'm not afraid of interrupting the king's sleep. So if you'll prevent him from taking opium tonight, assuming I'll be sleeping in the cabinet of echoes, all these pearls and diamonds will be yours."

The servant agreed to do it and gave her his word. A few minutes afterward, Truitonne arrived. She noticed Florine with her pie, which she pretended to be eating. "What are you doing there, Mie Souillon?"

"Madame," replied Florine, "I am eating astrologers, musicians, and physicians."

At that moment, all the birds began to sing more melodiously than sirens and then to cry, "Give us a piece of silver, and we'll tell you your fortune." A duck that was particularly prominent called out in a voice louder than any of the others, "Quack! Quack! Quack! Quack! I'm a physician; I cure all disorders and every sort of madness, except that of love."

Truitonne was most surprised by so many wonders. Indeed, she had never seen so many in her entire life. Thinking it an excellent pie, she coveted it. "Come, come, Mie Souillon, what shall I give you for it?"

"The usual price," answered Florine, "permission to sleep in the cabinet of echoes—nothing more."

"Why," said Truitonne generously (for she was in a good mood due to her acquisition of such a pie), "you will have a gold coin as part of the bargain."

Florine was now happier than she had been for some time because she hoped the king would hear her. Therefore, she took her leave of Truitonne with many thanks. As soon as night came, she requested to be led to the cabinet, ardently hoping that

the servant would keep his word, and that instead of giving the king his opium, he would substitute something that would keep his majesty awake. When she thought everybody else was asleep, she began her usual lamentations. "How many dangers did I confront searching for you," she said, "while you fled from me and sought to marry Truitonne? What did I do to you, you cruel person, to make you forget your vows? Remember your transformation, my favors, and our tender conversations."

She repeated nearly all of them, her memory sufficiently proving that nothing was dearer to her than such recollections. The king was not asleep and heard Florine so distinctly that he could not imagine where they came from. But his heart, pierced by tenderness, brought back the image of his incomparable princess so vividly that he felt his separation from her just as keenly as he had at the moment the knives had wounded him in the cypress tree. He began to speak aloud on his part, as the queen had done on hers. "Ah, princess," he said, "too cruel to a lover who adored you. Is it possible that you would have sacrificed me to our mutual enemies?"

Florine heard what he said and replied that if he would grant Mie Souillon an audience, he would learn about all the mysteries he had been unable to grasp until now. At these words, the impatient king called one of his servants and asked him if he could find a Mie Souillon and bring her to him. The servant answered that nothing could be easier: she was sleeping in the cabinet of echoes.

The king did not know what to think. How could such a great queen as Florine be disguised as a scullion? And yet, how could Mie Souillon have the queen's voice and know such particular secrets unless she were not Florine herself? In his uncertainty, he arose and dressed himself in the greatest haste. He descended by a back staircase to the door of the cabinet of echoes. Florine had taken the key out of the lock, but the king had a master key that unlocked every door in the palace.

A lamp at some distance cast a faint light on the scene. Lying on a couch, she was dressed in a light robe of white taffeta, which she wore beneath her coarse disguise, and her beautiful hair bathed her shoulders. The king entered in a rush, his love getting the better of his anger. The moment he saw for certain it was Florine, he flung himself at her feet, bathed her hands with his tears, and felt he would die of joy, grief, and a thousand different emotions that swirled inside of him.

The queen was no less moved. Her heart seemed to stop beating; she could scarcely

breathe. She looked earnestly at the king without saying a word, and when she found the strength to speak to him, she had no power to reproach him, for the joy of beholding him again made her forget all of her groundless complaints. At length they explained to each other what had happened and justified what they had done. Their tender feelings were revived more strongly than ever, and the only obstacle that remained was the fairy Soussio.

However, at this moment the enchanter, who was so fond of the king, arrived with a famous fairy, who was none other than the one who had given the four eggs to Florine. After initial compliments were exchanged, the enchanter and the fairy declared that their power had united in favor of the king and queen and that Soussio could do nothing against them. Consequently, their marriage could take place without delay.

We may readily imagine the delight of these two young lovers. As soon as it was daytime, the news spread throughout the palace, and everybody was enchanted at the sight of Florine. When the tidings reached Truitonne, she ran to the king's apartments. To her surprise, she found her beautiful rival there, and the moment she attempted to open her mouth to abuse her, the enchanter and the fairy appeared and changed her into a sow. Since Truie in French means sow, she still retained part of her name, plus her natural disposition to grumble. She ran out of the room grunting and then into the kitchen courtyard, where long peals of laughter greeted her and completed her despair.

Now that King Charmant and Queen Florine had been rescued from such a hideous person, they thought of their wedding and how elegant and magnificent it would be. Indeed, it is easy to judge how great their happiness was after so many prolonged misfortunes.

When Truitonne tried to force that charming
king
To tie a knot which death alone could sunder,
Regardless of the consequences it would bring,
She certainly committed a great blunder.
Of course, if possible she did not know, a
marriage
Unblessed by mutual love is wretched slavery.
But Charmant's bold, uncompromising
carriage,
Showed as much prudence, I maintain, as
bravery.
Better to be a bird of any hue
A raven, crow, an owl, I do protest,
Than stick for life to a partner like glue
Who scorns you, or whom you detest.
Too many matches of this sort I've seen,
And wish that now there were some king
magician
To stop these ill-matched souls at once and lean
On them with force to keep his prohibition.
He must be vigilant and forbid the banns,
Whenever true affection might be slighted.
And Hymen must be prevented from joining
hands,
Whenever hearts have not first been united.

The Ram

N THOSE happy times when fairies still existed, a king reigned, and he had three daughters. Young and beautiful, all three possessed considerable talents, but the youngest was the most charming and the favorite by far. Indeed, they called her Merveilleuse. Her father gave her more gowns and ribbons in a month than he gave the others in a year, and she was so good-natured that she shared everything with them so that there might be no misunderstandings.

Now, the king had some evil neighbors who grew tired of keeping peace with him. Therefore, they formed a powerful alliance and compelled him to arm his country in self-defense. Once he had raised a large army, he assumed command and rode off to do battle. The three princesses remained with their tutors in a castle, and every day they received good news about the king's exploits. One time he took a city, another he won a battle. Finally, he succeeded in routing his enemies and driving them out of his dominions. Then he returned to the castle as fast as he could to see his little Merveilleuse, whom he adored so much.

The three princesses had ordered three satin gowns to be made for themselves—one green, one blue, one white. Jewels were selected to match their dresses—the green enriched with emeralds, the blue with turquoises, and the white with diamonds. Thus attired, they went to meet the king, singing the following verses, which they had written to celebrate his victories:

"With conquest crowned on many a glorious
plain,
What joy to greet our king and sire again!
Welcome him back, victorious, to these halls,
With new delights and countless festivals.
Let shouts of joy and songs of triumph prove
His people's loyalty, his daughters' love!"

When the king saw his lovely daughters in such splendid attire, he embraced them all tenderly, but caressed Merveilleuse more than the others. A magnificent banquet was arranged, and the king and his three daughters sat down to eat. Since it was his habit to draw inferences from everything, he said to the eldest, "Tell me, please, why have you put on a green gown?"

"Sire," she answered, "having heard of your achievements, I imagined that green would express the joy and hope with which your return inspired me."

"That is very prettily said!" the king exclaimed. "And you, my child," he continued, "why are you wearing a blue gown?"

"My liege," the princess said, "I want to indicate that we should constantly implore the gods to protect you. Moreover, your sight is to me like that of Heaven and all the Heavenly Host."

"You speak like an oracle," the king said. "And you, Merveilleuse, why have you dressed yourself in white?"

"Because, sire," she answered, "it becomes me better than any other color."

"What?" the king cried, very much offended. "Was that your only motive, you little coquette?"

"My motive was to please you," said the princess. "It seems to me that I ought to have no other."

The king, who loved her dearly, was so perfectly satisfied with this explanation that he declared himself quite pleased by the little turn she had given to her meaning and the art with which she had at first concealed the compliment.

"Now, then," he said, "I've had an excellent supper, but I won't go to bed yet. Tell me what you all dreamed of the night before my return."

The eldest said she had dreamed that he had brought her a gown with gold and jewels that glistened brighter than the sun. The second said she had dreamed he had brought her a golden distaff to spin herself some shifts. The youngest said she had dreamed that he had married off her second sister and on the wedding day, he had offered her a golden vase and said, "Merveilleuse, come here. Come here so you can wash."

Infuriated by this dream, the king knit his brow and made such an exceedingly wry face that everybody saw he was enraged. He retired to his room and flung himself onto the bed, but he could not forget his daughter's dream. "This insolent creature," he said, "she wants to turn me into her servant. I wouldn't be surprised at all if she put on that white satin dress without thinking of me at all. She doesn't take me seriously. But I'll frustrate her wicked designs while there's still time."

He arose in a fury, and though it was still dark outside, he sent for the captain of his guards and said, "You heard Merveilleuse's dream. It forecasts strange things against me. I command you to seize her immediately, take her into the forest, and kill her. Afterward, you're to bring me her heart and tongue so I'll be sure you haven't deceived me. If you fail, I'll have you put to death in the cruelest manner imaginable."

The captain of the guards was astounded by this barbarous order. He did not dare argue with the king, however, for fear of increasing his rage and causing him to give the horrifying order to someone else. Therefore, he assured him he would take the princess, kill her, and bring him her heart and tongue.

The captain strode directly to the princess's apartment, where he had some difficulty in obtaining permission to enter because it was still quite early. He informed Merveilleuse that the king desired to see her. She arose immediately, and a tiny Moorish girl named Patypata carried her train. A young ape and a little dog that always accompanied her also ran after her. The ape was called Grabugeon and the little dog, Tintin. The captain of the guards made Merveilleuse descend into the garden, where he told her the king was taking in the fresh morning air. She entered it, and the captain pretended to look for the king. When he did not find him, he said, "No doubt his majesty has walked farther on into the woods."

He opened a small gate and led the princess into the forest. It was just getting light, and the princess saw that her escort had tears in his eyes and was so dejected that he could not speak.

"What's the matter?" she inquired kindly. "You seem very much distressed."

"Ah, madame," he exclaimed, "how could I be otherwise, for I've been given the most dreadful order that has even been given! The king has commanded me to kill you in this forest and to take your heart and tongue to him. If I fail to do so, he will put me to death."

Turning pale with terror, the poor princess began to weep softly, like a lamb about to be sacrificed. Then she turned her beautiful eyes to the captain of the guards and looked at him without anger. "Do you really have the heart to kill me?" she asked. "I've never done you any harm, and I've always spoken well of you to the king. If I really deserved my father's hate, I'd suffer the consequences without a murmur. But alas, I've always shown him so much respect and affection that he has no just reason to complain."

"Fear not, beautiful princess," said the captain, "I'm incapable of such a barbarous act. I'd rather have him carry out his threat and kill me. Nevertheless, if I were to kill myself, you wouldn't be much better off. We must find some way that will enable me to return to the king and convince him you're dead."

"What way is there?" asked Merveilleuse. "He's ordered you to bring him my heart and tongue, and if you don't, he won't believe you."

Patypata had witnessed everything, though neither the captain nor the princess was aware of her presence because they were so overcome by sadness. Advancing courageously, she threw herself at Merveilleuse's feet. "Madame," she said, "I want to offer you my life. You must kill me. I'd be most happy to die for such a good mistress."

"Oh, I could never permit it, my dear Patypata," the princess said, kissing her. "After such an affectionate proof of your friendship, your life is as dear to me as my own."

Then Grabugeon stepped forward and said, "You have good reason, princess, to love such a faithful slave as Patypata. She can be of much more use to you than I am. Now it's my turn to offer you my heart and tongue with joy, for I wish to immortalize myself in the annals of the empire of monkeys."

"Ah, my darling Grabugeon," Merveilleuse replied, "I can't bear the idea of taking your life."

"I'd find it intolerable," exclaimed Tintin, "good little dog as I am, if anyone but myself were to sacrifice his life for my mistress! Either I die or nobody dies."

Upon saying this, a great dispute arose between Patypata, Grabugeon, and Tintin, and they exchanged a great many harsh words. At last, Grabugeon, who was quicker than the others, scampered up to the top of a tree and flung herself down headfirst, killing herself on the spot. As much as the princess grieved over her loss, she agreed to let the captain of the guards cut out her tongue since the poor thing was dead. To their dismay, however, it was so small (for the creature was not much bigger than one's fist) that they felt certain the king would not be deceived by it.

"Alas, my dear little ape," cried the princess, "there you lie, and your sacrifice hasn't saved my life!"

"That honor has been reserved for me," interrupted the Moor, and as she spoke, she snatched the knife that had been used on Grabugeon and plunged it into her bosom. The captain of the guards would have taken her tongue, but it was so black that he knew he would not be able to deceive the king with it.

"Look at my misfortune!" the princess said tearfully. "I lose all those I love, and yet my fate remains unchanged."

"Had you accepted my offer," Tintin said, "you would have only had to mourn my loss, and I would have had the satisfaction of being the only one mourned."

Merveilleuse kissed her little dog and wept such bitter tears over him that she became quite exhausted. She turned hastily away, and when she ventured to look around again, her escort was gone, and she found herself alone with the dead bodies of her Moor, her ape, and her little dog. She could not leave the spot until she had buried them in a hole that she found by chance at the foot of a tree. Afterward, she scratched these words into the tree:

Three faithful friends lie
buried in this grave.
They saved my life with deeds
most brave.

Then she began to think about her own safety. It was certainly dangerous for her to remain in that forest, especially since it was so close to her father's castle. The first person who saw her would recognize her. Then again, she might be attacked and devoured like a chicken by the lions and wolves that infested it. So, she set off walking as fast as she could.

The forest was so enormous, however, and the sun so strong that she was soon about ready to collapse from heat, fear, and exhaustion. She looked around in every direction, but was unable to see an end to the woods. Every movement frightened her. She continually imagined that the king was in hot pursuit, seeking to kill her. Indeed, she uttered so many cries of woe that it is impossible to repeat them all here.

As she walked on, not following any particular path, the thickets tore her beautiful dress and scratched her ivory skin. At last, she heard some sheep bleating. "It is probably some shepherds with their flocks," she said. "Perhaps they'll be able to direct me to a village where I can disguise myself in peasant garb. Alas, kings and queens are not always the happiest people in the world! Who in all this kingdom would have ever believed that I'd become a fugitive, that my father would want to take my life without reason, and that I'd have to disguise myself to save my neck?"

Even as she made these remarks, she was approaching the spot where she had heard the bleating. Upon reaching an open glade encircled by trees, she was astonished to see a large ram with gilded horns and fleece whiter than snow. He had a garland of flowers around his neck, his legs were entwined with ropes of enormous pearls, and chains of diamonds hung about him. As he lay on a couch of orange blossoms, a pavilion of gold cloth suspended in the air sheltered him from the rays of the sun. There were a hundred brightly decked sheep all around him, and instead of browsing on grass, some were having coffee, sherbet, ices, and lemonade; others, strawberries and cream, and preserves. Some were playing at basset, others at a game of cards. Several wore collars of gold ornamented with numerous fine emblems, earrings, ribbons, and flowers. Merveilleuse was so astounded that she remained stock-still. Her eyes were roving in search of the shepherd in charge of this extraordinary flock when the beautiful ram ran over to her in a sprightly manner. "Approach, divine princess," he said. "You have nothing to fear from such gentle and peaceful animals of our kind."

"What a miracle! A talking ram!" the princess exclaimed.

"What's that, madame?" the ram replied. "Your ape and your little dog spoke very prettily. Why weren't you surprised by that?"

"A fairy endowed them with the gift of speech, which made everything less miraculous," Merveilleuse stated.

"Perhaps we had a similar experience," the ram answered, smiling sheepishly. "But what caused you to come our way, my princess?"

"A thousand misfortunes, my lord ram," she said to him. "I'm the most unhappy person in the world. I'm seeking a place of refuge from my father's fury. "

"Come, madame," the ram replied, "come with me. I can offer you one that will be known only by you, and you will be completely in charge of everything there."

"I can't follow you," Merveilleuse said. "I'm about to die from exhaustion."

The ram with golden horns called for his chariot, and immediately six goats were led forward, harnessed to a pumpkin of such tremendous size that two persons could sit in it with the greatest ease. The hollowed-out pumpkin was dry inside and fitted with splendid down cushions and lined all over with velvet. Getting into the pumpkin, the princess was astounded by such a unique equipage. The master ram seated himself in the pumpkin beside her, and the goats took them at full gallop to a cave. A large stone blocked the entrance, but the golden-horned ram touched the stone with his foot, and it fell away at once. He told the princess, "Enter without fear."

She imagined that the cave would be a horrible place, and if she had not been so afraid of being captured, nothing would have induced her to go into it, but her fear was so great that she would have thrown herself even into a well to avoid capture.

Consequently, she followed the ram without hesitation. He walked in front of her to show her the way down, which ran so very deep that she thought she was going at least to the other end of the earth. At moments, she feared he was leading her to the region of the dead.

Suddenly, she came upon a vast meadow bursting with a thousand different flowers, whose sweet aroma surpassed that of any she had ever smelled. A broad river of orange-flower water flowed around it; fountains of Spanish wine, rossolis, hippocras, and a thousand other liqueurs formed charming cascades and rivulets. The meadow was home to entire avenues of unusual trees, and partridges greased and dressed better than those eaten at the restaurant La Guerbois hung from the branches. In other avenues, the branches were festooned with quails, young rabbits, turkeys, chickens, pheasants, and songbirds. In certain parts, where from afar the atmosphere appeared hazy, it rained bisques of crayfish and other soups, foie gras, ragouts of sweetbreads, white puddings, sausages, tarts, patties, jam, and marmalade. There were also gold coins, pearls, and diamonds. Showers so rare—and so useful—would no doubt have attracted excellent company if the great ram had been more inclined to mix in general society, but all the chronicles in which he is mentioned concur in assuring us that he was as reserved as a Roman senator.

Merveilleuse had arrived in this beautiful region during the finest time of the year. Thus, she was fortunate to see that there was also a palace, surrounded by long rows of orange trees, jasmines, honeysuckles, and tiny musk roses, whose interlaced branches formed cabinets, halls, and chambers, all hung with gold and silver gauze and furnished with large mirrors, chandeliers, and remarkable paintings. The master ram told the princess to consider herself the sovereign of this realm. "I have been suffering from grief for many years, and it is now up to you to make me forget all my misfortunes."

"Your behavior is so generous, charming ram," she said, "and everything I see appears so extraordinary that I don't know what to make of it."

No sooner had she uttered these words than a group of the most remarkable and beautiful nymphs appeared before her. They gave her fruit in baskets of amber, but when she stepped toward them, they shrank back slightly. When she extended her hands to touch them, she felt nothing—they were only phantoms.

"What does this mean?" she exclaimed. "Who are these things around me?" She began to weep, and King Ram (for so they called him), who had left her momentarily, returned and found her in tears, causing him such despair that he felt he would die at her feet.

"What's the matter, lovely princess?" he inquired. "Has anyone here been disrespectful to you?"

"No," she answered, "I can't complain. It's only that I'm not accustomed to living among the dead and with sheep that talk. Everything here frightens me, and though I'm greatly obliged to you for bringing me here, I'd be even more obliged if you'd bring me back into the world."

"Don't be alarmed," the ram replied. "Please deign to listen to me calmly, and you shall hear my sad story":

I was born to inherit a throne. A long line of kings, my ancestors, had ensured that the kingdom I'd be taking over was the finest in the universe. My subjects loved me. Feared and envied by my neighbors, I was thus justly respected. It was said that no king had ever been more worthy of such homage, and my physical appearance was not without its attractions as well.

I was extremely fond of hunting, and once, when I was zealously pursuing a stag, I became separated from my attendants. Suddenly, seeing the stag plunge into a pond, I spurred my horse in after him. This was as unwise as it was bold. But instead of the coldness of water, I felt an extraordinary heat. The pond dried up, and through an opening gushing with terrible flames I fell to the bottom of a precipice, where nothing was to be seen but fire.

I thought I was lost when I suddenly heard a voice saying, "No less fire could warm your heart, ungrateful one!"

"Hah! Who is it that complains of my coldness?" I said.

"An unfortunate who adores you without hope," the voice replied.

Just then, the flames were extinguished, and I perceived a fairy whose age and ugliness had horrified me ever since I had known her in my early childhood. She was leaning on a young slave of incomparable beauty, and the golden chains she wore sufficiently indicated who she was.

"What miracle is this, Ragotte?" I asked her (since that was the fairy's name). "Have you really ordered this?"

"Who else should have ordered it?" the fairy replied. "Has it taken you this long to learn the way I feel? Must I undergo the shame of explaining myself? Have my eyes, once so certain of their power, lost all their influence? Just look how low I'm stooping! I'm the one who's confessing my weakness to you, who, great king though you may be, are less than an ant compared to a fairy like me."

"I am whatever you please," I said impatiently, "but what is it you demand of me? Is it my crown, my cities, my treasures?"

"Ah, wretch," she replied disdainfully, "if I so desired it, my scullions would be more powerful than you. No, I demand your heart! My eyes have asked you for it thousands and thousands of times. You haven't understood them, or rather, you don't want to understand them. If you had been desperately in love with someone else," she continued, "I wouldn't have interrupted the progress of your ardor, but I had too great an interest in you not to discover the indifference that

reigned in your heart. Well, then, love me!" she added, rolling her eyes and pursing her mouth to make it look more pleasant. "I'll be your little Ragotte, and I'll add twenty kingdoms to what you possess already, a hundred towers filled with gold, five hundred filled with silver—in a word, all you can wish for."

"Madame Ragotte," I said to her, "I would never think of declaring myself to a person of your merit at the bottom of a pit in which I expect to be roasted. I implore you, by all the charms that you possess, to set me free, and then we'll consider together what we can do to satisfy you."

"Ha, traitor!" she exclaimed, "if you loved me, you wouldn't seek the road back to your kingdom. You'd be happy in a grotto, in a foxhole, in the woods or the desert. Don't think that I'm so naïve. You hope to escape, but I warn you that you'll remain here. Your first task will be to tend my sheep. They are intelligent animals and speak just as well as you do."

Upon saying this, she took me to the plain where we now stand and showed me her flock. I paid scant attention to them, for I was struck by the marvelous beauty of the slave beside her. My eyes betrayed me. The cruel Ragotte noticed my admiration and attacked her. She plunged a bodkin into one of her eyes with such violence that the adorable girl fell dead on the spot. At this horrible sight, I threw myself on Ragotte, and with my sword in hand, I would have made her into a sacrificial victim for the spirits of the underworld if she hadn't used her power to freeze me as I stood. All my efforts were in vain. I fell to the ground and sought some way to kill myself and end my agony. But the fairy said to me with an ironical smile, "I want you to become acquainted with my power. You're a lion right now, but soon you'll become a sheep."

As she pronounced this sentence, she touched me with her wand, and I found myself transformed as you now behold me. I haven't lost the faculty of speech, nor the sense of torment caused by my condition. "You are to be a sheep for five years," she said, "and absolute master of this beautiful realm. Meanwhile, I'll move far from here so I won't have to see your handsome face. But I'll brood over the hate I owe you."

Then she disappeared and, in truth, if anything could have relieved my misfortune, it would have been her absence. The talking sheep you see here acknowledged me as their king, and they informed me that they were unfortunate mortals who had in various ways offended the vindictive fairy. They had been changed into a flock, and some had to serve longer penances than others. In fact, every now and then, they become what they were before and leave the flock. As for the shadows you've seen, they are Ragotte's rivals and enemies whom she has deprived of life for a century or so and who will return to the world later on. The young slave I mentioned is among them. I've seen her several times with great pleasure, although she didn't speak to me. When first I approached her, I was disturbed to discover it was nothing but her shadow. However, I noticed that one of my sheep was giving this phantom a lot of attention and learned that he was her lover. Ragotte had separated them out of jealousy, and this is the reason why I've avoided the shadow of the slave since then. During the past three years, I've longed only for my freedom.

"In the hope of regaining it, I frequently wander into the forest," he continued. "It was there that I saw you, beautiful princess. Sometimes you were in a chariot that you drove yourself with more skill than Apollo does his own. Sometimes you followed the chase on a steed that seemed would obey no other rider, or you were in a race with the ladies of your court, flying lightly over the plain, and you won the prize like another Atalanta. Ah, princess, if I had dared to speak to you during this time in which my heart paid you secret homage, what wouldn't I have said? But how would you have received the declaration of an unhappy sheep like me?"

Merveilleuse was so stirred by all she had heard that she scarcely knew how to answer him. She said something civil, however, which gave him some hope, and also told him that she was less alarmed by the ghosts now that she knew their owners would revive again.

"Alas," she continued, "if my poor Patypata, my dear Grabugeon, and the pretty Tintin, who died to save me, could have met with a similar fate, I wouldn't be so melancholy here."

Despite the disgrace of the royal ram, he still possessed some remarkable prerogatives. "Go," he said to his grand equerry (a splendid-looking sheep), "go fetch the Moor, the ape, and the little dog. Their shadows will amuse our princess."

A moment later, they appeared, and although they did not approach near enough for Merveilleuse to touch them, their presence was a great consolation to her.

The royal ram possessed all the intelligence and refinement required for pleasant conversation, and he adored Merveilleuse so much that she began to have some regard for him and soon after came to love him. A pretty sheep, so gentle and affectionate, is not a displeasing companion, particularly when one knows that he is a king and that his transformation will eventually end. Thus, the princess spent her days peacefully, awaiting a happier future. The gallant ram devoted himself entirely to her. He gave fetes, concerts, and hunts in which his flock aided him and even the shadows played their part.

One day when his couriers arrived—for he regularly sent out couriers for news and always obtained the best—he learned that the eldest sister of Princess Merveilleuse was about to marry a great prince, and the most magnificent preparations were being made for the wedding.

"Ah," the young princess said, "how unfortunate I am to be deprived of witnessing so many fine things! Here I am underground, among ghosts and sheep, while my sister is about to be made a queen. Everybody will pay their respects to her, and I'm the only one who won't be able to share in her joy."

"What reason do you have to complain, madame?" asked the king of the sheep. "Have I refused you permission to attend the wedding? Depart as soon as you please.

Only give me your word that you'll return. If you don't agree to that, I'll perish at your feet, for my love for you is too passionate and I'd never be able to live if I lost you."

Touched, Merveilleuse promised the ram that nothing in the world could prevent her return. Therefore, he provided her with an equipage befitting her birth. She was superbly attired, and nothing was omitted to embellish her beauty. She got into a chariot of mother-of-pearl drawn by six Isabella-colored hypogriffins that had just arrived from the other end of the earth. She was accompanied by a great number of exceedingly handsome, richly attired officers. These the royal ram had ordered to come from a distant land to form the princess's train.

She arrived at her father's court at the moment the marriage was being celebrated. As soon as she appeared, she dazzled everyone by her glittering beauty and the jewels that adorned her. She heard nothing but acclamation and praise. The king gazed at her with such zeal and pleasure that she was afraid he would recognize her, but he was so convinced that his daughter was dead that he did not have the least inkling who she was.

Nevertheless, she was so afraid she might be detained that she did not stay to the end of the ceremony. She departed abruptly, leaving a small coral box garnished with emeralds, on which was written in diamonds: "JEWELS FOR THE BRIDE." They opened it immediately, and what extraordinary things they found! The king, who was burning to know who she was, was despondent about her departure. He gave strict orders that if she ever returned, they were to shut the gates and detain her.

Brief though the absence of Merveilleuse had been, it had seemed like ages to the ram. Waiting for her by the side of a fountain in the thickest part of the forest, he had immense treasures displayed there with the intention of giving them to her in gratitude for her return. As soon as he saw her, he ran toward her, romping and frisking like a real sheep. He lay down at her feet, kissed her hands, and told her all about his anxiety and impatience. His love for her so inspired him that he managed to speak with an eloquence that completely captivated the princess.

A short time afterward, the king was to marry off his second daughter, and Merveilleuse heard about it. Once again, she asked the ram for permission to attend a fete in which she took the closest interest. Of course, he felt a pang he could not suppress when he heard her request,

for a secret presentiment warned him of a catastrophe. But since we cannot always avoid evil, and since his consideration for the princess overruled any other feeling, he did not have the heart to refuse her. "You desire to leave me, madame," he said, "and I must blame my sad fate for this unfortunate situation more than you. In consenting to your wish, I'll never make you a greater sacrifice."

She assured him that she would return as quickly as she had the first time. "I would be deeply grieved if anything were to keep me from you. I beg you, don't worry about me."

She went in the same pomp as before and arrived just as they were beginning the marriage ceremony. Although everyone was following the nuptials, her presence caused exclamations of joy and admiration that drew the eyes of all the princes to her. They could not stop gazing at her: her beauty, they felt, was so extraordinary that they could easily have been convinced that she was more than mortal.

The king was charmed to see her once more, and he never took his eyes off her, except to order all the doors to be closed to prevent her departure. When the ceremony was nearly concluded, the princess rose hastily in order to disappear in the throng, but was shocked and distressed to find that all the gates were locked against her.

The king approached with a respectful, submissive air that reassured her. He begged her not to deprive them so soon of the pleasure of admiring her and requested that she remain and grace the banquet he was about to give the princes and princesses who had honored him with their presence on this occasion. He led her into a magnificent salon, in which the entire court was assembled, and offered her a golden basin and a vase filled with water so that she might wash her beautiful hands. No longer could she restrain her feelings. She flung herself at his feet, embraced his knees, and exclaimed, "Look, my dream has come true! You've offered me water to wash with on my sister's wedding day without anything evil happening to you."

The king had no difficulty recognizing her, for he had been struck by her strong resemblance to Merveilleuse more than once. "Ah, my dear daughter!" he cried, embracing her with tears in his eyes. "Can you ever forgive my cruelty? I wanted to take your life because I thought your dream predicted I would lose my crown. Indeed, it did just that, for now that your two sisters are married, each has a crown of her own. Therefore, mine shall be yours." Upon saying this, he rose and placed his crown on the princess's head, crying, "Long live Queen Merveilleuse!"

The entire court took up and shouted. The two sisters threw their arms around her neck and kissed her a thousand times. Merveilleuse was so happy she could not express her joy. She cried and laughed at the same time. She embraced one, talked to another, thanked the king, and in the midst of all this, she recalled the captain of the guard, to whom she was so much indebted. When she asked eagerly to see him, however, they informed her he was dead, and she felt a pang of sorrow.

After they sat down to dinner, the king asked her to relate all that had happened to her ever since the day he had given his fatal orders. She immediately began telling the story with the most remarkable grace, and everybody listened to her attentively.

While she was engrossed in telling her story to the king and her sisters, though, the enamored ram watched for the princess as the hour set for her return passed. Indeed, his anxiety became so extreme that he could not control it. "She'll never come back!" he cried. "My miserable sheep's face disgusts her. Oh, unfortunate lover that I am, what will become of me if I lose Merveilleuse? Ragotte! Cruel fairy! How you have avenged yourself for my indifference to you!"

He indulged in such lamentations for hours, and then, as night approached without any signs of the princess, he ran to the city. When he reached the king's palace, he asked to see Merveilleuse, but since everybody was now aware of her adventures and did not want her to return to the ram's realm, they harshly refused to let him see her. He uttered cries and lamentations capable of moving anyone except the Swiss guard who stood sentry at the palace gates. At length, broken-hearted, he flung himself to the ground and breathed his last sigh.

The king and Merveilleuse were completely unaware of the sad tragedy that had taken place. The king suggested to his daughter that she ride in a triumphal coach and show herself to everyone in the city by the lights of thousands and thousands of torches illuminating the windows and all the great squares. But what a horrible spectacle she encountered as she left the palace gates—her dear ram stretched out breathless on the pavement! Jumping out of the coach and running to him, she wept and sobbed, for she knew that her delay in returning had caused the royal ram's death. In her despair, she felt she would die herself.

Now we know that people of the highest rank are subject, like all others, to the blows of fortune, and that they frequently experience the greatest misery at the very moment they believe themselves to have attained their heart's goal.

The choicest blessings sent by Heaven
Often tend to cause our ruin.
The charms, the talents, that we're given,
May often end on a sad tune.
The royal ram would have surely seen
Happier days without the charms that led
The cruel Ragotte to love, then hurl her mean
But fatal vengeance on his head.
In truth, he should have had a better fate,
For spurning a sordid Hymen's chains;
Honest his love—unmasked his hate—
How different from our modern swains!
Even his death may well surprise
The lovers of the present day:
Only a silly sheep now dies,
Because his ewe has gone astray.

The Green
Serpent

O NCE upon a time, there was a great queen who gave birth to twin daughters. Soon after, she invited twelve fairies, who lived nearby, to come and bestow gifts upon them, as was the custom in those days. Indeed, it was a very useful custom because the power of the fairies generally compensated for the deficiencies of nature. Sometimes, however, they also spoiled what nature had done its best to make perfect, as we shall soon see.

When the fairies had all gathered in the banquet hall, they were about to sit at the table and enjoy a magnificent meal when suddenly the fairy Magotine entered. She was the sister of Carabossa and no less malicious. The queen shuddered when she saw her. She feared some disaster because she had not invited her to the celebration. However, she carefully concealed her anxiety, personally looked for an armchair for the fairy, and found one covered with green velvet and embroidered with sapphires. Since Magotine was the eldest of the fairies, all the rest made way for her to pass and whispered to one another, "Let us quickly endow the infant princesses, sister, so that we may get the start on Magotine."

When the armchair was set up for her, she rudely declined it, saying that she was big enough to eat standing. She was mistaken in this, however, because the table was rather high, and she was not tall enough to see over it. This annoyance increased her foul mood even more.

"Madame," the queen said, "I beg you to take your seat at the table."

"If you had wished me to do so," the fairy replied, "you would have sent an invitation to me as you did to the others, but you only want beauties with fine figures and fine dresses like my sisters here. As for me, I'm too ugly and old. Yet, despite it all, I have just as much power as they have. In fact, without boasting about it, I may even have more."

All the fairies urged her strongly to sit at the table, and eventually, she consented. A golden basket was placed before them, containing twelve bouquets composed of jewels. The fairies who had arrived first each took a bouquet, leaving none for Magotine. As she began to mutter between her teeth, the queen ran to her room and brought her a casket of perfumed Morocco leather covered with rubies and filled with diamonds, and asked her to accept it. But Magotine shook her head and said, "Keep your jewels, madame. I have more than enough to spare. I came only to see if you had thought of me, and it's clear you've neglected me shamefully."

Thereupon, she struck the table with her wand, and all the delicacies heaped on it were turned into fricasseed serpents. This sight horrified the fairies so much that they threw down their napkins and fled the table. While they talked with one another about the nasty trick Magotine had played on them, that cruel fairy approached the cradle in which the princesses, the loveliest children in the world, were lying wrapped in golden swaddling. "I endow you with perfect ugliness," she quickly said to one of them, and she was about to utter a malediction on the other when the fairies, who were greatly disturbed, ran and stopped her. Then the mischievous Magotine broke one of the window panes, dashed through it like a flash of lightning, and vanished from sight.

Not all the good gifts that the benevolent fairies proceeded to bestow on the princess alleviated the misery of the queen, who found herself the mother of the ugliest being in the universe. Taking the infant in her arms, she had the misfortune of watching her grow more hideous by the moment. She struggled in vain to suppress her tears in the presence of their fairy ladyships, whose compassion is impossible to imagine.

"What shall we do, sisters?" they said to one another. "How can we ever console the queen?"

They held a grand council about the matter, and at the end, they told the queen not to give into her grief since a time would come when her daughter would be very happy.

"But," the queen interrupted, "will she become beautiful again?"

"We can't give you any further information," the fairies replied. "Be satisfied, madame, with the assurance that your daughter will be happy."

She thanked them very much and did not forget to give them many presents. Although the fairies were very rich, they

always liked people to give them something. Throughout the world, this custom has been passed down from that day to our own, and time has not altered it in the least.

The queen named her elder daughter Laidronette and the younger Bellotte. These names suited them perfectly because Laidronette, despite her boundless intelligence, became too frightful to behold, whereas her sister's beauty increased hourly until she looked thoroughly charming.

After Laidronette turned twelve, she went to the king and queen and threw herself at their feet. "Please, I implore you! Allow me to shut myself up in a desolate castle so that I will no longer torment you with my ugliness."

Despite her hideous appearance, they could not help being fond of her, and it was not without some pain that they consented to let her depart. However, since Bellotte remained with them, they had ample consolation.

Laidronette begged the queen not to send anyone except her nurse and a few officers to wait on her. "You needn't worry, madame, about my being abducted. I can assure you that, looking as I do, I shall avoid even the light of day."

After the king and queen had granted her wishes, she was conducted to the castle she had chosen. It had been built many centuries before, and the sea crashed beneath its windows and served it as a moat. Nearby there was a large forest in which one could stroll, and in several fields leading to the forest, the princess played various instruments and sang divinely.

She spent two years in this pleasant solitude; even writing several volumes recording her thoughts, but the desire to see her father and mother again induced her to take a coach and revisit the court. She arrived just as they were to celebrate her sister Bellotte's marriage. Everyone had been rejoicing, but the moment they saw Laidronette, their joy turned to distress. She was neither embraced nor hugged by any of her relatives. Indeed, the only thing they said to her was that she had grown a good deal uglier, and they advised her not to appear at the ball.

"However, if you wish to see it, we shall find some hole for you to peep through."

She replied that she had come there neither to dance nor to hear the music, and that she had been in the desolate castle so long that she had felt a longing to pay her respects to the king and the queen. She was painfully aware that they could not endure the sight of her. Therefore, she told them that she would return to her wilderness, where the trees, flowers, and springs that she frequented did not reproach her for her ugliness. When the king and queen saw how hurt she was, they told her reluctantly that she could stay with them two or three days. Good-natured as always, she replied, "It would be harder for me to leave you if I were to spend so much time in your good company."

Since they were all too eager for her to depart, they did not press her to stay, but coldly remarked that she was quite right. Meanwhile, Princess Bellotte gave her a gift of an old ribbon for coming to her wedding that she had worn all winter in a bow on her muff, and Bellotte's fiancé gave her some gingeolin taffeta to make a petticoat. If she had expressed what she thought, she would have surely thrown the ribbon and gingeolin rag in her generous donors' faces, but she had such good sense, prudence, and judgment that she revealed none of her bitterness. With her faithful nurse at her side, she left the court to return to her castle. Her heart was filled with so much grief that she did not say a word during the entire journey.

One day as she was walking on one of the gloomiest paths in the forest, she saw a large green serpent at the foot of a tree. As it reared its head, it said to her, "Laidronette, you aren't the only unhappy creature in the world. Look at my horrible form. And yet, at birth I was even handsomer than you."

Terrified, the princess turned without listening anymore to the serpent and fled from the spot, and for many days thereafter did not dare to leave the castle because she was afraid of another such encounter. Eventually, she tired of sitting alone in her room, and one evening she went for a walk along the beach. As she was strolling slowly, pondering her sad fate, she noticed a small gilt barque painted with a thousand different emblems gliding toward her. It had a sail made of gold brocade, a mast of cedar, and oars of eagle wood, and it appeared to be drifting at random. When it landed on the shore, the curious princess stepped on board to inspect all of its beautiful decorations. She found its deck laid with crimson velvet and gold trimmings, and all the nails were diamonds.

Suddenly, the barque drifted out to sea again, and the princess, alarmed at her impending danger, grabbed the oars and endeavored in vain to row back to the beach. But the wind rose, and the waves became high. She lost sight of land and, seeing nothing around her but sea and sky, she resigned herself to her fate, fully convinced not only that it was unlikely to be a happy one, but also that this was another one of the fairy Magotine's mean tricks. "If I must die, why do I have such a secret dread of death?" she asked. "Indeed, have I ever enjoyed any of the pleasures of life so much that I should now feel regret at dying? My ugliness disgusts even my family. My sister is a great queen, and I'm consigned to exile in the depths of a wilderness where the only companion I've found is a talking serpent. Wouldn't it be better for me to perish than to drag out such a miserable existence?"

After having reflected this way, she dried her tears and courageously peered out to discover where death would appear and welcomed its speedy approach. Just then, however, she saw a serpent riding the billows toward the vessel, and as it approached her, it said: "If you're willing to be helped by a poor green serpent like me, I have the power to save your life."

"Death is less frightful to me than you are!" the princess exclaimed. "If you want to do me a kind favor, never let me set eyes on you again."

The green serpent gave a long hiss (the manner in which serpents sigh), and without saying a word it immediately dove under the waves.

"What a horrible monster!" the princess said to herself. "He has green wings, a body made of a thousand colors, ivory claws, fiery eyes, and a bristling mane of long hair on his head. Oh, I'd much rather die than owe my life to him! But what motive does he have in following me? How did he obtain the power of speech that enables him to talk like a rational creature?"

As she was entertaining these thoughts, a voice answered her: "You had better learn, Laidronette, that the green serpent is not to be despised. I don't mean to be harsh, but I assure you that he's less hideous in the eyes of his species than you are in the eyes of yours. However, I do not desire to anger you but to lighten your sorrows, provided you consent."

The princess was dumbfounded by this voice, and the words it uttered seemed so unjust to her that she could not suppress

her tears. Suddenly, though, a thought occurred to her. "What am I doing? I don't want to cry about my death just because I'm reproached for my ugliness!" she exclaimed. "Alas, shouldn't I perish as though I were the grandest beauty in the world? My demise would be more of a consolation to me."

Completely at the mercy of the winds, the vessel drifted on until it struck a rock and immediately shattered into pieces. The poor princess realized that mere philosophizing would not save her in such a catastrophe. She grabbed onto some pieces of the wreck, so she thought, for she felt herself buoyed in the water and fortunately reached the shore, coming to rest at the foot of a towering boulder. To her dismay, she was horrified to discover that her arms were wrapped tightly around the neck of the green serpent! When he realized how appalled she was, he retreated from her and said, "You'd fear me less if you knew me better, but it is my hard fate to terrify all those who see me."

Upon saying this, he plunged into the surf, and Laidronette was left alone by the enormous rock. No matter where she looked, she could see nothing that might alleviate her despair. Night was approaching. She was without food and did not know where to go. "I thought I was destined to perish in the ocean," she said sadly, "but now I'm sure that I'm to end my days here. Some sea monster will come and devour me, or I'll die of hunger."

After she stood up, she climbed to the top of the crag and sat down. As long as it was light, she gazed at the ocean, and when it became dark, she took off her taffeta petticoat, covered her head with it, and waited anxiously for whatever was to happen next. Eventually, she fell asleep and seemed to hear the music of some instruments. She was convinced that she was dreaming, but a moment later she heard someone sing the following verse, which seemed to have been composed expressly for her:

"Let Cupid make you now his own.
Here he rules with gentle tone.
Love with pleasure will be sown.
On this isle no grief is known."

The attention she paid to these words caused her to wake up. "What good or bad luck shall I have now?" she exclaimed. "Might happiness still be in store for someone so wretched?"

She opened her eyes timidly, fearing

that monsters would surround her, but she was astonished to find that, in place of the rugged, looming rock, there was a room with walls and ceiling made entirely of gold. Moreover, she was lying in a magnificent bed that perfectly matched the rest of this palace, which was the most splendid in the universe. She began asking herself a hundred questions about all of this, unable to believe she was wide awake. Finally, she got up and ran to open a glass door that led onto a spacious balcony, from which she could see all the beautiful things that nature, with some help from art, had managed to create on earth: gardens filled with flowers, fountains, statues, and the rarest trees; distant woods; palaces with walls ornamented with jewels, and roofs composed of pearls so wonderfully constructed that each was an architectural masterpiece. A calm, smiling sea strewn with thousands of vessels, whose sails, pendants, and streamers fluttered in the breeze, completed the charming view.

"Gods! You just gods!" the princess exclaimed. "What am I seeing? Where am I? What an astounding change! What has become of the terrible rock that seemed to threaten the skies with its lofty pinnacles? Am I the same person who was shipwrecked last night and saved by a serpent?"

Bewildered, she continued talking to herself, first pacing, and then stopping. Finally, she heard a noise in her room. Reentering it, she saw a hundred pagods advancing toward her. They were dressed and made up in a hundred different ways. The tallest pagods were a foot high, and the shortest no more than four inches. Some were beautiful, graceful, pleasant; others hideous, dreadfully ugly. Their bodies were made of diamonds, emeralds, rubies, pearls, crystal, amber, coral, porcelain, gold, silver, brass, bronze, iron, wood, and clay. Some were without arms, others without feet; some had mouths extending to their ears, eyes askew, and noses broken. In short, nowhere in the world could a greater variety of people be found than among these pagods.

Those pagods who presented themselves to the princess were the deputies of the kingdom. After a speech containing some very judicious ideas, they informed her that they had traveled about the world for some time past, but in order to obtain their sovereign's permission to do so, they had to take an oath not to speak during their absence. Indeed, some were so scrupulous that they would not even shake their heads or move their hands or feet, but the majority of them could not help it. This was how they had traveled about the universe, and when they returned, they amused the king by telling him everything that had occurred, even the most secret transactions and adventures in all the courts they had visited.

"This is a pleasure, madame," one of the deputies added, "which we shall have the honor of occasionally affording you, for we have been commanded to do all we can to entertain you. Instead of bringing you presents, we now come to amuse you with our songs and dances."

They began immediately to sing the following verses while simultaneously dancing to the music of tambourines and castanets:

"Sweet are pleasures after pains,
Lovers, do not break your chains;
Trials though you may endure,
Happiness they will ensure.
Sweet are pleasures after pains,
Joy from sorrow luster gains."

When they stopped dancing and singing, their spokesman said to the princess, "Here, madame, are a hundred pagodines, who have the honor of being selected to wait on you. Any wish you may have in the world will be fulfilled, provided you consent to remain among us."

The pagodines appeared in their turn. They carried baskets cut to their own size and filled with a hundred different articles so pretty, so useful, so well made, and so costly that Laidronette never tired of admiring and praising them, uttering exclamations of wonder and delight at all

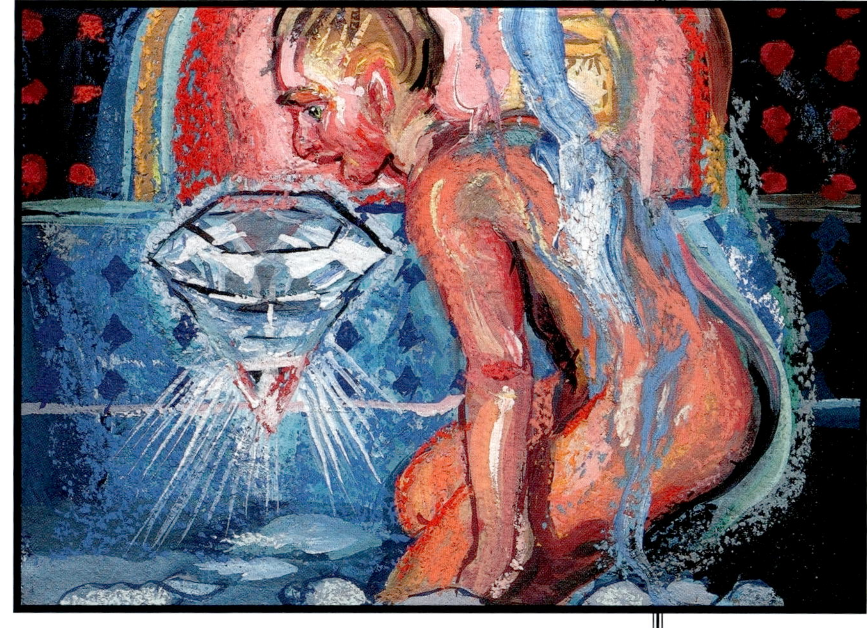

the marvels they showed her. The most prominent pagodine, a tiny figure made of diamonds, advised her to enter the grotto of the baths, since the heat of the day was increasing. The princess proceeded in the direction indicated between two ranks of bodyguards, whose appearance was enough to make one die with laughter.

She found two baths of crystal in the grotto ornamented with gold and filled with scented water so delicious and uncommon that she marveled at it. Shading the baths was a pavilion of green and gold brocade. When the princess inquired why there were two, they answered that one was for her, and the other for the king of the pagods.

"But where is he, then?" the princess asked.

"Madame," they replied, "he is presently with the army waging war against his enemies. You'll see him as soon as he returns."

Then the princess inquired if he were married. They answered no. "Why, he is so charming that no one has yet been found who would be worthy of him."

She indulged her curiosity no further, but disrobed and entered the bath. All the pagods and pagodines began to sing and play on various instruments. Some had lutes made out of nutshells; others, bass viols made out of almond shells, for it was, of course, necessary that the instruments fit the size of the performers. However, all the parts were arranged in such perfect harmony that nothing could surpass the delight their concert gave her.

When the princess emerged from her bath, they gave her a magnificent dressing gown. A pair of pagods playing a flute and oboe marched before her, and a train of pagodines singing songs in her praise trailed behind. In this state, she entered a room where her toilet was laid out. Immediately, the pagodines in waiting, and those of the bedchamber, bustled about, dressed her hair, put on her robes, and praised her. There was no longer talk of her ugliness, of gingeolin petticoats, or greasy ribbons.

The princess was truly taken aback. "To whom am I indebted for such extraordinary happiness?" she asked herself. "I was on the brink of destruction. I was waiting for death to come and had lost hope, and yet I suddenly find myself in the most magnificent place in the world, where I've been welcomed with the greatest joy!"

Since the princess was endowed with a great deal of good sense and breeding, she conducted herself so well that all the wee creatures who approached her were enchanted by her behavior. Every morning when she arose, she was given new dresses, new lace, and new jewels. Though it was a great pity that she was so ugly, she who could not abide her looks began to think they were more appealing because of the great pains they took in dressing her. She rarely spent an hour without some pagods coming to visit and recounting to her the most curious and private events of the world: peace treaties, offensive and defensive alliances, lovers' quarrels and betrayals, unfaithful mistresses, distractions, reconciliations, disappointed heirs, matches broken off, old widows remarrying foolishly, treasures discovered, bankruptcies declared, fortunes made in a minute, favorites disgraced, office seekers, jealous husbands, coquettish wives, naughty children, and ruined cities. In short, they told the princess everything under the sun to entertain her. She occasionally saw some pagods who were so corpulent and had such puffed out cheeks that they were wonderful to behold. When she asked them why they were so fat, they answered, "Since we're not permitted to laugh or speak during our travels and are constantly witnessing all sorts of absurdities and the most intolerable follies, our inclination to laugh is so great that we swell up when we suppress it and cause what may properly be called risible dropsy. Then we cure ourselves as soon as we get home."

The princess admired the good sense of the pagodine people, for we too might burst with laughter if we laughed at all the silly things we see every day. Scarcely an evening passed without a performance of one of the best plays by Corneille or Molière. Balls were held frequently, and the smallest pagods danced on a tightrope in order to be better seen. What's more, the banquets in honor of the princess might have served for feasts on the most solemn occasions. They also brought her books of every description—serious, amusing, and historical. In short, the days passed like minutes, although, to tell the truth, all these sprightly pagods seemed insufferably little to the princess. For instance, whenever she went out walking, she had to put some thirty or so into her pockets in order for them to keep up. It was the most amusing thing in the world to hear the chattering of their little voices, shriller than those of puppets in a show at the fair.

One night when the princess was unable to fall asleep, she said to herself, "What's to become of me? Am I to remain here forever? My days are more pleasant than I could have dared to hope, yet my heart tells me something's missing. I don't know what it is, but I'm beginning to feel that this unvarying routine of amusements is rather insipid."

"Ah, princess," a voice said, as if answering her thoughts, "isn't it your own fault? If you'd consent to love, you'd soon discover that you can abide with a lover for an eternity without wishing to leave. I speak not only of a palace, but even the most desolate spot."

"Who is this pagodine speaking to me?" the princess inquired. "What pernicious advice are you giving me? Why are you trying to disturb my peace of mind?"

"I am not a pagodine, madame, but a person who forewarns you of what will sooner or later come to pass," the voice replied. "I am the unhappy ruler of this realm, who adores you, madame, and who can't tell you this without trembling."

"A king who adores me?" the princess replied. "Does this king have eyes or is he blind? Doesn't he know that I'm the ugliest person in the world?"

"I've seen you, madame," the invisible being answered, "and have found you're not what you represent yourself to be. Whether it's for your person, merit, or misfortunes, I repeat: I adore you. But my feeling of respect and timidity oblige me to conceal myself."

"I'm indebted to you for that," the princess responded. "Alas, what would befall me if I were to love anyone?"

"You'd make a man who can't live without you into the happiest of beings," the voice said. "But he won't venture to appear before you without your permission."

"No, no," the princess said. "I wish to avoid seeing anything that might arouse my interest too strongly."

The voice fell silent, and the princess continued to ponder this incident for the rest of the night. No matter how strongly she vowed not to say the least word to anyone about it, she could not resist asking the pagods if their king had returned. They answered in the negative. Since this reply did not correspond in the least with what she had heard, she was quite disturbed. She continued making inquiries: Was their king young and handsome? They told her he was young, handsome, and very charming. She asked if they frequently received news about him.

They replied, "Every day."

"But," she added, "does he know that I reside in his palace?"

"Yes, madame," her attendants answered, "he knows everything that occurs here concerning you. He takes great interest in it, and every hour a courier is sent off to him with an account about you."

Lapsing into silence, she became far more thoughtful than she had ever been before. Whenever she was alone, the voice spoke to her. Sometimes she was alarmed by it, but at other times she was pleased, for nothing could be more polite than its manner of address.

"Although I've decided never to love," the princess said, "and have every reason

to protect my heart against an attachment that could only be fatal to it, I nevertheless confess to you that I yearn to see a king who has such strange tastes. If it's true that you love me, you're perhaps the only being in the world guilty of such weakness for a person so ugly."

"Think whatever you please, adorable princess," the voice replied. "I find that you have sufficient qualities to merit my affection. Nor do I conceal myself because I have strange tastes. Indeed, I have such sad reasons that if you knew them, you wouldn't be able to refrain from pitying me."

The princess urged him to explain himself, but the voice stopped speaking, and she heard only long, heavy sighs. All these conversations made her very uneasy. Although her lover was unknown and invisible to her, he paid her a thousand attentions. Moreover, the beautiful place she inhabited led her to desire companions more suitable than the pagods. That had been the reason why she had begun feeling bored, and only the voice of her invisible admirer had the power to please her.

One very dark night, she awoke to find somebody seated beside her. She thought it was the pagodine of pearls, who had more wit than the others had and sometimes came to keep her company. The princess extended her arm to her, but the person seized her hand and pressed it to a pair of lips. Shedding a few tears on it, the unseen person was evidently too moved to speak. She was convinced it was the invisible monarch.

"What do you want of me?" she sighed. "How can I love you without knowing or seeing you?"

"Ah, madame," he replied, "why do you make conditions that thwart my desire to please you? I simply cannot reveal myself. The same wicked Magotine, who's treated you so badly, has condemned me to suffer for seven years. Five have already elapsed. There are two remaining, and you could relieve the bitterness of my punishment by allowing me to become your husband. You may think that I'm a rash fool, that I'm asking an absolute impossibility. But if you knew, madame, the depth of my feelings and the extent of my misfortunes, you wouldn't refuse this favor I ask of you."

As I have already mentioned, Laidronette had begun feeling bored, and she found that the invisible king certainly had all the intelligence she could desire. Therefore, she was swayed by love, which she disguised to herself as pity, and replied that she needed a few days to consider his proposal.

The celebrations and concerts recommenced with increased splendor, and only songs about marriage were heard. Presents were continually brought to her that surpassed all that had ever been seen. The enamored voice assiduously wooed her as soon as it turned dark, and the princess retired at an earlier hour in order to have more time to listen to it. Finally, she consented to marry the invisible king and promised him that she would not attempt to look upon him until the full term of his penance had expired.

"It's extremely important," the king said, "both for you and me. Should you be imprudent and succumb to your curiosity, I'll have to begin serving my sentence all over again, and you'll have to share in my suffering. But if you can resist the evil advice that you will soon receive, you'll have the satisfaction of finding in me all that your heart desires. At the same time, you'll regain the marvelous beauty that the malicious Magotine took from you."

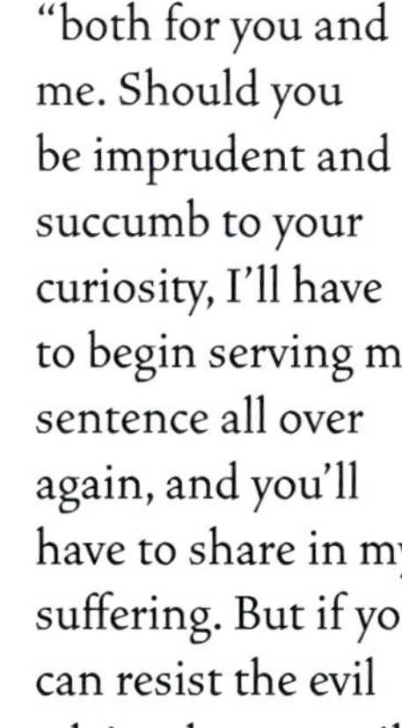

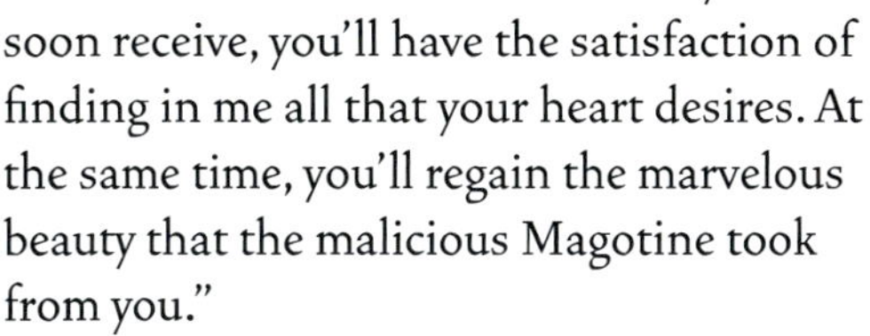

Delighted by this new prospect, the princess vowed a thousand times that she would never indulge her curiosity without his permission. So, the wedding took place without any pomp and fanfare, but the modesty of the ceremony did not at all affect their hearts.

Since all the pagods were eager to entertain their new queen, one of them brought her the history of Psyche, written in a charming style by one of the most popular authors of the day. She found many passages in it that paralleled her own adventures, and they aroused in her a strong desire to see her father, mother, sister, and brother-in-law. Nothing the king could say to her sufficed to quell this whim.

"The book you're reading reveals the terrible ordeals Psyche experienced. For mercy's sake, try to learn from her experiences and avoid them."

After she promised to be more than cautious, a ship manned by pagods and loaded with presents was sent with letters from Queen Laidronette to her mother, imploring her to come and pay a visit to her daughter in her own realm. (The pagods assigned to this mission were permitted, on this one occasion, to speak in a foreign land.)

In fact, the princess's disappearance had affected her relatives. They believed she had perished, and consequently, her letters made them very happy. The queen, who was dying to see Laidronette again, did not lose a moment in departing with her other daughter and son-in-law. The pagods, the only ones who knew the way to their kingdom, safely conducted the entire royal family, and when Laidronette saw them, she thought she would die from joy. She had read the story of Psyche over and over again to be completely on her guard regarding any questions that they might put to her and to make sure she would have the right answers. However, the pains she took were all in vain. Indeed, she made a hundred mistakes. Sometimes she reported that the king was with the army; sometimes he was ill and in no mood to see anyone; sometimes he was on a pilgrimage; and at other times, hunting or fishing. In the end, it seemed that the barbarous Magotine had unsettled her wits and doomed her to say nothing but nonsense.

When her mother and sister discussed the matter together, they concluded that she was deceiving them and perhaps herself as well. With misguided zeal, they told her what they thought and in the process skillfully plagued her mind with a thousand doubts and fears. After refusing for a long time to acknowledge the justice of their suspicions, she confessed at last that she had never seen her husband, but his conversation was so charming that just listening to him was enough to make her happy.

"What's more," she told them, "he has only two more years to spend in this state of penance, and at the end of that time, I shall not only be able to see him, but I myself shall become as beautiful as the orb of day."

"Oh, unfortunate creature!" the queen exclaimed. "What a devious trap they've set for you! How could you have been so naïve to listen to such tales? Your husband is a monster, and that's all there is to it. Moreover, all the pagods he rules are downright monkeys."

"I believe differently," Laidronette replied. "I think he's the god of love himself."

"What a delusion!" Princess Bellotte cried. "They told Psyche that she had married a monster, and she discovered that it was Cupid. You're positive that Cupid is your husband, and yet it's certain he's a monster. At the very least, put your mind to rest. Clear up the matter. It's easy enough to do."

This was what her sister had to say, and her husband was even more emphatic. Poor Laidronette was so confused and disturbed that, after having sent her family home loaded with presents that sufficiently repaid the gingeolin taffeta and muff ribbon, she decided to catch a glimpse of her husband, come what may. Oh, fatal curiosity, which never improves in us despite a thousand dreadful examples, how dearly you are about to make

this unfortunate princess pay! Laidronette became convinced that it would be a great pity not to imitate her predecessor, Psyche. Consequently, she shone a lamp on their bed and gazed upon the invisible king so dear to her heart. When she saw, however, the horrid green serpent with his long, bristling mane instead of a tender Cupid young, white, and fair, she let out the most frightful shrieks causing the serpent to awake in a fit of rage and despair.

"Cruel woman," he cried, "is this the reward for all the love I've given you?"

The princess did not hear a word. She had fainted from fright. Within seconds, the serpent was far away. Some of the pagods heard the uproar caused by this tragic scene, and they ran to Laidronette's apartment. Then they carried the princess to her couch and did all they could to revive her. No one can possibly fathom Laidronette's profound despair upon regaining consciousness. Indeed, she reproached herself a thousand times for the misfortune she had brought upon her husband! She loved him tenderly, but she abhorred his form and would have given half her life if she could have taken back what she had done.

These sad reflections were interrupted by several pagods who entered her room with fear written on their faces. They came to warn her that several ships of puppets with Magotine at their head had entered the harbor without encountering any resistance. Puppets and pagods had been enemies for ages and had competed with each other in a thousand ways because the puppets had always enjoyed the privilege of talking wherever they went—a privilege denied the pagods. Magotine was the queen of the puppets, and her hatred for the poor green serpent and the unfortunate Laidronette had prompted her to assemble her forces in order to torment them just when their suffering was most acute.

She accomplished this goal easily because the queen was in such deep despair. Although the pagods urged her to give the necessary orders, she refused, insisting that she knew nothing of the art of war. Nevertheless, she ordered them to convene all those pagods who had been in besieged cities or on the councils of the greatest commanders and told them to take the proper steps. Then she shut herself up in her room and regarded everything happening around her with utter indifference.

Magotine's general was the celebrated puppet Punch, and he knew his business well. He had a large body of wasps, mayflies, and butterflies in reserve, and they performed wonders against

some lightly armed frogs and lizards. The latter had been in the pay of the pagods for many years and were, if truth be told, much more frightening in name than in action.

Magotine amused herself for some time by watching the combat. The pagods and pagodines outdid themselves in their efforts, but the fairy dissolved all their superb edifices with a stroke of her wand. The charming gardens, woods, meadows, and fountains were soon in ruins, and Queen Laidronette could not escape the sad fate of becoming the slave of the most malignant fairy that ever was or will be. Four or five hundred puppets forced her to go before Magotine.

"Madame," Punch said to the fairy, "here is the queen of the pagods, whom I have taken the liberty of bringing to you."

"I've known her a long time," Magotine said. "She was the cause of my being insulted on the day she was born, and I'll never forget it."

"Alas, madame," the queen said, "I believed you were sufficiently avenged. The gift of ugliness that you bestowed on me to such a supreme degree would have satisfied anyone less vindictive than you."

"Look how she argues," the fairy said. "Here is a learned doctor of a new sort. Your first job will be teaching philosophy to my ants. I want you to get ready to give them a lesson every day."

"How can I do it, madame?" the distressed queen replied. "I know nothing about philosophy, and even if I were well versed in it, your ants are probably not capable of understanding it."

"Well now, listen to this logician," exclaimed Magotine. "Very well, Queen. You won't teach them philosophy, but despite yourself you'll set an example of patience for the entire world that will be difficult to imitate."

Immediately thereafter, Laidronette was given a pair of iron shoes so small that she could fit only half her foot into each one. Nevertheless, she was compelled to put them on, and the poor queen could only weep in agony.

"Here's a spindle of spider webs," Magotine said. "I expect you to spin it as fine as your hair, and you have but two hours to do it."

"I've never spun, madame," the queen said. "But I'll try to obey you even though what you desire strikes me to be impossible."

She was immediately led deep into a dark grotto, and after they gave her some brown bread and a pitcher of water, they closed the entrance with a large

rock. In trying to spin the filthy spider webs, she dropped her spindle a hundred times because it was much too heavy. Even though she patiently picked it up each time and began her work over again, it was always in vain.

"Now I know exactly how bad my predicament is. I'm wholly at the mercy of the implacable Magotine, who's not just satisfied with having deprived me of all my beauty, but wants some pretext for killing me."

She began to weep as she recalled the happiness she had enjoyed in the kingdom of Pagodia. Then she threw down her spindle and exclaimed, "Let Magotine come when she will! I can't do the impossible."

"Ah, queen," a voice answered her. "Your indiscreet curiosity has caused you these tears, but it's difficult to watch those we love suffer. I have a friend whom I've never mentioned to you before. She's called the Fairy Protectrice, and I trust she'll be of great service to you."

All at once, she heard three taps, and without seeing anyone, she found her web spun and wound into a skein. At the end of the two hours, Magotine, who wanted to taunt her, had the rock rolled from the grotto mouth and entered it, followed by a large escort of puppets.

"Come, come, let us see the work of this idle hussy who doesn't know how to sew or spin."

"Madame," the queen said, "it's quite true I didn't know how, but I was obliged to learn."

When Magotine saw the extraordinary result, she took the skein of spider web and said: "Truly, you're too skillful. It would be a great pity not to keep you employed. Here, Queen, make me some nets with this thread strong enough to catch salmon."

"For mercy's sake!" the queen replied. "You see that it's barely strong enough to hold flies."

"You're a great casuist, my pretty friend," Magotine said, "but it won't help you a bit."

She left the grotto, had the stone replaced at the entrance, and assured Laidronette that if the nets were not finished in two hours, she was a lost creature.

"Oh, Fairy Protectrice!" the queen exclaimed, "if it's true that my sorrows can move you to pity, please don't deny me your assistance."

No sooner had she spoken than, to Laidronette's astonishment, the nets were made. With all her heart, she thanked the friendly fairy who had granted her this favor, and it gave her pleasure to think that it must have been her husband who had provided her with such a friend.

"Alas, green serpent," she said, "you're much too generous to continue loving me after the harm I've done you."

No reply was forthcoming, for at that moment, Magotine entered. She was puzzled to find the nets finished. Indeed, they were so well made that common hands could not have done the work.

"What?" she cried. "Do you have the audacity to maintain that it was you who wove these nets?"

"I have no friend in your court, madame," the queen said. "And even if I did, I'm so carefully guarded that it would be difficult for anyone to speak to me without your permission."

"Since you're so clever and skillful, you'll be of great use to me in my kingdom."

She immediately ordered the captains of her fleet to make the sails ready and all the puppets to prepare themselves to board. At the same time, she commanded that they chain down Laidronette because she feared that she might fling herself overboard in some fit of despair.

One night when the unhappy princess was deploring her sad fate, she perceived by the light of the stars that the green serpent was silently approaching the ship.

"I'm always afraid of alarming you," he said, "and despite the reasons I have for not sparing you, you're extremely dear to me."

"Can you pardon my indiscreet curiosity?" she replied. "Would you be offended if I said:

"Is it you? Is it you? Are you again near?
My own royal serpent, so faithful and dear!
May I hope to see my fond husband again?
Oh, how I've suffered since we were parted then!"

The serpent replied as follows:

"To hearts that love truly, to part causes pain,
With hope even to whisper of meeting again.
In Pluto's dark regions what torture above
Our absence forever from those whom we love?"

Magotine was not one of those fairies who fall asleep, because the desire to do mischief kept her continually awake. Thus, she was able to overhear the conversation between the serpent king and his wife. Flying like a Fury to interrupt it, she said, "Aha, you amuse yourselves with rhymes, do you? And you complain about your fate in bombastic tones? Truly, I'm delighted to hear it. Proserpine, who is my best friend, has promised to pay me if I lend her a poet. Not that there is a dearth of poets below, but she simply wants more. Green serpent, I command you to go finish your penance in the dark manor of the underworld. Give my regards to the gentle Proserpine!"

Uttering long hisses, the unfortunate serpent departed, leaving the queen in the depths of sorrow.

"What crime have we committed against you, Magotine?" she exclaimed heatedly. "No sooner was I born than your infernal curse robbed me of my beauty and made me horrible. How can you accuse me of any crime when I wasn't even capable of using my mind at that time? I'm convinced that the unhappy king whom you've just sent to the infernal regions is as innocent as I am. But finish your work. Let me die this instant. It's the only favor I ask of you."

"You'd be too happy if I granted your

request," Magotine said. "You must first draw water for me from the bottomless spring."

As soon as the ships had reached the kingdom of puppets, the cruel Magotine took a millstone and tied it around the queen's neck, ordering her to climb to the top of a mountain that soared high above the clouds. Upon arriving there, she was to gather enough four-leaf clovers to fill a basket, descend into the depths of the next valley to draw the water of discretion in a pitcher with a hole in the bottom, and bring her enough to fill her large glass. The queen responded that it was impossible to obey her: the millstone was more than ten times her weight and the pitcher with a hole in it could never hold the water she wished to drink. "No, I cannot be induced to attempt anything so impossible."

"If you don't," Magotine said, "rest assured that your green serpent will suffer for it."

This threat so frightened the queen that she tried to walk despite her handicap. But, alas, the effort would have been for naught if the Fairy Protectrice, whom she invoked, had not come to her aid.

"Now you can see the just punishment for your fatal curiosity," the fairy said. "Blame no one but yourself for the condition to which Magotine has reduced you."

After saying this, she transported the queen to the top of the mountain. Terrible monsters that guarded the spot made supernatural efforts to defend it, but one tap of the Fairy Protectrice's wand made them gentler than lambs. Then she proceeded to fill the basket for her with four-leaf clovers.

Protectrice did not wait for the grateful queen to thank her, for to complete the mission, everything depended on her. She gave the queen a chariot drawn by two white canaries who spoke and whistled in a marvelous way. She told her to descend the mountain and fling her iron shoes at two giants armed with clubs who guarded the fountain. Once they were knocked unconscious, she had only to give her pitcher to the canaries, who would easily find the means to fill it with the water of discretion. "As soon as you have the water, wash your face with it, and you will become the most beautiful person in the world." She also advised her not to remain at the fountain, or to climb back up the hill, but to stop at a pleasant small grove she would find on her way. She could remain there for three years because Magotine would merely suppose that she was either still trying to fill her pitcher with water or had fallen victim to one of the dangers during her journey.

Embracing the knees of the Fairy Protectrice, the queen thanked her a

hundred times for the special favors she had granted her. "But, madame," the queen added, "neither the success I may achieve nor the beauty you promise me will give me the least pleasure until my serpent is transformed."

"That won't occur until you've spent three years in the mountain grove," the fairy said, "and until you've returned to Magotine with the four-leaf clovers and the water in the leaky pitcher."

The queen promised the Fairy Protectrice that she would scrupulously follow her instructions. "But, madame," she added, "must I spend three years without hearing any news of the serpent king?"

"You deserve never to hear any more about him for as long as you live," the fairy responded. "Indeed, can anything be more terrible than having made him begin his penance all over again?"

The queen made no reply, but her silence and the tears flowing down her cheeks amply showed how much she was suffering. She got into her little chariot, and the canaries did as commanded. They conducted her to the bottom of the valley, where the giants guarded the fountain of discretion. She quickly took off her iron shoes and threw them at their heads. The moment the shoes hit them, they fell down lifelessly like colossal statues. The canaries took the leaky pitcher and mended it with such marvelous skill that there was no sign of its having ever been broken.

The name given to the water made her eager to drink some. "It will make me more prudent than I've been," she said. "Alas, if I had possessed those qualities, I'd still be in the kingdom of Pagodia." After she had taken a long drink of the water, she washed her face with some of it and became so very beautiful that she might have been mistaken for a goddess rather than a mortal.

The Fairy Protectrice immediately appeared and said, "You've just done something that pleases me very much. You knew that this water could embellish your mind as well as your person. I wanted to see to which of the two you would prefer the most, and it was your mind. I praise you for it, and this act will shorten the term of your punishment by four years."

"Please don't reduce my sufferings," the queen replied. "I deserve them all. But comfort the green serpent, who doesn't deserve to suffer at all."

"I'll do everything in my power," the fairy said, embracing her. "But since you're now so beautiful, I want you to drop the name of Laidronette, which no longer suits you. You must be called Queen Discrète."

After she vanished, the queen found she had left a pair of dainty shoes that were so pretty and finely embroidered that she thought it almost a pity to wear them. Soon she got back into her little chariot with her pitcher full of water, and the canaries flew directly to the grove of the mountain.

Never was a spot as pleasant as this. Myrtle and orange trees intertwined their branches to form long arbors and bowers that the sun could not penetrate. A thousand brooks running from gently flowing springs brought a refreshing coolness to this beautiful abode. But most curious of all were the animals there, which gave the canaries the warmest welcome in the world.

"We thought you had deserted us," they said.

"The term of our penance is not over yet," the canaries replied. "But here is a queen whom the Fairy Protectrice has ordered us to bring to you. Try to do all you can to amuse her."

She was immediately surrounded by all sorts of animals, who paid her their best compliments. "You shall be our queen," they said to her. "You shall have all our attention and respect."

"Where am I?" she exclaimed. "What supernatural power has enabled you to speak to me?"

One of the canaries whispered in her ear, "You should know, madame, that several fairies were distressed to see various persons fall into bad habits on their travels. At first, they imagined that they needed merely to advise them to correct themselves, but their warnings were paid no heed. Eventually, the fairies became quite upset and imposed punishments on them. Those who talked too much were changed into parrots, magpies, and hens. Lovers and their mistresses were transformed into pigeons, canaries, and lapdogs. Those who ridiculed their friends became monkeys. Gourmands were made into pigs, and hotheads into lions. In short, the number of persons they punished was so great that this grove has become filled with them. Thus, you'll find people with all sorts of qualities and dispositions here."

"From what you've just told me, my dear canary," the queen said, "I've reason to believe that you're here only because you loved too well."

"It's quite true, madame," the canary replied.

I'm the son of a Spanish grandee. Love in our country has such absolute power over our hearts that one cannot resist it without being charged with the crime of rebellion. An English ambassador arrived at the court. He had a daughter who was extremely beautiful, but insufferably haughty and sardonic. In spite of all this, I was attracted to her. My love, though, was greeted with so much disdain that I lost all patience. One day, when she had exasperated me, a venerable old woman approached and reproached me for my weakness. Yet, everything she said only made me more obstinate. When she perceived this, she became angry. "I condemn you," she said, "to be a canary for three years, and your mistress to be a wasp." Instantly, I felt an indescribable change come over me. Despite my affliction, I could not restrain myself from flying into the ambassador's garden to determine the fate of his daughter. No sooner had I arrived than I saw her approach in the form

of a large wasp buzzing four times louder than all the others. I hovered around her with the devotion of a lover that nothing can destroy, but she tried several times to sting me. "If you want to kill me, beautiful wasp," I said, "it's unnecessary to use your sting. You only have to command me to die, and I'll obey you." The wasp did not reply, but landed on some flowers that had to endure her bad temper.

Overwhelmed by her contempt and the condition to which I was reduced, I flew away without caring where my wings would take me. I eventually arrived at one of the most beautiful cities in the universe, which they call Paris. Wearily, I flung myself on a tuft of large trees enclosed within some garden walls, and before I knew who had caught me, I found myself behind the door of a cage painted green and ornamented with gold. The apartment and its furniture were so magnificent that I was astounded. Soon a young lady arrived. She caressed me and spoke to me so sweetly that I was charmed by her. I did not live there long before learning who her sweetheart was. I witnessed this braggart's visits to her, and he was always in a rage because nothing could satisfy him. He was always accusing her unjustly, and one time he beat her until he left her for dead in the arms of her women. I was quite upset at seeing her suffer this unworthy treatment, and what distressed me even more was that the blows he dealt the lovely lady served only to increase her affection.

Night and day, I wished that the fairies who had transformed me into a canary would come and set to rights such ill-suited lovers. My wish was eventually fulfilled. The fairies suddenly appeared in the apartment just as the furious gentleman was beginning to make his usual commotion. They reprimanded him severely and condemned him to become a wolf. The patient lady who had allowed him to beat her, they turned into a sheep and sent her to the grove of the mountain. As for myself, I easily found a way to escape. Because I wanted to see the various courts of Europe, I flew to Italy and fell into the hands of a man who had frequent business in the city. Since he was very jealous of his wife and did not want her to see anyone during his absence, he took care to lock her up from morning until night, and I was given the honor of amusing this lovely captive. However, she had other things to do than to attend to me. A certain neighbor who had loved her for a long time came to the top of the chimney in the evening and slid down it into the room, looking blacker than a devil. The keys that the jealous husband kept with him served only to keep his mind at ease. I constantly feared that some terrible catastrophe would happen, when one day the fairies entered through the keyhole and surprised the two lovers. "Go and do penance!" the fairies said, touching them with their wands. "Let the chimney sweeper become a

squirrel and the lady an ape, for she is a cunning one. And your husband, who is so fond of keeping the keys of his house, shall become a mastiff for ten years."

"It would take me too long to tell you all the various adventures I had," the canary said. "Occasionally I was obliged to visit the grove of the mountain, and I rarely returned there without finding new animals, for the fairies were always traveling and were continually upset by the countless faults of the people they encountered. But during your residence here you'll have plenty of time to entertain yourself by listening to the accounts of all the inhabitants' adventures."

Several of them immediately offered to relate their stories whenever she desired. She thanked them politely, but since she felt more inclined to meditate than to talk, she looked for a spot where she could be alone. As soon as she found one, a little palace arose on it, and the most sumptuous banquet in the world was prepared for her. It consisted only of fruits, but they were of the rarest kind. They were brought to her by birds, and during her stay in the grove, there was nothing she lacked.

Occasionally, she was pleased by the most unique entertainments: lions danced with lambs; bears whispered tender things to doves; serpents relaxed with linnets; a butterfly courted a panther. In short, no amour was categorized according to species, for it did not matter that one was a tiger or another a sheep, but simply that they were people whom the fairies had chosen to punish for their faults.

They all loved Queen Discrète to the point of adoration, and everyone asked her to arbitrate their disputes. Her power was absolute in this tiny republic, and if she had not continually reproached herself for causing the green serpent's misfortunes, she might have accepted her own misfortune with some degree of patience. However, when she thought of the condition to which he was reduced, she could not forgive herself for her indiscreet curiosity.

Finally, the time came for her to leave the grove of the mountain, and she notified her escorts, the faithful canaries, who wished her a happy return. She left secretly during the night to avoid the farewells and lamentations, which would have cost her some tears, for she was touched by the friendship and respect that all these rational animals had shown her.

She did not forget the pitcher of discretion, the basket of four-leaf clovers, or the iron shoes. Just when Magotine believed her to be dead, she suddenly appeared before her, the millstone around her neck,

the iron shoes on her feet, and the pitcher in her hand. Upon seeing her, the fairy uttered a loud cry. "Where have you come from?"

"Madame," the queen said, "I've spent three years drawing water into the broken pitcher, and I finally found the way to make it hold water."

Magotine burst into laughter, thinking of the exhaustion the poor queen must have experienced. But when she examined her more closely, she exclaimed, "What's this I see? Laidronette has become quite lovely. How did you get so beautiful?"

The queen informed her that she had washed herself with the water of discretion and that this miracle had been the result. At this news, Magotine dashed the pitcher to the ground. "Oh, you powers that defy me," she exclaimed, "I'll be revenged. Get your iron shoes ready," she said to the queen. "You must go to the underworld for me and demand the essence of long life from Proserpine. I'm always afraid of falling ill and perhaps dying. Once I have that antidote in my possession, I won't have any more cause for alarm. Take care, therefore, that you don't uncork the bottle or taste the liquor she gives you, or you'll reduce my portion."

The poor queen had never been so taken aback as she was by this order. "Which way is it to the underworld?" she asked. "Can those who go there return? Alas, madame, won't you ever tire of persecuting me? Under what unfortunate star was I born? My sister is so much happier than I am! Ah, the stars above are certainly unfair."

As she began to weep, Magotine exulted at her tears. She laughed loudly and cried, "Go! Go! Don't put off your departure a single moment, for your journey promises to benefit me a great deal."

Magotine gave her some old nuts and black bread in a bag, and with this handsome provision, the poor queen started on her journey. She was determined, however, to dash her brains out against the first rock she saw to put an end to her sorrows. She wandered at random for some time, turning this way and that, thinking it most extraordinary to be sent like this to the underworld. When she became tired, she lay down at the foot of a tree and began to think of the poor serpent, forgetting all about her journey. Just then, the Fairy Protectrice appeared and said to her, "Don't you know, beautiful queen, that if you want to rescue your husband from the dark domain where he is being kept under Magotine's orders, you must seek the home of Proserpine?"

"I'd go much farther, if it were possible, madame," she replied, "but I don't know how to descend into that dark abode."

"Wait," said the Fairy Protectrice.

"Here's a green branch. Strike the earth with it and repeat these lines clearly." The queen embraced the knees of her generous friend and then said after her:

"You who can wrest from mighty Jove the
thunder!
Love, listen to my prayer!
Come, save me from despair,
And calm the pangs that rend my heart
asunder!
As I enter the realm of Tartarus, be my guide.
Even in those dreary regions you hold sway.
It was for Proserpine, your subject, that Pluto
sighed;
So open the path to their throne and point
the way.
A faithful husband from my arms they tear!
My fate is harder than my heart can bear;
More than mortal is its pain;
Yet for death it sighs in vain!"

No sooner had she finished this prayer than a young child more beautiful than anything we shall ever see appeared in the midst of a gold and azure cloud. He flew down to her feet with a crown of flowers encircling his brow. The queen knew by his bow and arrows that it was Love. He addressed her in the following way:

"I have heard your tender sighs,
And for you have left the skies.
Love will chase your tears away,
And try his best in every way.
Shortly shall your eyes be blest
With his sight you love the best.
Then the penance will be done,
And your foe will be overcome."

The queen was dazzled by the splendor that surrounded Love and delighted by his promises. Therefore, she exclaimed:

"Earth, my voice obey!
Cupid's power is like my sway.
Open for him and point the way
To Pluto's dark and gloomy throne!"

The earth obeyed and opened her bosom. The queen went through a dark passage, in which she needed a guide as radiant as her protector, and finally she reached the underworld. She dreaded meeting her husband there in the form of a serpent, but Love, who sometimes employs himself by doing good deeds for the unfortunate, had foreseen all that was to be foreseen: he had already arranged that the green serpent become what he was before his punishment. Powerful as Magotine was, there was nothing she could do against Love.

The first object the queen's eyes encountered was her charming husband. She had never seen him in such a handsome form, and he had never seen her as beautiful as she had become. Nevertheless, a presentiment, and perhaps Love, who made up the third in the party, caused each of them to guess who the other was. With extreme tenderness, the queen said to him:

"I come to share your prison and your pain.
Though doomed no more the light of heaven
to see,
Here let but love unite our hearts again,
No terrors these sad shades will have for me!"

Carried away by his passion, the king replied to his wife in a way that demonstrated his ardor and pleasure. However, Love, who is not fond of losing time, urged them to approach Proserpine. The queen offered Magotine's regards and asked her for the essence of long life. Proserpine immediately gave the queen a phial very badly corked in order to induce her to open it. Love, who is no novice, warned the queen against indulging a curiosity that would again be fatal to her. Quickly, the king and queen left those dreary regions and returned to the light of day with Love accompanying them. He led them back to Magotine and hid himself in their hearts so that she would not see him. His presence, however, inspired the fairy with such humane sentiments that she received these illustrious unfortunates graciously, even though she did not know why. With a supernatural effort of generosity, she restored the kingdom of Pagodia to them, and they returned there immediately and spent the rest of their days in as much happiness as they had previously endured trouble and sorrow.

Too oft is curiosity
The cause of fatal woe.
A secret that may harmful be,
Why should we seek to know?

It is a weakness of womankind,
For witness the first created,
From whom Pandora was designed,
And Psyche imitated.

Each one, despite a warning, on the same
Forbidden quest intent,
Did bring about her misery and become
Its fatal instrument.

Psyche's example failed to save
Poor Laidronette from erring.
Like warning she was led to brave.
Like punishment incurring.

Alas, for human common sense,
No tale, no caution, schools!
The proverb says, Experience
Can make men wise, and change dumb fools.

But when we're told, yet fail to listen
To the lessons of the past,
I fear the proverb lies quite often,
Despite the shadows forward cast.

The White Cat

NCE upon a time, there was a king who had three brave, handsome sons, and he grew afraid that they were becoming eager to reign during his lifetime. He had even heard rumors that they were seeking to win over adherents to help them take over the kingdom. The king knew he was growing old, but his mind was still alert, and he had no desire to yield the throne when he was still competent to rule. Consequently, he thought the best way to keep them from growing restive was to tantalize them with promises that he would always avoid fulfilling.

One day, he called his sons into his room and spoke to them kindly: "You'll agree with me, my dear sons, that my great age prevents me from managing the affairs of state as assiduously as before. I fear my subjects may suffer from this circumstance, and I want to transfer my crown to one of you. To deserve such a gift, however, it is only just that you, in turn, try to please me. Now, since I contemplate retiring to the country, I believe that a pretty, faithful, and intelligent little dog would make an excellent companion. So, instead of showing preference to the eldest among you, I declare that whoever brings me the handsomest little dog will immediately become my heir."

The princes were exceedingly surprised by the king's inclination to possess a little dog, but the two younger sons realized they could profit from this proposition and gladly accepted the task, while the eldest was too timid or too respectful to stand up for his rights. Therefore, they took leave of the king, who distributed money and jewels among them and added, "Return without fail next year on the same day and hour, and bring me your little dogs."

Before setting out, they withdrew to a castle a mile from the city and gathered their most intimate friends for several splendid banquets. During this time, the three brothers pledged eternal friendship to one another. They declared that they would act without jealousy or regrets in this particular affair, and the successful candidate was to share his fortune with the others. Finally, they departed, agreeing to meet at the same castle on their return before proceeding together to the king. Since they did not want to be recognized by anyone, they refused to take any assistants with them and even changed their names.

Each took a different road. The two elder met with many adventures, but let me recount only those of the youngest. He was well mannered and possessed a gay, cheerful temperament, even though his courage was most intrepid. He had a noble figure, a striking face, regular features, and fine teeth. He was very talented in all those skills that a prince was expected to demonstrate: he could paint and sing with a pleasant voice, and he played the lute with a sensitivity that charmed everyone. In short, he was a highly accomplished young fellow.

There was hardly a day that passed that he did not purchase some dogs. They were big and little: greyhounds, mastiffs, bloodhounds, pointers, spaniels, water dogs, and lapdogs. The instant he found one handsomer than the next, he let the previous one go, since he could not have possibly led around thirty or forty thousand dogs by himself, and he remained firm in his determination not to have gentlemen, servants, or pages in his company.

One day, as he was traveling without any fixed destination, he was surprised at nightfall by a thunderous rainstorm in a forest, and he lost the path he was following. So, he took the first he could find, and after having walked a long way, he saw a glimmer of light that indicated there was some habitation nearby in which he might find shelter until morning. Guided by the light, he came to the gate of the most magnificent castle you could ever imagine. This gate was made of gold and covered with carbuncles, and their pure, vivid light illuminated everything in the vicinity. It was this light that the prince had perceived from a distance. The walls were transparent porcelain of various colors, and the histories of all the fairies from the beginning of time were painted there. The famous adventures of Donkey-Skin, Finette, the Orange Tree, Gracieuse, Sleeping Beauty, the Green Serpent, and a hundred others, were all included. He was delighted to see Prince Sprite among them, for he was his uncle, according to the legends of Brittany. The rainstorm prevented him from lingering before this mural because he was being drenched to the skin. Besides, he could hardly see anything beyond the rays cast by the gate's carbuncles. So, he returned to the golden gate, where he saw a goat's foot dangling from a chain of diamonds. He admired all the magnificence and apparent security in which the owners of the castle seemed to live. "Indeed," he said to himself, "what's to prevent thieves from cutting off this chain and pulling the carbuncles off the gate? They could make themselves rich for the rest of their lives."

Pulling the goat's foot, he immediately heard a bell ring, which by its sound seemed to be made of gold or silver. A moment later, the gate was opened without his seeing anything but a dozen hands, each holding torches, suspended in midair. He was so astonished that he hesitated to move forward. However, he felt other hands that gently pushed him forward. Therefore, he advanced with some distrust, and to be on the safe side, he kept his hand on the hilt of his sword. On entering a vestibule entirely decorated with porphyry and lapis lazuli, he heard two enchanting voices raised in song:

"Be not offended by the hands you see.
Have no fear in this beautiful place.
There's nothing here except a lovely face,
Nothing at all that your heart might flee."

Unable to believe that he was being invited so graciously for the purpose of eventually being harmed, he let himself be pushed toward a large coral gate that opened before his eyes. Then he entered into a salon of mother-of-pearl and then passed through several apartments variously ornamented with such an abundance of paintings and jewels that he was captivated by the sight of them. Thousands and thousands of lights, from the vaulted roof of the salon down to the floor, illuminated parts of the other apartments, which were also filled with chandeliers, girandoles, and stages lined with wax candles. Such magnificence was so resplendent that he had difficulty imagining how all this had been made possible.

After passing through sixty rooms, he was stopped by the hands that had been guiding him and watched as a large easy chair moved by itself toward the fireplace. At the same moment, a fire was ignited, and the hands, which appeared to him handsome, white, small, plump, and well shaped, began to undress him, for he was soaked, as I have already told you, and they were afraid he would catch cold. Although they did not reveal themselves, they gave him a splendid shirt suitable for a wedding day and a morning gown made of rich golden material embroidered with emerald ciphers. The bodiless hands carried over a dressing table that had everything he needed. Nothing could be more magnificent. They combed his hair with a lightness and pleasant skill. Finally, they dressed him again, not in his own clothes, but with others much richer. He observed all that took place with silent wonder and a certain alarm that he could not altogether conquer.

After they had powdered, curled, perfumed, attired, and adorned him to look handsomer than Adonis, the hands led him into a hall that was superbly gilt and furnished. All around were paintings of the stories about all the most famous cats: Rodilardus hung by the heels in the Council of Rats, Puss in Boots, Marquis of Carabas, The Writing Cat, The Cat That Became a Woman, Witches in the Shape of Cats, and their Sabbath and all its ceremonies. In a word, these paintings were highly unusual.

A table was set with two places, each with a golden cadenas. The buffet astonished him, for it held innumerable cups of rock crystal studded with a thousand rare stones. The prince was trying to figure out why there were two place settings when he saw several cats take their places in a small orchestra that had been designed expressly for them. One held a music book with the most extraordinary notes, another held a roll of paper with which to beat time, and the rest had miniature guitars.

Suddenly, each cat began to mew in a different tone and strummed the strings of their guitars with their claws, producing the strangest music that he had ever heard. The prince would have thought he was in the lower regions if he had not found the palace so marvelously beautiful; this fact alone prevented him from making such an error. He was, however, obliged to stuff his ears, and he laughed heartily at the sight of the various postures and grimaces of these novel musicians.

As he pondered the odd things that had already happened to him in the chateau, he saw a figure scarcely a foot tall enter the hall. This puppet was draped with a long black crepe veil, and the two cats preceding it, wearing cloaks and swords, were also dressed in deep mourning. A large retinue of cats followed, some carrying rat traps filled with rats, and others, mice in cages. The prince could not get over his astonishment. He did not know what to think. The little black figure approached, and as it lifted its veil, he perceived the most beautiful white cat that ever has been or ever will be seen. In a very youthful, melancholy air, she began mewing so softly and sweetly that it went straight to his heart.

"Prince," she said, "you are welcome. My mewing majesty regards you with pleasure."

"Madame cat," the prince said, "it's very generous of you to receive me with so much ceremony, but you don't appear to me to be any ordinary little animal. Your gift of speech and the superb castle you inhabit are sufficient evidence that confirms my view."

"Prince," the white cat replied, "please forgo paying me these compliments. I'm plain in my speech and my manners, though I have a generous heart. Come, let them serve supper and put an end to

the concert, for I am certain that you do not understand what they are singing."

"Are they actually singing words, madame?" he inquired.

"Yes, indeed," she answered. "We have poets here of considerable talent, and if you remain among us for long, you'll become convinced of this fact."

"You need only say so, and I'll believe it," the prince responded politely. "All the same, madame, I regard you as a most unusual cat."

The supper was placed on the table by the hands of invisible bodies. First, there were two soups, one of pigeons and the other of very plump mice. The sight of the mice prevented the prince from touching his dish, believing that the same cook had concocted both, but the cat, who guessed from his face what was going on in his mind, assured him that their meals had been cooked separately and that he could eat it with the perfect assurance that it contained neither rats nor mice. The prince did not wait to be told twice, for he felt that the pretty cat had no wish to deceive him.

At that moment, he noticed to his surprise that she had a miniature set in a bracelet on her paw. He begged her to show it to him, supposing it to be that of some Master Minagrobis. He was astonished to find the portrait of an extraordinarily handsome young man who resembled himself so nearly that he could not have asked for a better likeness. Sighing, the white cat became even more melancholy, lapsing into a profound silence. The prince saw clearly that there was some unusual story connected with the portrait, but did not venture to ask any questions for fear of displeasing her. Instead, he entertained her by telling all the news he had and in the process found her well acquainted with the various concerns of princes and other events occurring in the world.

After supper, the white cat invited her guest to enter a salon with a theater where twelve cats and twelve monkeys danced a ballet. One party was dressed as Moors, the other as Chinese. You can easily imagine the leaps and capers they performed, and every now and then they gave each other a scratch or two. Soon the evening came to an end, and the white cat bade "Good night" to her guest.

The invisible hands, which had been his guides so far, took hold of him again and led him into an apartment quite different from any he had seen, for it was not so much magnificent as it was elegant. All the decorations were made of the wings of butterflies whose various colors formed a thousand different flowers. There were also the feathers of exceedingly rare birds that perhaps have never been seen anywhere else. The furnishings of the bed were made of and tied with a thousand bows of ribbon. Large mirrors hung from the ceiling to floor in frames of chased gold representing a thousand tiny cupids.

The prince went to bed without saying a word, for there were no means of talking with the hands that waited upon him. He slept but little and was wakened early by a muffled noise. The hands immediately lifted him out of bed and dressed him in hunting attire. Looking into the castle courtyard, he saw more than five hundred cats, some of whom led greyhounds in the slips, while others blew horns. It was a grand holiday. The white cat was going to hunt and wanted the prince to accompany her. The officious hands gave him a wooden horse, and though he made some objection to mounting it, saying that he could never become a knight-errant like Don Quixote, his resistance was useless. The horse had a bridle and saddle embroidered with gold and diamonds, and in fact, it went at full gallop and kept pace wonderfully. The white cat rode a monkey, the handsomest and proudest ever seen. She had thrown off her long veil in favor of a dragoon's cap, which made her look so bold that she frightened all the mice in the vicinity. Never was there a more charming hunting party. The cats outran the rabbits and hares, and as fast as they caught them, the white cat had a curée made in her presence, and a thousand skillful feats were performed to the great delight of the whole company. The birds, in turn, were by no means safe, for the kittens climbed the trees, and a great monkey carried the white cat up even to the nests of

the eagles so that their eaglets were at her mercy.

Once the hunt was over, the white cat took a horn, and though it was about the length of one's finger, it emitted a call so clear and loud that it was easily heard ten miles away. As soon as she had sounded two or three flourishes, she was surrounded by all the cats in the country. Some rode chariots through the air, and others came in boats by water. Never before had so many cats been gathered, nearly all dressed in different fashions. Attended by this splendid entourage, the white cat returned to the castle, requesting the prince to accompany her. He was perfectly willing to do so, even though all this caterwauling smacked of a witch's festival.

As soon as they reached home, she put on her long black veil and dined with the prince, who was hungry and did justice to the good meal. They brought him some liqueurs, which he sipped with great satisfaction, and they soon made him forget all about the little dog he was to find for the king. He no longer thought of anything but mewing with the white cat—that is to say, remaining her kind and faithful companion. He spent his days by amusing himself in pleasant ways, followed by ballets, carousals, and a thousand other events that provided him with a good deal of entertainment. Even the beautiful cat herself frequently composed verses and sonnets so full of passionate tenderness that made him suspect she had a susceptible heart, for no one could speak as she did without being in love. Unfortunately, her secretary, who was an old cat, wrote in such a vile scrawl that it is impossible to read them today, even though her works have been preserved.

The prince had forgotten all about the land of his birth. The hands continued to wait upon him, and he regretted sometimes that he was not a cat so he could spend his whole life long in such excellent company. "Alas," he said to the white cat, "how wretched I'll be when I must leave you! I love you so dearly! Either become a woman or make me a cat."

Amused by his wish, she gave him some mysterious answers that he did not understand in the least. A year flies by quickly when one has neither care nor pain, when one is merry and in good health. The white cat knew when the prince was supposed to return, and since he had forgotten it, she reminded him. "Don't you know," she asked, "that you have only three days left to look for the little dog that your father desires? Your brothers have already found several that are very beautiful."

The prince's memory of his task returned to him, and his negligence astonished him. "What secret spell could have made me forget the most important thing in the world?" he exclaimed. "My honor and fortune are at stake. Where shall I find a dog that can win the kingdom for me, or a horse swift enough to complete the journey in such a short time?"

Seeing him become so anxious and sad, the white cat said to him sweetly, "Prince,

do not be distressed. I'm your friend, and you may stay here one more day. Although it's five hundred miles from here to your country, the good wooden horse will carry you there tomorrow in less than twelve hours."

"I thank you, beautiful cat," the prince said, "but I cannot simply return to my father without bringing him a little dog."

"Wait," said the white cat, "here's an acorn that contains one more beautiful than the Dog Star."

"Oh, madame cat," the prince cried, "your majesty is jesting with me."

"Put the acorn to your ear," she replied, "and you'll hear it bark."

He obeyed her, and immediately the little dog went "bow-wow."

The prince was extremely delighted, for any dog that could be kept in an acorn was bound to be quite diminutive. Since he was so eager to see the dog, he wanted to open the acorn, but the white cat told him that the dog might catch cold on the journey, and it would be better for him to wait until he was in his royal father's presence. He thanked her a thousand times and bade her a most tender farewell.

"I assure you," he said, "that the days I have spent with you have flown by so quickly that I deeply regret leaving you behind. Although you're the sovereign here and all the cats that compose your court possess much more wit and gallantry than ours, I'd be honored if you came with me."

The cat replied to this invitation only with a deep sigh: "Prince, depart."

The prince was the first to reach the castle where he had agreed to meet his brothers. Arriving shortly thereafter, they were surprised to see a wooden horse in the courtyard that curvetted with more grace than the horses in the riding schools. When the prince came forward to receive them, they embraced several times and recounted their travels to one another, though our prince kept the bulk of his adventures a secret from his brothers. As he showed them an ugly turnspit, he remarked, "I think it's so beautiful that I've selected it for the king."

Despite the close friendship of the brothers, the two elder felt a secret joy at their young brother's awful taste. Since they were sitting at a table, they nudged each other's feet by way of signifying that they did not have much to fear from him.

The next morning, they set out together in the same coach. The king's two elder sons carried a few little dogs in baskets so beautiful and delicate that everyone was afraid to touch them. The youngest son carried the poor turnspit, which was so filthy that nobody could bear the sight of it. As soon as they set foot in the palace, everybody surrounded them and welcomed them back to the court. Once they had entered the king's apartment, he was at a loss to make a decision, for the little dogs given to him by his two elder sons were nearly equal in beauty. In fact, the two brothers had already begun to dispute the right of succession when their younger brother reconciled them by taking out of his pocket the acorn that the white cat had given him. He opened it immediately, and everybody saw a tiny dog lying on cotton. He got up and jumped through a ring without touching any part of it. The prince placed it on the floor, and instantly it began dancing a sarabande with castanets that was as sprightly as the most celebrated Spanish dancer. It was a thousand different colors, and its hair and ears swept the ground. The king was dumbfounded and wondered how could he possibly criticize the beauty of Toutou?

Nevertheless, he was by no means inclined to bestow his crown on his youngest son, for the smallest fleur-de-lis in its circlet was dearer to him than all the dogs in the universe. Therefore, he told his sons that he was gratified by the trouble they had taken. Indeed, they had succeeded so well in fulfilling his first request that he wanted to test their ability again before he fulfilled his promise. "You have a year to travel over land and sea in quest of a piece of cloth so fine that it will pass through the eye of a needle used to make Venetian point lace."

All three were extremely disappointed to learn that they were obliged to undertake a new voyage of discovery, but the two elder princes, whose dogs were less beautiful than that of the youngest, readily consented. Both went their own ways without declaring their friendship to him as they had done before because the trick of the turnspit had rather cooled their ardor.

Our prince remounted his wooden horse, and since he did not wish for any assistance other than that obtained from the friendship of the white cat, he set off at a gallop toward the castle where she had so kindly received him. He found all the doors open, and the windows, roofs, towers, and walls were all illuminated by a hundred thousand lamps, which produced a brilliant effect. The hands that had attended him so well advanced to meet him and took the bridle of the excellent wooden horse, which they led to the stable while the prince entered the white cat's apartments.

Wearing her morning cap, she was lying in a little basket on a fine mattress of white satin. She seemed in low spirits until she saw the prince. Then she cut a thousand capers and played as many gambols to show him her delight. "Whatever hope I had that you'd return," she said, "I confess, prince, that I didn't want to deceive myself by indulging in it. I'm generally so unfortunate in matters that concern me that this is a pleasant surprise."

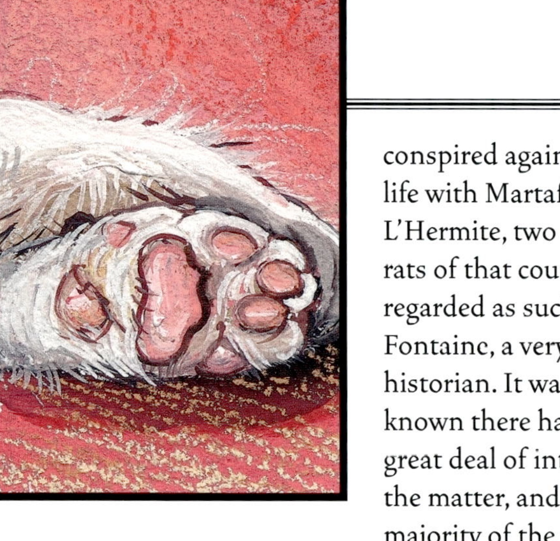

The grateful prince caressed her a thousand times and told her about the success of his journey, which she knew perhaps better than he did. "Only now the king wants a piece of cloth that can pass through the eye of a needle."

In truth, he believed it was impossible to find such a thing, but he did not hesitate to ask her to make the attempt, relying implicitly upon her friendship and assistance. Becoming more serious, the white cat told him it was a matter that demanded consideration. Fortunately, there were some cats in her castle who spun extremely well. She intended to put a claw to it herself and speed up the work as much as possible. "Rest assured that you have no need of searching any farther for what you will more readily find in my castle than in any other place in the world."

The hands appeared bearing torches, and the white cat and prince followed them. They entered a magnificent arbor running along the side of a large river, over which an astonishing display of fireworks was to be produced. Four cats were to be burnt there simultaneously because they had been tried and sentenced in due form for having eaten the roast meat, cheese, and milk, provided for the white cat's supper. They were even charged of having conspired against her life with Martafax and L'Hermite, two famous rats of that country, and regarded as such by La Fontaine, a very dutiful historian. It was well known there had been a great deal of intrigue in the matter, and that the majority of the witnesses had been bribed. Despite all this, the prince managed to obtain their pardon. The fireworks did not harm anyone, and never had such splendid skyrockets been seen before.

Afterward, a splendid supper was served. This gratified the prince more than the fireworks because he was famished. The wooden horse had carried him at such a rapid pace that he had never ridden so hard before in his life. The following days were spent like those of the previous year, and the ingenious white cat set forth a thousand diverse entertainments to regale her guest. Our prince was probably the first mortal who ever found so much amusement among cats without human company.

The truth is, the white cat possessed charming, sweet, and well-rounded qualities. She was wiser than a cat is allowed to be, and the prince was sometimes astonished by her knowledge.

"No," he said, "it's not natural for you to possess all these wonderful qualities I've discovered in you. If you love me, charming pussy, explain to me what miracle has enabled you to think and speak so perfectly that you might be elected a member of the most famous Academy of Arts and Sciences?"

"Stop questioning me, prince," she said. "I'm not allowed to answer, and you may conjecture as much as you like without the least contradiction from me. Let it suffice that I'll always have a velvet paw for you, that I take a tender interest in all that concerns you."

The second year slipped away like the first—without their being aware of it at all. The prince could scarcely think of anything he desired without the diligent hands instantly providing him with it, whether it be a book, jewel, picture, or antique medal. He had but to say, "I want a certain gem in the cabinet of the Great Mogul or of the King of Persia, or such a statue in Corinth or any part of Greece," and it was instantaneously before him, without his knowing how it came or who brought it. This pastime was not without its charms, for it is sometimes very pleasant to possess the finest treasures in the world.

The white cat, who constantly attended to the prince's welfare, warned him that the hour of departure was approaching. There was no need to worry, however, about the piece of cloth he needed. She had made a most wonderful one for him, and she added that she intended this time to furnish him with an equipage worthy of his birth. Without waiting for his reply, she told him to look into the great courtyard of the castle. He saw an open carriage made of gold and enameled in scarlet with a thousand gallant emblems that stimulated the mind as much as the eye. It was drawn by twelve horses as white as snow, four-and-four abreast, bearing harnesses of scarlet velvet embroidered with diamonds and plated with gold. The carriage was lined to match, and a hundred coaches followed in its train. Each was led by eight horses and filled with superbly attired nobles of high bearing. There was as well an escort of a thousand bodyguards, whose uniforms were covered so much with embroidery that you could not see the stuff of which they were made. Most striking about this cavalcade was the portrait of the white cat, which could be seen on the emblems on the carriage or the uniforms of the bodyguards or attached by a ribbon to the doublets of those who formed the train, as if it were a new order with which she had decorated them.

"Go," she said to the prince. "Appear at the court of your father in such a sumptuous state that your magnificence may make an impression on him and prevent him from refusing again to bestow you with the crown you deserve. Here's a walnut. Crack it only in his presence, and you'll find in it the piece of cloth you asked of me."

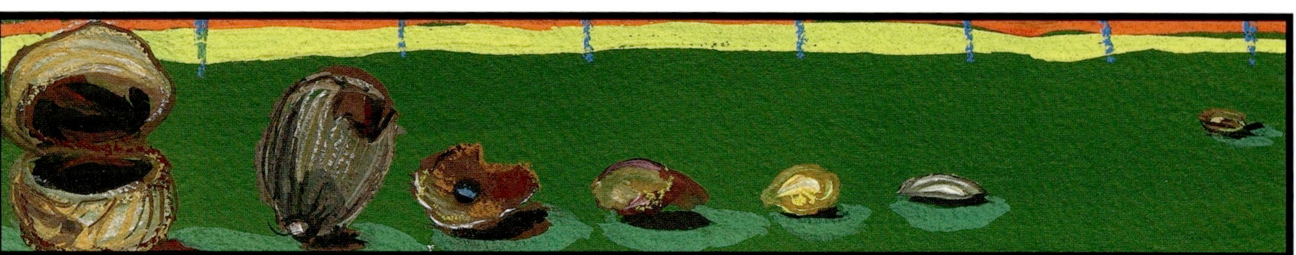

"Charming white cat," he said, "I must confess that your kindness has exhilarated me so much that, if you consent, I'd prefer spending my life here with you than enjoying all the grandeur that I have reason to expect elsewhere."

"Prince," she replied, "I'm convinced that you have a good heart, a rare quality among princes. Usually they want to be loved by everyone. Rarely do they want to love anyone themselves. You're proof that the rule has its exception. I give you credit for the affection you've demonstrated for a white cat that, after all, is good for nothing but catching mice."

The prince kissed her paw and departed. We would have some difficulty in believing the speed with which he traveled if we were not already aware of the pace at which the wooden horse had previously covered the five-hundred-mile distance from the castle. Impelled by a similar power, these swift steeds traveled for twenty-four hours straight and stopped only when they reached the king's palace.

The two elder brothers had already arrived, and when they did not see the youngest prince, they congratulated themselves on his negligence. "Here's a piece of good luck!" one whispered to the other. "He's either dead or very ill. He won't be our rival in the important business about to be decided."

They immediately displayed their cloths, which were so fine that they could pass through the eye of a large needle, though not that of a small one. Elated by this, the king used it as a pretext to deny their claims. He ordered the magistrates to bring the needle that he had selected out of the city treasury, where it had been carefully kept during the princes' absence. There was a good deal of murmuring when he did this. The friends of the princes, particularly those of the eldest, whose cloth was made of the finer material, protested, "It's downright chicanery. The king is too cunning and deceptive."

The king's followers contended that he was merely bound by the conditions he had proposed. The matter seemed settled when suddenly they heard a loud flourish of trumpets, kettle drums, and oboes, announcing the arrival of our prince in all his pomp and accoutrements. The king and his two other sons were all equally thunderstruck by such splendor.

After the prince had respectfully greeted his father and embraced his brothers, he revealed a box dotted with rubies. In it was the walnut. He cracked it expecting to find the boasted piece of cloth, but instead found a hazel nut, which he also cracked and was surprised to find a cherrystone! Everybody looked at one another, and the king laughed up his sleeve at his son, who had been naïve enough to believe he could bring a whole piece of cloth in a walnut. Yet, why shouldn't the prince have believed it when he had already given the king a dog that had emerged from an acorn? Therefore, he cracked the cherrystone and found a kernel. A great murmur arose in the room. Everyone was convinced that the young prince had been duped in this adventure, but he did not respond to the courtiers' raillery. Opening the kernel, he found in it a grain of wheat, and in the grain of wheat a millet seed. In truth, he began to have doubts himself and muttered between his teeth, "White cat, white cat, you've fooled me!" Instantly, he felt a cat's claw on his hand give him such a scratch that blood began to flow. He knew not whether this scratch was given to encourage or to dishearten him, but he nevertheless opened the millet seed, and the entire company was astonished when he drew out a piece of cloth four hundred yards long, so wonderfully wrought that all the birds, beasts, and fish were depicted in their natural colors along with the trees, fruits, and plants of the earth; rocks, rare gems, and shells of the ocean; the sun, the moon, the great and lesser heavenly bodies. There were also portraits of all the kings and lesser sovereigns reigning in the world at that time, with those of their wives, mistresses, children, and all their subjects, not omitting the smallest urchin—everyone in his particular walk of life accurately represented and dressed in the garb of his country.

When the king saw this piece of cloth, he became as pale as the prince had become red with bewilderment when he had not at first found it. The needle was produced, and the prince passed and repassed the cloth through the eye of it six times. The king and the two elder princes looked on in sullen silence, except at those moments when the beauty and uniqueness of the cloth forced them to acknowledge that nothing in the universe could compare to it.

The king heaved a deep sigh and, turning toward his sons, he said, "Nothing gives me as much consolation in my old age as observing the deference paid by you to my wishes. Consequently, I want to put your obedience to a new test. Go and travel for another year, and he who at the end of it brings back the most beautiful maiden shall marry her and be crowned king on his wedding day. It's necessary anyway that my successor should marry, and I faithfully pledge that I'll no longer defer bestowing the reward I have promised."

This unjust decision went especially against our prince, for the little dog and piece of cloth were worth more than ten kingdoms. He was so well bred, though, that he would not contest his father's will, and he promptly climbed back into his carriage. His whole entourage followed

him, and he took the road back to his dear white cat. She knew the day, the very moment he would arrive. The entire way was strewn with flowers; thousands of vases exuded perfume everywhere and particularly within the castle. The white cat was seated on a Persian carpet under a pavilion of cloth of gold in a gallery, and from there she saw him approach, received by the hands that had always attended him. All the cats climbed up into the gutters to welcome him with a desperate squalling.

"So, prince," the white cat said, "you've returned once more without a crown."

"Madame," he replied, "your generosity placed me in a position to obtain it, but I'm convinced that it would have given the king more pain to part with it than the pleasure I would have gained from acquiring it."

"It doesn't matter at all," she said. "Nothing will be overlooked if you want to win it, for I'll help you in this affair. Since you're obliged to return with a beautiful maiden to your father's court, I'll find one who'll help you obtain the prize. In the meantime, let us be merry. I've ordered a naval combat between my cats and the terrible rats of this country. My cats will perhaps be embarrassed a little because they're afraid of water. On the other hand, they would have too much of an advantage, and one ought to equalize matters as much as possible."

Admiring the prudence of madame puss, the prince heaped praises on her and accompanied her to a terrace that overlooked the sea. The ships in which the cats embarked were large pieces of cork, on which they managed to sail conveniently enough, and the rats had bound several eggshells together for their navy. The battle was long and cruel. The rats flung themselves into the water and swam much better than the cats so that they triumphed and were defeated alternately twenty times. However, Minagrobis, admiral of the feline fleet, reduced the rattish race to utmost despair when he devoured the general of their forces, an old rat of great experience, who had been around the world three times in splendid ships on which he had been neither captain nor common sailor but simply a lickspittle. The white cat would not permit the utter destruction of all these poor unfortunate creatures. A smart politician, she calculated that if there were no more rats or mice left in the country, her subjects would live in a state of idleness that might work to her disadvantage.

The prince spent this year as he had the two previous ones, hunting, fishing, or playing chess, which the white cat did extremely well. He could not help occasionally questioning her as to the miraculous power that enabled her to speak. He asked her whether she was a fairy, or had been transformed into a cat, but since she never said anything but what she chose, she never gave answers that did not wholly suit her. Consequently, her replies consisted of a number of fragments that signified nothing in particular, and he clearly perceived she was not inclined to share her secret with him.

Nothing flies faster than time spent without trouble or sorrow, and if the cat had not been careful to remember the day when the prince had to return to court, he certainly would have forgotten it. On the eve of his departure, she told him that everything depended on him taking home one of the most beautiful princesses in the world. "The hour to destroy that fatal work of the fairies has finally arrived. You must cut off my head and tail and fling them quickly into the fire."

"Me?" the prince exclaimed. "Blanchette, my love! I can't be so barbarous as to kill you! Ah, you undoubtedly mean to test my heart. But rest assured that it is incapable of forgetting the love and gratitude it owes you."

"No, prince," she replied, "I don't suspect you of ingratitude. Well I know your worth. Neither you nor I control our destiny in this matter. Do as I bid you, and then we'll both begin to be happy. On my word of honor as a noble cat, you'll discover that I'm truly your friend."

The eyes of the young prince welled up with tears at the mere thought of being obliged to cut off the head of his little kitten, so pretty and so charming. He said all the most tender things he could think of in order to induce her to spare him such a trial. However, she persisted in replying that she wanted to die by his hand, and that only this way would he prevent his brothers from obtaining the crown. In a word, she urged him so earnestly that he drew his sword tremblingly, and with a faltering hand he sliced off the head and tail of his dearly beloved cat.

The very next moment he beheld the most charming transformation imaginable. The body of the white cat swelled in size and changed suddenly into that of an indescribably perfect young maiden. Her eyes enthralled everyone's heart, and her sweetness held them captive. Her form was majestic, her demeanor noble and modest, her spirit, gentle, her manners, engaging. She was, in sum, the most charming being in the world.

The prince was so struck with amazement at the pleasant sight of her that he thought he was enchanted. He could not speak or open his eyes wide enough to take her in. His astonishment became even greater when he saw an extraordinary number of lords and ladies enter the room. Each had his or her cat's skin flung over a shoulder as they advanced and threw themselves at the feet of their queen. "How great is our pleasure at seeing you restored to your natural form!" She received them with signs of affection that clearly indicated the goodness of her heart, and after spending a short time in their company, she requested that they leave her alone with the prince, to whom she told the following tale:

I don't want you to think, my lord, that I've always been a cat, or that my birth was an obscure one in the eyes of men. My father was king of six realms. He loved my mother tenderly and gave her complete liberty to do whatever she liked. Her great love was traveling, and shortly before I was born, she took a journey to a certain mountain about which she had heard the most extraordinary tales. While traveling there, she was told that she was then passing near an ancient fairy castle, the most beautiful in the world. At least this is what people believed according to legend. Since nobody ventured there, they could not know for certain, but they did know that the fairies had in their garden the finest, most delicious, and most delicate fruit that one could ever eat.

My mother immediately had such an overwhelming desire to taste some that she turned her steps toward the castle. She arrived at the gate of that superb edifice, which blazed with gold and azure on all sides, but when she knocked, nobody appeared to answer. It seemed as if everyone in the castle were dead. Her desire grew in proportion to the obstacle. She sent for ladders so that her attendants might climb over the garden walls, and they would have succeeded had not the said walls visibly increased in height, even though no one was seen to cause this. They lengthened the ladders by tying two or three together, but they broke under the weight of those who mounted them, and the attendants were either crippled or killed.

The queen was in despair. She saw the large trees laden with what looked like delicious fruit, and was determined to eat some or die. Ordering several splendid tents to be pitched before the castle, she remained there six weeks with her entire entourage. She neither slept nor ate, but sighed unceasingly and talked of nothing but the fruit in the inaccessible garden. Eventually, she fell dangerously ill without anyone being able to find a cure for her illness, for the inexorable fairies had never appeared so much as once since she had set up the tents. All her officers were deeply troubled. Nothing was to be heard but sobs and sighs, and the dying queen kept asking for fruit from her attendants and cared only for that which was denied her.

One night, awakening from a doze, she opened her eyes and saw a decrepit old woman seated in an armchair at the head of her bed. Even as she stared, shocked that her women had allowed a stranger to come so near her, the old woman said, "We think your majesty is very obstinate in persisting in your desire to eat our fruit, but since your life is precariously hanging on this, my sisters and I consent to give you as much as you can eat on the spot as well as whatever you can carry away with you. However, you must give us something in exchange."

"Ah, heavens! I can't purchase such fruit at too high a price."

"We wish to have the daughter whom you are about to bring into the world," she said. "As soon as she is born, we'll come and fetch her, and she'll be brought up among us. There are no virtues, charms, or accomplishments with which we shall not endow her. In a word, she'll be our child, and we'll make her happy. But be advised that your majesty will not be allowed to see her anymore until she is married. If this proposal is agreeable to you, I'll cure you instantly and lead you into our orchard. Even though it's night, you'll be able to see well enough to pick whatever fruit you desire. If what I have said does not please you, then good night, queen, I'm going to bed."

"Hard as the condition may be that you impose upon me," the queen replied, "I shall accept it rather than die, for I know I cannot live another day, and my infant would therefore perish with me. Cure me, wise fairy," she continued, "and don't postpone for one moment the opportunity of enjoying the privilege you've promised."

The fairy touched her with a golden wand, saying, "Let your majesty be free from all the ills that confine you to this bed!"

It seemed to the queen that someone had instantaneously stripped off a heavy, stiff robe that had oppressed her, though some portions of it still clung to her, apparently in the places most affected by her disorder. Sending for all her ladies, she told them with a smiling countenance that she was quite well and was going to get up. "Soon those gates of the fairy palace, so well bolted and barred, will be opened for me to enter, and I'll be able to eat the fine fruit and take away as much as I like."

All of her ladies thought the queen was seeing things in her delirium because she wanted the fruit so much. Instead of replying, they began to weep, and some went to waken all the physicians to come and see their majesty's condition.

This delay exasperated the queen, but when she ordered them to bring her clothes to her instantly, they refused. She flew into a passion, turning red with rage. They attributed all this to fever, but once the physicians arrived, felt her pulse, and went through the usual ceremonies, they could not deny that she was in perfect health. Her women, who realized the mistake, caused by their zeal, tried to atone for it by asking her majesty's pardon and dressing her as quickly as possible. Peace was restored, and the queen quickly followed the old fairy, who was still waiting for her.

She entered the palace, which required nothing to make it the most beautiful place in the world. Two other fairies, somewhat younger than the one who conducted my mother, received her at the gate and welcomed her graciously. She asked them to lead her straight into the garden and to those espaliers where she would find the best fruit.

"Everything is equally good," they said to her, "and if it weren't for the fact that you desire the pleasure of picking it yourself, we need only call the fruit we wish for, and it will come to us here."

"I implore you, ladies," the queen said, "to show me such an extraordinary sight."

The eldest fairy put her finger into her mouth and whistled three times. Then she cried, "Apricots, peaches, nectarines, sherries, plums, pears, cherries, melons, muscatel grapes, apples, oranges, lemons, gooseberries, strawberries, raspberries, come at my call!"

"But," the queen said, "all the fruit that you've summoned cannot be found at the same season."

"In our orchard," they replied, "we have all the fruits of the earth. They're always ripe, always excellent, and they never spoil."

Meanwhile, the fruit rolled in over the floor

pell-mell, but without being bruised or dirtied. So, the queen, eager to satisfy her longing, threw herself on them and took the first that came to hand, devouring rather than eating it.

After having partly satisfied her appetite, she begged the fairies to let her proceed to the espaliers so that she might have the pleasure of choosing the fruit on the tree and then gathering it. "We freely give you permission," they said, "but remember the promise you've made us. You won't be allowed to rescind it!"

"I'm convinced," she said, "that you live so well here, and this palace appears to me so beautiful that if I did not love my husband dearly, I'd propose remaining here with you along with my daughter. Therefore, you need have no fear about by retracting my word."

Completely satisfied, the fairies opened all their gardens and enclosures to her. She remained there three days and three nights without wishing to go out again because she found everything so delicious. She gathered the fruit to take home with her, and since it did not spoil, she had four thousand mules loaded with the fruit. In addition, the fairies gave her the most exquisite golden baskets in which to carry it and many other precious items. They promised her that I would be educated like a princess and that they would make me a model of perfection and choose a husband for me. "You will receive notice of the wedding, and we hope you will attend."

The king was delighted by the queen's return, and the entire court rejoiced as well. There were nothing but balls, masquerades, ring games, and banquets, at which the queen's fruit was served as a delicious treat. The king preferred to eat the fruit more than anything else offered him, but he was unaware of the bargain the queen had made with the fairies.

He often asked her where she had traveled to find such good things. One time, she told him that she had found them on an almost inaccessible mountain. Another time, she said they grew in various valleys. Other times, she named a garden or great forest. Surprised by so many contradictions, the king questioned those who had accompanied her, but she had so strictly forbidden them to tell anyone of her adventure that they dared not talk about it. Eventually, the queen became uneasy about the promise she had made the fairies, and as the time for her to give birth approached, she fell into an alarming state of melancholy. She kept sighing constantly and looked worse and worse every day. After a great deal of probing, she informed him of everything that had occurred with her and the fairies, and how she had promised to give them the daughter she was about to bring into the world.

"What?" said the king. "We have no other children. You know how much I want some, and for the sake of eating two or three apples you gave away our daughter? You have no feelings for me!"

He overwhelmed her with a thousand reproaches, which were almost the death of my poor mother, but that did not satisfy him. He had her locked up in a tower and surrounded it with soldiers to prevent her from having communication with anyone except the officers of her household. These, too, he changed so they were not the same as those who had been with her at the fairy castle.

The misunderstanding between the king and the queen threw the whole court into consternation, and everybody changed into clothes more suitable to the general sorrow. The king, for his part, appeared inexorable. He never visited his wife, and as soon as I was born, he had me brought into the palace to be nursed, while she remained a most unhappy prisoner.

The fairies were aware of all that took place and became annoyed. They regarded me as their property and my detention as a theft. Before seeking vengeance in keeping with their anger, they sent a grand embassy to the king to warn him that he had better set the queen free, restore her to his favor, and surrender me to their ambassadors so that I could be nursed and brought up by the fairies. The ambassadors were so little and deformed (for they were hideous dwarfs) that they did not have the power to persuade the king to comply with their request. He refused bluntly, and if they had not taken their departure instantly, something worse might have befallen them. When the fairies heard of my father's conduct, they were highly indignant, and after demolishing his six kingdoms by inflicting every ill on them that they could devise, they released a terrible dragon that poisoned the air wherever it breathed, wilting all the trees and plants. Moreover, the dragon devoured man and child.

In the throes of despair, the king consulted all the wise men in his dominions as to what he might do to protect his subjects from the misfortune that was overwhelming them. On the one hand, they advised him to seek out the best physicians and the most excellent remedies throughout the world, and on the other, to offer a free pardon to all criminals under the death penalty who would agree to fight the dragon. The king approved of this advice and acted on it immediately, but without success, for the pestilence continued, and the dragon devoured all those who attacked him. Finally, the king turned to a fairy who had been his friend from childhood. She was very old and rarely left her bed. Going to see her, he reproached her a thousand times for permitting fate to persecute him without coming to his rescue.

"What would you have me do?" she said. "You've irritated my sisters. They're as powerful as I am, and we rarely act against one another. Try to appease them by giving them your daughter. The little princess rightfully belongs to them. You've put the queen in prison. What has that charming woman done for you to treat her so severely? It would be best if you decided to keep your wife's pledge to the fairies. I assure you, you'll be rewarded greatly if you do."

My father loved me dearly, but seeing no other way of saving his kingdoms from the lethal dragon, he told his friend that he would take her advice. He was willing to surrender me to the fairies since she had assured him that I'd be cherished and treated as a princess of my rank ought to be. He also agreed to allow the queen to come back to the court. Finally, he told the fairy that she should name the person who should carry me to the fairy castle, and it would be done.

"You may even remain in its vicinity, if you desire, to witness the celebration that will take place there."

The king told her that he would go there with the queen within a week's time and asked her to notify her sister fairies of his intention so that they might make the necessary arrangements.

As soon as he returned to the palace, he sent for the queen and received her with as much affection and regard as he had exhibited rashness

and anger when he imprisoned her. She was so changed and melancholy that he would hardly have recognized her if his heart had not assured him that she was the same person he had formerly loved so tenderly. With tears in his eyes, he implored her to forget the misery he had caused her and assured her she would never again experience anything like that on his account.

"I brought it upon myself by my imprudence in promising our daughter to the fairies," she replied. "If anything could excuse my actions, it was the condition to which I had been reduced at the time."

The king then informed her that he had decided to place me in the hands of the fairies. The queen, in her turn, opposed this intention. It seemed as if some fatality was hanging over this affair, and that I was forever doomed to be a subject of dissension between my father and mother. After she groaned and wept for a considerable time without obtaining her goal (for the king saw too clearly the fatal consequences of hesitating, and our subjects continued to perish as if they were answerable for the faults of our family), she consented to all he desired, and everything was prepared for the leave taking.

I was placed in a mother-of-pearl cradle ornamented with the most elegant things that art could ever conceive. Hanging from every side were garlands and festoons of flowers made of jewels, whose different colors reflected the rays of the sun with such dazzling splendor that you could scarcely look upon them. The magnificence of my swaddling surpassed that of the cradle, if that were possible, for all the bands of my clothes were formed of large pearls. Twenty-four princesses of royal blood carried me on a delicate litter. Though their dresses were all different, they were not allowed to wear any color but white in token of my innocence. The entire court accompanied me according to rank.

While we were climbing the mountain, we heard a melodious symphony more and more distinctly. At length, thirty-six fairies appeared, for the trio of fairies had invited their friends to accompany them. Each was seated in a pearl shell larger than that in which Venus arose from the ocean. Seahorses, which seemed rather awkward in getting overland, drew these pearl cars, and though the occupants wore more sumptuous finery than the greatest queens in the universe, they were at the same time old and ugly hags.

The dragon who had been their instrument of vengeance followed them in chains of diamonds. They carried olive branches to signify to the king that his submission had found favor with them, and when I was presented, their caresses were so extraordinary that they seemed to have no other goal in life except to make me happy. They took me in their arms, kissed me a thousand times,

endowed me with various gifts, and then began to dance the fairy brawl. It is a very lively dance, and it's hard to imagine how well these old ladies jumped and capered. Afterward, the dragon that had devoured so many people crawled forward, and the three fairies to whom my mother had promised me seated themselves upon it. Then they placed my cradle between them and struck the dragon with a wand. It immediately spread its great, scaly wings, which were finer than gauze and glittered with all sorts of extraordinary colors, and in this way did they return to their castle. On seeing me aloft on this terrible dragon, my mother could not help shrieking over and over again. The king consoled her, saying, "My friend the old fairy has assured me that no misfortune will befall her. She'll be as well taken care of as if she had remained in our own palace."

The queen was calmed by this assurance, though she continued to be distraught at the idea of being separated from me for such a long time. She felt she was to blame for everything, for if she had not insisted on eating the fruit of that garden, I would have been brought up in my father's realm and would never have suffered the misfortunes that I still must relate to you.

Know, then, prince, that my guardians had built a tower expressly for my abode, and it had a thousand beautiful apartments suitable for each season of the year, magnificent furniture, and amusing books. But it was without doors so that one could only enter it by the windows, which were set very high. Atop this tower was a beautiful garden ornamented with flowers, fountains, and green arbors, where you could remain cool on the hottest of dog days. Here was the place where I was brought up by the fairies, and the care they took of me even exceeded what they had promised the queen. She would have thought every day was my wedding day. I was taught everything befitting my age and rank. I didn't give them much trouble because I learned almost everything with the greatest ease. My docility pleased them, and since I never saw another soul, I might have lived there in perfect tranquility for the rest of my life.

When the fairies came to see me, they were always mounted on the terrible dragon I have already mentioned. Since they never mentioned the king or queen and called me their daughter, I believed myself to be so. Nobody lived with me in the tower except a parrot and a small dog that they had given me to amuse myself, for the creatures were endowed with reason and conversed remarkably well.

On one side of the tower was a path lined with deep ruts and trees that so choked the road that I had never seen anyone pass by since I had been shut up there. But one day when I was at the window talking with my parrot and my dog, I heard a noise. As I looked around, I noticed a young chevalier who had stopped to listen to our conversation. I had never seen a young man before but in a painting, and I was happy that chance provided me with this opportunity. Not dreaming of the danger that accompanies the pleasure of contemplating such a charming object, I leaned forward to gaze at him, and the more I looked, the more was I delighted. He made a deep bow, stared at me, and seemed frustrated that he could not find a way to converse with me, for my window was very high, and he feared being overheard, since he knew well enough that I was in the castle of the fairies.

The night came suddenly upon us, or, to be more precise, it came without our noticing it. He blew his horn two or three times, entertaining me with a few flourishes. Then he took his leave, and I was unable to ascertain which way he had gone because the night was so dark. I remained steeped in contemplation, no longer feeling the same pleasure in talking to my parrot and dog that I had felt before. They said the prettiest things in the world to me, for fairy creatures are very witty, but my mind was preoccupied, and I was too naïve to conceal it. Perroquet noticed it, and since he was a shrewd bird, he revealed no sign of what was going on in his mind.

As soon as it was light, I got up and ran to my window. Of course, I was most pleasantly surprised to see the young knight at the foot of the tower. He was so magnificently dressed that I imagined that it must be partly on my account, and I wasn't mistaken. He addressed me through a sort of speaking horn, informing me that until then he had been indifferent to the charms of all the beautiful women he had seen, but now he was so overwhelmed by my beauty that he could not imagine how he could live without seeing me every day. Greatly pleased by this compliment, I was at the same time so very disturbed that I dared not reply, for I would have been compelled to cry out with all my might and run the risk of being better heard by the fairies than by him. I threw him some flowers I had in my hand that he received as a favorable sign. Kissing them several times and thanking me, he asked me if I would approve of his standing under my window every day at the same hour, and if so, to throw him something else. Consequently, I immediately pulled off a turquoise ring I had on my finger and flung it to him. Then I gave him a signal to depart as quickly as possible because I heard the fairy Violente mounting her dragon on the other side of the tower to bring me my breakfast.

The first words she uttered on entering my room were "I smell the voice of a man here. Search, dragon!"

Oh, how upset I was! My heart was sinking, for I was afraid the monster would fly out through the opposite window and follow the chevalier. "Indeed, my good mama," I said (for the old fairy liked me to call her so), "you're jesting, surely, when you say you smell the voice of a man. Is it possible to smell a voice? And if so, what mortal would be rash enough to venture to climb this tower?"

"What you say is true, daughter," she replied. "I'm delighted to hear you reason so nicely, and I suppose the hatred I bear all men sometimes makes me imagine they're near." Giving me my breakfast and my spindle, she said, "After you've had your breakfast, don't forget to spin, for you did nothing yesterday, and my sisters will be angry with you."

In fact, I had been so preoccupied by the stranger that I had found it quite impossible to spin.

As soon as the fairy was gone, I rebelliously tossed my spindle aside and climbed up to the terrace to look out as far as I could see. I had an excellent telescope, and there was nothing to interrupt the view. So, I looked in every direction until I discovered my chevalier on the summit of a mountain. He was resting beneath a rich pavilion of gold cloth and surrounded by a large entourage. I was convinced that he was the son of some king who reigned in the vicinity. Since I feared that if he returned to the tower, he would be discovered by the terrible dragon, I fetched my parrot and told him to fly to the mountain. "There you will find the person who had spoken to me. Beg him in my name never to come again, for I fear my vigilant guardians will surely do him harm."

Perroquet carried out his task like a clever parrot. The courtiers were all surprised to see him flying at full speed and watched him perch on their master's shoulder and whisper in his ear. The king (for that's what he proved to be) was both delighted and troubled by this message. He found my anxiety on his account encouraging, but the many obstacles barring him from speaking to me distressed him. Still, he was bent on wooing me and asked Perroquet a hundred questions. Perroquet asked him as many in return, for he was naturally inquisitive. The king gave him a ring to bring to me in return for my turquoise. It was a turquoise as well, but much finer than mine, for it was shaped like a heart and encircled by diamonds. "It's fitting," he told the parrot, "that I treat you as an ambassador. Therefore, let me give you my portrait. Show it to no one but your charming mistress." He tied the miniature under the bird's wing, and he brought the ring back to me in his beak.

I awaited the return of my little green courier with an impatience I had never known before. He told me that the person to whom I had sent him was a great king. "I was most kindly received by him, and you may rest assured he lives only for your sake. Despite the grave danger in coming to the foot of the tower, he is determined to brave everything rather than renounce the pleasure of seeing you."

These tidings greatly troubled me, and I began to weep. Perroquet and my little dog Toutou did their best to console me because they loved me with a great deal of tenderness. Then Perroquet gave me the king's ring and showed me his portrait. I confess I was tremendously delighted to be able to regard the king's image closely, especially since I had seen him only at a distance. He appeared to me much more charming than I had supposed. My mind began to project a hundred different scenarios, some pleasant, some distressing, and my conflict made me appear extraordinarily anxious.

The fairies who came to see me noticed it. They remarked to one another that I had undoubtedly become tired of my dull life. "It's time we find her a husband of the fairy race for her."

Several were proposed, and eventually they settled on little King Migonnet. His kingdom was some five hundred miles away, but that was, of course, a trifle for them. Overhearing their discussion, Perroquet darted away to give me an account.

"Ah," he said, "how I'd pity you, my dear mistress, if you were to become Migonnet's queen. He's a frightful monkey. I'm sorry say this, but to tell you the truth, the king who loves you wouldn't condescend to have him for his footman."

"Have you seen him, Perroquet?"

"Indeed, I have," the bird continued. "I was brought up on the same branch with him."

"What? On a branch?" I exclaimed.

"Yes," he said, "he has talons like an eagle."

I was extremely disturbed by this account. I gazed at the charming portrait of the young king, certain that he had given it to Perroquet so I could have the opportunity of viewing him. When I compared it to the description of Migonnet, I felt I had nothing more to hope for in life, and I was determined to die rather than marry this creature.

I did not sleep a wink that night, talking matters over with Perroquet and Toutou. I dozed a little toward daybreak, and since my dog had a good nose, he smelled the king at the foot of the tower and woke Perroquet. "I'll wager," he said, "the king's below."

Perroquet replied, "Hold your tongue, babbler. Just because your eyes and ears are almost always open, you envy others their peace."

"Wager something, then," insisted good Toutou. "I'm sure he's there."

"And I'm sure he's not," replied Perroquet. "Didn't I forbid him to come here in my mistress's name?"

"Oh, you amuse me with your prohibitions!" my dog exclaimed. "A man in love consults only his heart."

All at once he began roughly tugging Perroquet by the wings, making him quite angry. The clamor they made woke me, and they told me what had started their quarrel. I ran, or rather flew, to my window, and I saw the king, who extended his arms toward me and said through his horn that he could no longer live without me.

"I implore you, find some way to escape from your tower, or find some way I can enter." He called upon all the gods and all the elements to witness that he would marry me immediately and make me one of the mightiest queens in the world.

In response, I ordered Perroquet to tell him that what he desired was quite impossible. Nevertheless, relying on his pledge and the oath he had taken, I was willing to attempt to carry out his wishes. But I implored him not to come every day since he might eventually be discovered, and the fairies would show him no mercy.

He withdrew filled with joy at the hope I had given him, and I found myself in a great quandary when I began to consider the promise that I had made to him. How was I to escape from a tower that had no doors? I had no one to help me but Perroquet and Toutou! I was so young

and inexperienced and timid! After considering this, I decided against an attempt that would never succeed, and I sent word to that effect by Perroquet to the king. At first, he was going to kill himself before the bird's eyes, but then he charged him to persuade me either to witness his death or to bring him some comfort.

"Sire," exclaimed my feathered ambassador, "my mistress is more than willing. She just lacks the means."

When the bird repeated to me all that had transpired, I felt more wretched than ever. The fairy Violente came to see me and noticed my eyes red and swollen. She observed that I had been crying and said, "Unless you tell me the cause, I shall burn you alive."

Her threats were always terrible, and I replied, trembling, that I was tired of spinning and wanted instead to make some nets to snare the young birds that pecked the fruit in my garden. "Cry no longer, my daughter," she said. "I'll bring you as much twine as you need."

Indeed, I received it that very evening, but she advised me to concern myself less about working than about my personal appearance, since King Migonnet was expected to arrive shortly. I shuddered when I heard these fateful tidings and gave no reply. As soon as she left, I began to make two or three pieces of net with the object of constructing a rope ladder, which I succeeded in doing very well, though I had never seen one. As it happens, the fairy never furnished me with as much twine as I needed and continually said to me, "Why, daughter, your work is like that of Penelope. You never make any progress, and yet you keep asking for more material."

"Oh, my good mama," I replied, "it's easy for you to talk. Don't you see I'm very awkward at my work and burn a good deal of it? Are you afraid I'll cause your ruin because of the thread?"

My naïve air amused her, though she was a very ill-tempered and cruel creature. I sent Perroquet to tell the king to be under the window of the tower on a certain evening, and he would find the ladder and learn the rest when he arrived. I fastened it as securely as possible since I was determined to make my escape with him. However, when he saw it, he did not wait for me to descend, but mounted it eagerly and jumped into my room just as I was preparing everything for my flight.

The sight of him so delighted me that I forgot all about the danger. He renewed all his vows and implored me not to postpone becoming his wife. We took Perroquet and Toutou as witnesses of our marriage. Never was a wedding between two persons of such exalted rank celebrated with less fanfare or commotion, and never were two hearts so perfectly happy as ours.

Day had not dawned when the king left me. I had told him of the dreadful intention of the fairies to marry me to little Migonnet, and my description of this creature horrified him as much as it had me. The hours seemed long years to me after the king's departure. Running to the window to follow him with my eyes despite the darkness, I saw to my astonishment a fiery chariot in the air being drawn by winged salamanders. It flew so fast that I could scarcely follow it, and it was escorted by several soldiers mounted on ostriches. I didn't have time to distinguish who the ugly creature was speeding through the sky, but I easily surmised that it must be either a fairy or an enchanter.

Shortly afterward, the fairy Violente entered

my room. "I bring you good news," she said. "Your lover has just arrived. Be prepared to receive him. Here are some dresses and jewels for you."

"And who has told you," I exclaimed, "that I desire to be married? It's not at all my desire. Send King Migonnet away again. I won't add a pin to my dress. I don't care whether he thinks I'm beautiful or ugly. I'm not going to be his."

"What's this I hear?" the fairy responded. "We have a young rebel here? We've a head without any brains in it! I won't be trifled with, I warn you—"

"What will you do to me?" I cried, blushing at the names she had called me. "Can you make life more miserable for me than it is already? I live in this tower with only a dog and a parrot, and I see only the horrible form of a dreadful dragon several times a day."

"Ha, you ungrateful little wretch," the fairy said, "you haven't deserved in the least all the care and consideration we've shown you. I've often told my sisters we'd reap nothing from all our labors!"

She departed to find them, and when she told them about our quarrel, they were just as taken aback as she was. Meanwhile, Perroquet and Toutou scolded me, vowing that if I continued to be so insolent, I'd suffer the terrible consequences. I felt so proud of possessing the heart of a great king that I despised the fairies and the advice of my poor little companions. I didn't dress myself, and I took pleasure in mussing my hair so that Migonnet might think me ugly.

Our meeting took place on the terrace. Arriving in his fiery chariot, he was tinier than the smallest dwarf I'd ever seen. Supporting himself on a pair of diamond crutches, he walked on his eagle's talons and on his knees at the same time because he had no bones in his legs. His royal mantle was only a half-yard long, and yet more than a third of it dragged on the ground. His head was as large as a peck measure, and his nose was so big that a dozen birds sat on it, warbling to entertain him. He had such a bushy beard that canaries made their nests in it. His ears rose more than a foot above his head, but they were not so noticeable because of the high-pointed crown that he wore to make him appear taller. The flames of his chariot roasted the fruit, scorched the flowers, and dried up the fountains, and his chief equerry was obliged to lift him. But as soon as he was brought near me, I fled into my room and locked the door and all the windows.

Extremely angry with me, Migonnet returned to the fairies, and they begged his pardon a thousand times for my rudeness. Since they feared him a great deal, they decided to appease him and to bring him into my room while I slept. Then they wanted to tie me hand and foot, place me in his fiery chariot, and send me away with him. After conceiving this plan, they scarcely said a cross word to me about my rude behavior. Instead, they merely advised me to think about making amends.

Perroquet and Toutou were astonished by such kindness on their part. "Do you know, mistress," my dog said, "I have some sneaking suspicions. My lady fairies are acting strangely, particularly Violente."

I laughed at these fears, while I awaited my dear husband's arrival with great anxiety. He was too impatient to keep me waiting long. I threw him the rope ladder, fully determined to flee with him. He mounted it sprightly and said such tender things that even now I don't dare recall them to mind.

While we were conversing together, as calmly as if we had been in his own palace, the windows of my room suddenly burst open. The fairies entered on their terrible dragon. Migonnet followed them in his fiery chariot flanked by all his guards on their ostriches. Fearlessly drawing his sword, the king thought only of rescuing me from the most dreadful fate that ever awaited a mortal. In brief—I don't know whether I should tell you this, my lord, those barbarous creatures set their dragon on him, and the beast devoured him before my eyes.

Driven to despair by his fate and my own, I flung myself at the jaws of the horrible monster, hoping he would swallow me along with all that I loved in the world. He was quite willing to comply, but the fairies were even crueler than the dragon and would not permit it.

"We must save her so that her agony will be prolonged," they cried. "A speedy death is too mild a punishment for this unworthy creature!"

They touched me, and I found myself immediately transformed into a white cat. Then they conducted me to this superb palace, which used to belong to my father. They transformed all the lords and ladies of the kingdom into cats, left only the hands visible of the rest of his court, and reduced me to the deplorable condition in which you found me. Finally, they informed me about my birth and the death of my father and mother, and told me, "You will be released from your cat-like form only by a prince who exactly resembles the husband we have just eliminated."

"It is you, my lord, who bear that resemblance," she concluded. "You have the same features, the same air, the same voice. I was struck by it the moment I saw you. I knew about everything that happened, and I'm equally aware of all that will happen. My troubles are about to end."

"And mine, lovely queen," said the prince, flinging himself at her feet. "How long will they last?"

"I already love you more than my life, my lord," the queen said. "You must return to your father, and we'll be able to ascertain there how he feels about me, and if he'll consent to what you desire."

Leaving the castle, the prince gave her his hand as she stepped into a chariot much more magnificent than those she had previously provided for him. The rest of the equipage matched the brilliance of the chariot, and even the hooves of the horses were shod with emeralds and nailed with diamonds. Such a thing has perhaps never been seen except on that occasion. I shall not repeat the pleasant conversation that took place between the queen and the prince on their journey. If her beauty was incomparable, her mind was no less superb, and the equally perfect young prince exchanged all sorts of charming thoughts with her.

As they neared the castle in which the prince was to meet his two elder brothers, the queen entered a little rock of crystal, the points of which were ornamented with gold and rubies. Completely surrounded by curtains that prevented people from seeing inside, it was carried by some handsome young men superbly attired. Meanwhile the prince remained in the chariot and watched his brothers walking with two extremely beautiful princesses. As soon as they caught sight of him, they greeted him and inquired, "Have you brought a lady with you?"

He replied that he had experienced bad luck on his journey and had encountered only surpassingly ugly hags. "The only rare item I've brought back is a little white cat."

They began to laugh at his naïveté. "A cat?" they exclaimed. "Are you afraid the mice will eat up our palace?"

The prince admitted that he had been rather unwise in selecting such a present for his father.

Thereupon, they continued on their way to the city. The elder princes rode with their princesses in open carriages made of gold and azure, and the heads of their horses were adorned with plumes of feathers and aigrettes. Nothing was more radiant than this cavalcade. Our young prince followed them, and behind him came the crystal rock, which everybody gazed at with wonder. Meanwhile, the courtiers hastened to inform the king that the three princes were coming.

"Are they bringing beautiful ladies with them?" the king asked.

"It would be impossible to find any that could surpass them," was the answer, which appeared to displease him.

The two princes eagerly ascended the palace stairs with their wonderful princesses. The king received them graciously and could not decide which deserved the prize. He looked at his youngest son and said, "Have you returned alone this time?"

"Your majesty will see a little white cat in this rock," the prince replied. "It meows so sweetly and has such velvet paws that you'll be delighted with it."

The king smiled and went to open the rock himself, but as soon as he approached it, the queen made it fly into pieces by means of a spring, and she suddenly appeared like the sun after it has been hidden in the clouds. Her hair fell in loose ringlets over her shoulders down to her very feet. She was crowned with flowers, and her gown was made of thin white gauze lined with rose-colored taffeta. As she made a most dignified curtsy to the king, he was

so overcome by this wondrous appearance that he could not resist exclaiming, "Behold the incomparable beauty who deserves the crown!"

"My liege," she announced, "I come not to deprive you of a throne you fill so worthily, for I was born the heiress to six kingdoms. Permit me to offer one to you and one to each of your elder sons. I ask of you no other recompense than your friendship and this young prince for my husband. Three kingdoms will be quite enough for us."

The king and the entire court joined in shouts of joy and astonishment. The marriage was celebrated immediately, as well as those of the other two princes, and the court subsequently spent several months enjoying entertainment and pleasures of every kind imaginable. Finally, each couple departed to reign over their own dominions. The beautiful white cat came to be immortalized in her realm due to her goodness and generosity as well as her rare talent and beauty.

The handsome young prince was fortunate to find
That beautiful princess hidden beneath a furry cat's skin,
Worthy to be adored and much inclined
To share the throne her affection won for him.

The willing heart is easily subdued
By enchanting eyes seeking conquest.
When love's soft flame is fanned by gratitude,
The charm will have more power and be full of zest.

I cannot overlook that mother
Who paid so dearly for her whim.
Like Eve before she did not care about the other,
And was selfishly prepared to sacrifice her kin.

Mothers beware and learn from this selfish queen!
Don't tamper with a daughter's lot
Or gratify the appetite and act so mean.
Condemn her conduct and remember what she got.